Aubrey De Vere

Legends and Records of the Church and the Empire

Aubrey De Vere

Legends and Records of the Church and the Empire

ISBN/EAN: 9783337152741

Printed in Europe, USA, Canada, Australia, Japan

Cover: Foto ©Andreas Hilbeck / pixelio.de

More available books at **www.hansebooks.com**

LEGENDS AND RECORDS

OF THE

CHURCH AND THE EMPIRE

BY

AUBREY DE VERE

LONDON

KEGAN PAUL, TRENCH & CO., 1, PATERNOSTER SQUARE

1887

TO

Ꞇhe Honourable Mrs. Robert O'Brien.

———•———

MY DEAREST SISTER,

To no one could this volume be so fitly dedicated as to you. It will remind you of the happy days when we read the great poets together, in our woods and on our lake, and when you welcomed my earliest poetic efforts with a sympathy but for which they would never have been repeated.

Your affectionate brother,

AUBREY DE VERE.

CURRAGH CHASE,
  Easter, 1887.

PREFACE.

———•◦•———

THE following poems are a few illustrations, however inadequate, of a historic period still more momentous than either the mediæval or the modern, each of which has found such enthusiastic admirers—the period which bridged the gulf between the ancient world and that in which we live. It begins with the Christian era, and extends to the coronation of Charlemagne. It prepared the way for that of the "Middle Ages;" and though it has till lately been less studied, it included a far greater number of elements and interests. A few remarks respecting it may be acceptable to some readers of this book. That intermediate and transitional period was enriched by the chief results of all the preceding ages, for it included the growth and decay of the Roman Empire, itself the heir of all the earlier empires. It held within it not less the germs of whatever of primary value was subsequently developed. The mediæval civilization matured those germs. It was, in its spirit, Christian doctrine embodied in kindred usages; while, in much beside, it was the ancient Roman Empire, her laws and language, widened by the moral influences derived from the barbaric races. But it was more than this. In it sacred antiquity as well as pagan antiquity lived again. In it the Hebrew Theism was lifted to and above the heights of man's intelligence and drawn closer to his heart by the mystery of the Holy Trinity; the Hebrew Hope was consummated by the Incarnation; the Hebrew moral law received a higher sanction when its spiritual scope had been revealed; the Psalms of David and the Songs of Prophets were the heritage of Christian churches and Christian cottages; and the great Book of the East became the foundation of mediæval letters. Notwithstanding it was not in the mediæval but in that earlier period that this wonderful process of expansion and assimilation first became palpable and visible. Much had to die before the loftier life was evolved; the husk of the seed had to perish before the time of flower and fruit had arrived. It was by the shock of rival races that the delusions of material prosperity were dispelled, crime punished, and the sterner lessons of true wisdom enforced. It was when Christian children faced the axe rather than worship false Gods, and bridegroom and bride walked side by side to the stake, that human ties came to be appreciated at once in their greatness and their littleness. Later, when emperors nominally Christian endeavoured to force upon the Christian Church an anti-Christian faith, her sons awoke to the full consciousness that spiritual freedom was a charge as sacred as the Truth which it alone could preserve. When genius and learning enlisted themselves on the side of error, the champions of that Truth took up in its defence the keenest weapons furnished by the armouries of Greek dialectics. The Neo-Platonists of Alexandria might imperil the philosophy of unwary Christians ; but the Christian creeds, successively defined in six General Councils, stood up like rock-fortresses to ward the Christian theology.

It was not, however, a Christian philosophy only which superseded or supplemented the earlier philosophy of Greece. A new literature sprang up also, the Patristic literature. It is thus that Mr. Allies remarks on it in his " Throne of the Fisherman," pp. 387–390.*

" Let us consider the interval of a hundred and fifty years between the end of the Pagan persecution, and the

---

* The latest volume of his "Formation of Christendom" (Burns and Oates), a work worthy of its high title, and one which brings before us the world's most momentous period (its history at once and its philosophy) with an insight and a comprehensiveness not combined in any other work with which I am acquainted. To it these slight poetic illustrations of the same subject are much indebted.

overthrow of the Western empire by the Northern tribes.
. . . It has often been remarked that after the failure of
the Persian attempt to enthrall Greece, a great outburst
of genius took place at Athens, which became the centre,
drawing to itself the greater minds of the larger Hellas.
The period begins with the dramas of Æschylus, and
may be said to end with the death of Aristotle. Thus it
lasted from the time that the independence of Greece
was saved from destruction by the Persian invader, until
a Grecian conqueror, in subjecting Persia, destroyed also
his country's freedom. There was no time like that
before it in Grecian history, and no time after it, for the
varied productions of genius. With the two exceptions
of Homer and Pindar, every poet, and almost every
historian and philosopher, who have made Greece illus-
trious, were born and flourished in this time. Similar
in duration, similar in exuberance of intellectual life, is
that space of the Church's history which begins with
Athanasius, the peerless confessor, and ends with Leo, the
peerless ruler, both great writers, but men in whom the
greatness of character surpasses the lustre of mind. . . .
Almost the whole wealth of Patristic literature lies between these two. . . . After Leo many hundred years
intervene before a similar period can be shown. As
soon as Paganism had been conquered in the conversion
of Constantine, and before the Northern barbarism broke

up the civilization of the West, and the Byzantine des-
potism quenched the genius of the East, this short time
was given by the Providence of God in which a Chrysos-
tom should use the language of Plato in its old age with
greater effect than Demosthenes in its prime : and in
which a rhetorician, of Thagaste, should take the worn-
out tongue of Cicero, and deposit in it treasures of
thought far beyond the range of Rome's 'least mortal
mind,' and mark out, almost single-handed, the ground-
work for the structure of theology and philosophy in the
Church, so that successors for fifteen centuries have
drawn upon his treasure, and sought to complete what
he had begun. . . . In this interval between Heathenism
and the Western Desolation with the Eastern enslave-
ment, the Church creates a greater intellectual Hellas,
and a greater intellectual Rome, than were their heathen
originals."

Mr. Allies proceeds to show how the great literature
thus rapidly produced had been furnished, not by a
single country, but by regions as numerous as those
which the martyrs had ennobled : in the East by
Antioch, Asia Minor, Jerusalem, Alexandria, and North
Africa ; in the West by Italy, Gaul, Dalmatia, and Spain ;
and how, notwithstanding, the whole of that literature
had breathed one harmonious spirit, as it drew its nurture
from a common Truth and Love. It thus became a

productive cause of that mediæval literature which rose up so many centuries later, to which the great scholastic and ascetic writers belonged, and which found its imaginative representatives in Dante, Chaucer, and the unknown authors of the ballads, in the chivalrous romances, and the heroic lays, like that far-famed "Chanson de Roland," recently added—a valuable accession—to English poetry by the translation of Judge O'Hagan. Before the literatures of "The Nations" had risen up, with all their varied powers, but contradictory tendencies, not all of them healthy, there had flourished that of a united Christendom; but its roots are to be found amid the rocks and ruins of an earlier and half-barbaric time, as the art of the mediæval ages was anticipated by the rough frescoes of the Catacombs. The visions of Hermas, and that Patmian vision associated with the Athenian Areopagite, were precursors of those later sung by the great Florentine, even as St. Athanasius and St. Augustine supplied the basis on which St. Thomas and Scotus built their fabrics of religious philosophy; and a monument had been raised to a mother, St. Monica, more touching than the love-sonnets addressed, centuries later, to Laura.

The profound interest of that earlier period proceeds mainly from the varying relations in which the old Roman Empire and the barbaric races stood to each other. That

Empire represented the whole civilization of the southern world in the East and West; while over the North the barbaric races roamed, exempt from its corruptions, if without its refinements, boundless in courage, faithful to domestic ties, loyal to kings, with a reverential habit, and spiritual capacities extinct along the luxurious shores of the Mediterranean. The eventual union of the southern with the northern races resulted in the Holy Roman Empire of Charlemagne. The memory of the earlier empire had not only survived, but impressed the barbaric races themselves with an awe which they could never shake off. Those who had not feared to storm the walls of Rome scarcely dared to look up at its monuments. Their chiefs were less proud of their triumph than of some titular decoration received from an emperor of the East, whose power did not extend beyond his palace. In spite of their wrongs at the hand of Rome, they felt that the Roman Empire was a thing too great to die. In Gaul, and especially along the borders of the Rhine, rose many a stately city, built by old Roman Coloni, which proved that the Roman civilization and the barbaric races were not incapable of coalescing. In proportion as the latter became Christian a disposition grew among them to regard a universal realm under an Emperor as the completed condition of humanity; for such a spiritual realm was presented to them in the Church, and such a spiritual head in the successor of St. Peter. A civil seemed the complement of an ecclesiastical unity to them, as, centuries later, it seemed to St. Bernard and Dante.

Still more were those who had once lived under the protection of the Empire reminded of their loss, while successively harried by the aggression of rival barbaric chiefs. They recalled to memory that wonderful "Pax Romana," which had given rest to the world for two centuries after Augustus, the prosperity which that peace had produced, and the security ensured by the Roman Law to all who were willing to worship the "Dea Roma." Could not such an Empire be restored under Christian conditions? The races of the South had expected to find in their barbaric conquerors nothing but that fierceness which had characterized their first invasions. But "out of the strong came sweetness." The Barbarians showed often that tenderness of heart which accompanies the spiritual nature, as hardness characterizes the materialistic. It was this union of the milder and the manlier qualities which enabled them, when converted, to infuse into the body with which they were incorporated that element needed in order at once to strengthen it and render it fruitful. Alexander the Great would have given by mandate to the whole world the intelligence and civilization of the Greeks. Had he succeeded, he must have also communicated the Greek levity and depraved morals to the barbaric races, and rendered them incapable of imparting to man any good gift ; a consideration which may qualify with hope our regret at the present slowness of many heathen nations to accept the Faith. It was the conquest of the South which converted the northern conquerors—" Grecia capta, Roman victricem cepit : "—while, on the other hand, it was the conversion of those victorious Barbarians which completed that of the Roman Empire, long re-calcitrant against the edicts of Constantine. It may be remarked, also, that, if the fusion of races had taken place when Rome was still dominant, the Roman Emperors would have continued to claim all that despotic power exacted by Constantine and his successors in religious matters, a power which commonly sides with error more readily than with Truth, because Truth is unbending.

This consideration is borne in upon us the more strongly since, humanly speaking, several centuries before Charle-magne, an Empire might have been erected more than once with far higher claims both to universality and permanence than were possessed by the pagan Roman Empire. If Augustus, or Trajan, had not elected to limit their empire, it could hardly have failed to include the whole of northern Europe within a moderate period, as it already included Gaul and Britain. Such an empire could hardly have fallen to pieces even among the Titanic convulsions of the barbaric invasions, and it might have averted them ; but it was not to be : and had it been created, however long it endured it could not have escaped the contagion of Roman materialism.

Again, Constantine, the first Christian Emperor, when substituting Byzantium for Rome as his capital, had apparently resolved to render his empire a universal one ; but it had been fashioned out of materials that lacked the solidity necessary for permanence, and in a few years the whole royal House had perished.   The next attempt was that of Stilicho.   That heroic man, although a Vandal, was devoted to the preservation of the Roman Empire ; and, to effect this end, his design seems to have been that of peaceably including the barbaric races within it, maintaining, however, the predominance of the Roman race, and the throne of his old master, the Emperor Theodosius.   His death frustrated that design. The enterprise of Theodoric, the Gothic King of Italy, was essentially different.   Its end was to create an empire in which, while the Italians were to be treated with social justice, the Goths were to constitute the predominant power, the throne remaining hereditary in Theodoric's house.   But the great Gothic race had been converted by Arian teachers ; and, at the close of his reign, Theodoric had entered on a war of persecution against the Church, thus fatally alienating both the clergy and people of Italy. His attempt failed like its predecessors, notwithstanding his many great qualities ; and in so many failures it is difficult not to recognize the hand of a Providence which had reserved a nobler gift for man. A Gothic Empire must have been one in which the civil and spiritual spheres were bitterly at variance. In the Frankish Empire they were at one, because each respected the limits of the other. But for that empire Christendom must, as far as we can see, have either drifted into an anarchy of warring races, speedily subjugated by the Caliphs of Islam, or else itself become an Arian Caliphate, the religious element in which must have waned in proportion as the despotic waxed.

Between the final fall of the Western Roman Empire under Augustulus (A.D. 476), and the coronation of Charlemagne (A.D. 800), three hundred and twenty-four years had elapsed, during which the need of a restored Imperial power had made itself more and more felt. The Emperors of the East had lost both the power and the will to protect the West, while they had often insulted her weakness and plotted against her peace. They had also for ninety years sided with the Iconoclasts. The Roman factions had become as dangerous to religion as the barbaric invasions. But above all a new and portentous Power threatened the whole Christian world with destruction—that of Islam. Its strength consisted chiefly in its unity; and only by unity in the Christian body, not alone ecclesiastical unity, but political also, could its progress be resisted. The Frankish chief, Charles Martel, had saved Europe by his victory over the Saracens, near Poitiers; his son and grandson, Pepin and Charlemagne, had equalled his renown. Charlemagne had gone to Rome, not as a conqueror, but as a deliverer. At his coronation he accepted passively what he had not sought. When Pope Leo III. dropped the imperial crown on his head, he acted unquestionably as the interpreter of the popular will at Rome, and of the Christian desire throughout the world.*

Regarded as an ideal the Holy Roman Empire was surely the highest of political ideals. Its aim was neither individual exaltation, nor "the greatest good of the greatest number," but the glory of God and peace among men. It was a supreme "magisterium," which was also a "ministerium;" an authority which was an obedience. Christianity had created a divine kingdom on earth; and its natural help and stay appeared to be a political one, recognizing the same sanction, and existing for the same aim, though for civil ends also. The two

---

* See "The Holy Roman Empire," pp. 56–59, by Professor Bryce, a far more candid authority on this subject than Gibbon. His work is one of great learning and interest.

kingdoms met in that principle of justice which was common to both; since justice at once witnesses to a spiritual law, and is the sole protection of material interests. The earlier Empires were from below; the new Empire was to be from above. They were shaped from the dust of the earth; the last was to be taken from the side of the Church, and to be "flesh of its flesh and bone of its bone." Its chief duty was to protect religion from tyranny and from anarchy; but it was bound no less to make Right, not Might, the arbiter among the kings of the earth, and thus create a peace to which the "Pax Romana" stood but in the same relation as the Roman Law stood to the Divine Law, and as material prosperity stands to the Beatitudes of the Gospel. Everywhere it had been felt that nations and states, high and venerable as they are, could not rightly be the ultimate tribunals among mankind without the perpetuation of wars; and Greece had endeavoured to avert unjust wars by her Amphyctionic Council, as Rome had, at a later time, by her Fecial Council. In the Holy Roman Empire the Emperor was the great arbiter; his office was regarded as a semi-sacred one. At his coronation he "is ordained a sub-deacon, assists the Pope in celebrating Mass," "receives a ring as a symbol of his faith," and "is admitted as a Canon of St. Peter's, and also of St. John Lateran."[*]

[*] "The Holy Roman Empire," p. 112.

His office was neither territorial, nor hereditary. It rested on election, and that election was to be determined by the repute of the candidate for wisdom and justice. Like the Pope, the Emperor might be a shepherd's son.

In one respect the two Roman Empires were striking contrasts. The ideal of the earlier one was comparatively low, but it was realized; the ideal of the Holy Roman Empire was sublime, but it was very imperfectly carried into effect, owing chiefly to personal ambitions, such as so largely frustrated the lofty aim of the Crusades. The comparative weakness of that empire had, however, its compensating advantages. The lightness of its sway, even where that sway was recognized, enabled the nations to develop their several energies in freedom. On one side of that empire the Saracen dominion, which had had nearly two centuries' start of it, burned like a volcano; and on another, the Byzantine Empire mouldered like a mummy; but the Holy Roman Empire did a great work, though imperfectly, averting injustice, how often we cannot know, consolidating the European body, and assisting in the amalgamation of the northern and southern races, and the preservation of the ancient literature, art, and philosophy. If on many occasions despotic Emperors waged war on religious freedom, they never succeeded in subjugating it; nor was it from them that the chief scandals which afflicted religion proceeded, but from the feuds of Roman factions shortly before the Empire of Charlemagne was restored under Otho the Great.

The two Roman Empires were contrasts no less in their bequests to mankind. As the glory of the pagan Empire was a false glory, so its " Pax Romana " was a false peace. It corrupted man, and necessitated the terrible penance which followed when the judgment had at last fallen, and for centuries humanity staggered amid the barbaric irruptions. The chosen people had escaped from the House of Bondage, but had not reached the Promised Land. It wandered long in the desert. When, on the other hand, the Holy Roman Empire fell into abeyance, it left behind it a noble bequest—the Modern Nations. They had grown mature beneath its care ; they had grown strong as it declined ; but between them and it a bond remained in the Christian civilization which it had helped to extend or had protected among them. Those nations are still but fragments both of the Holy Roman Empire and of that earlier Empire, which had unwittingly aided in the creation of one with aims so much more elevated than its own, and done so by its persecutions.

The two periods of the ancient Roman Empire, and of the Holy Roman Empire, were complete periods, and ran, each, its unbroken course : that intermediate Romano-

Barbaric period was one shattered and imperfect, made up of adverse forces and rival tendencies borne forward with precipitous current and in a direction not easily predicted. It was Christianity which determined that direction. It had raised the old Pagan Empire into the Christian Empire, as Michael Angelo lifted the dome of the Pantheon to the summits of St. Peter's. It had flashed into the blind bosom of the barbaric races a beam that developed their vast latent capacities. An eminent German philosopher has remarked that it was not by any material antagonist of its own order that pagan Rome was overthrown : it was by a power of a sort wholly alien, and one which Rome had at once recognized as her foe. It was Christian Love. That principle had taught the martyrs to die while the philosophers could only dispute ; it had made a Thecla face the lions, and St. Jerome find a palace in his cell. A Divine Love had added tenfold to the strength of human love (while apparently restricting it) by redeeming it from the bondage of self-love through the discipline of self-sacrifice. As a consequence, the Family had once more asserted its primal dignity as the unit of all social existence, and the root of all political order : the " Kingdom of Christ," the great representative of Divine Love, stood up thus as the universal Family of Man ; and the only truly universal empire revealed itself as a spiritual empire. " The Cross had conquered," for from it alone could have issued forth that divine love, the principle of life in a new-created world. The commotions of that world, while it was gradually taking shape are, as we revert to them in remembrance, but the storm-lights and shadows which chase each other over a plain, while the real life works on in the herbage beneath.*   History, as written without the insight of Faith, regards chiefly those tumultuous apparitions, and strives to make a picture of the splendid yet tragic pageant : but Christian philosophy has a keener insight; and the reverent tradition of early days dwelt often both fondly and wisely even on trivial incidents associated with that wonderful period. It was not surprised by the supernatural element included in them, because it regarded all that belongs to Christianity as supernatural. The highest authorities among those who disbelieve modern miracles have commonly maintained, when commenting on the frequent statements of the fathers, that miracles were not confined to the Apostolic age, but were vouchsafed in the following ages also because then required for the conversion of the Nations.†

---

* See Wordsworth's poem, entitled " Rural Illusions."

† Thus " the judicious Hooker " : " If the fire have proclaimed itself unable so much as singe a hair of his head ; if lions, beasts ravenous by nature and keen with hunger, being set to devour, have, as it were, religiously adored the very flesh of the faithful man," etc.—Sermon on Faith.

The early legends of the nations are not poetic fictions: they rest on facts, a few that survived when myriads were forgotten because in them there lay a deep spiritual significance. As little are they unquestionable historical records; because, as Cardinal Newman has well remarked, it would have been an impossibility that they should have descended to us traditionally through the ages without catching an atmospheric colouring from the fancy of successive generations. They are not the less worthy of being remembered because much that was admirable in early days would be unfit for imitation in ours; and to look with contempt even on the illusions sometimes connected with them is the error of a narrow as well as an ungenial intellect, or of a nature surrendered less pardonably to the illusions of a later day.

The old Roman Empire passed away; so passed the Holy Roman Empire; so passed the barbaric kingdoms; the Empire of the East; Feudalism;—that terrible Caliphate. What remains are Christianity, and the Nations evolved by its influence out of the warring elements which preceded their genesis. Those nations, too, are in "a transitional" period: they, too, are advancing they know not whither—through a desert, though one which the labours of forgotten sages, and yet more, the martyrdoms of peasants and of children, have caused " to blossom as the rose." If they are advancing towards a

"Holy Land," their way, too, not improbably, may traverse large regions of cleansing persecutions and strange convulsions ; but their Holy Land will not be confined, like the mediæval, to half of Europe, but will extend over the whole earth. They have all the aids vouchsafed to the pilgrims of that earlier transitional period, and, in addition to them, many others derived from Inductive Science, universal Commerce, constitutional Freedom, diffused Education, and a world's experience. These are true aids, provided that the chief of aids is not for their sake neglected. We have much to remind us, no doubt, that the greatest helps to progressive civilization may be changed by misuse into its greatest hindrances : but the lessons from so great a past teach us anything rather than despondency as regards the present, or distrust as regards the future. We are " Stepping Westward ; " but that high spirit of virtuous knowledge and beneficent power which broke like a sunrise from the East, and still " rejoices to run its course," has not yet completed a single circuit of the earth ; and how many such circuits may have to be completed, we know not.

A. DE VERE.

CURRAGH CHASE, *May* 7, 1887.

NOTE.

"History as Written," etc., p. xxiii. line 7—Coleridge expresses himself thus on Gibbon's "Decline and Fall of the Roman Empire :"

"No distinct knowledge of the actual state of the empire can be obtained from Gibbon's rhetorical sketches. He takes notice of nothing but what may produce an effect ; he skips on from eminence to eminence, without ever taking you through the valleys between. . . . When I read a chapter in Gibbon, I seem to be looking through a luminous haze or fog ; figures come and go, I know not how or why, all larger than life, or distorted, or discoloured. Nothing is real, vivid, true ; all is scenical, and, as it were, exhibited by candle-light. And that poor scepticism which Gibbon mistook for Socratic philosophy has led him to misstate and mistake the character and influence of Christianity in a way which even an avowed infidel or atheist would not and could not have done. Gibbon was a man of immense reading, but he had no philosophy."—Coleridge's "Table Talk," vol. ii. p. 231, 232.

CONTENTS.

———◦◦◦———

		PAGE
THE LEGEND OF SAINT THECLA	... ...	1
SAINT DIONYSIUS, THE AREOPAGITE	... ...	19
THE LEGEND OF SAINT LONGINUS	... ...	38
THE LEGEND OF SAINT PANCRATIUS	... ...	50
THE LEGEND OF SAINT DOROTHEA	... ...	80
CONSTANTINE IN THRACE	... ...	95
CONSTANTINE AT CONSTANTINOPLE	... ...	112
THE LEGEND OF SAINT ALEXIS	... ...	132
SAINT AGATHA	... ...	191
SAINT LUCY	... ...	194
SAINT ANASTASIA AT AQUILEIA	... ...	197
THE FEAST OF SAINT PETER'S CHAINS	... ...	203
SAINT PERPETUA	... ...	206
SAINTS VALERIAN AND CECILIA	... ...	207
SAINT EMMELIA	... ...	208
THE ALEXANDRIAN VERSION OF THE SCRIPTURES ...	210
SAINT LEO THE GREAT	... ...	211

Contents.

	PAGE
EUSTOCHIUM, OR SAINT JEROME'S LETTER	212
THE DEATH OF SAINT JEROME	223
STILICHO	244
THE LEGEND OF SAINT GENEVIEVE	258
AMALASUNTA	273
SAINT BONIFACE	285
THE CROWNING OF CHARLEMAGNE; AND THE HOLY ROMAN EMPIRE; AN ODE	302

THE LEGEND OF SAINT THECLA.

ARGUMENT.

Saint Paul preaches Christ at Iconium, standing on a stone where many ways meet; and Thecla, a noble virgin, sees him not, but hears his discourse daily for three days, standing at a window. She believes gladly; and hearing that the Apostle has been scourged and commanded to depart from that city, she desires of him two things, namely, baptism at his hand, and admission among them who minister to him. St. Paul baptizes her, but denies her second request, announcing that God has reserved for her a higher task. Thecla is sentenced to be thrown to wild beasts, but is saved from death. She journeys southward to Mount Taurus; and there, being led by the Holy Spirit into all knowledge, she preaches to the shepherd race, and after many years brings them into the obedience of Christ. Her task fulfilled, she departs to Seleucia on the sea; and she is named " The eldest daughter of Saint Paul." In Seleucia she dies; and to this day a singular honour is accorded to her at Christian death-beds.

WHEN holy Paul westward had made his way

    From Antioch to Iconium, he abode

With Onesiphorus, preaching day by day

    In market-place, or on the common road,

Or standing on a stone, with feet firm-set,

Where four long streets, by plaintains bordered, met.

B

It chanced that in a house that stone hard by
   There dwelt a damsel, Thecla, young and fair,
Dear to the poor for heart and lineage high,
   Dear to the rich, for she was richest there :
And so for her great riches and sweet face
Iconium's proudest sons besought her grace.

Thecla was not to marriage rites inclined,
   For from her childhood she had treasured still
The dream of some Deliverer, conquering, kind,
   Courteous in word, resistless in his will,
In act heroic, and august in thought,
Yet nothing seen like that her fancy wrought.

To festal games that maid would seldom go,
   Never to fanes where pagan dance and song
Surprised with painful blush a cheek of snow,
   And did to heathen rites themselves a wrong :
Her more it pleased in fragrant glades to roam
Than sit at Circus or at Hippodrome.

Alone beside that poplar-girded lake,
   Iconium's mirror-bath, she paced at noon ;
At eve o'er rocky heights her path would take,
   And watch far flashes from the ascended moon,
Like sea-gleams glimmering from a sea-bird's wings,
Illume remoter Halys' mountain springs.

With laughing girls alone she twined the dance
  Where leaned the green reed 'gainst the silvered rill:
There, if wild youths in frolic or by chance
  Broke on them, through the thickets green and still
They fled, far scattered like the pearls that gem,
Ere the cord bursts, some queenly diadem.

Of all the Olympian choir she loved but one,
  The Queen of Night, and ofttimes frowned, aggrieved
At that strange legend of Endymion:
  At most its merest outline she believed;
" The boy was good: she kissed him as he slept;
Then passed: he woke; found no one near, and wept."

A youth with manors broad but ill of life,
  In part his wasted fortunes to repair,
In part from love this fair one sought for wife:
  Urgent and loud her parents propp'd his prayer:
" Iconium's best has proffered you his hand:"
Her "no" meant that they could not understand.

They pressed her oft: weariness too can jest:—
  One eve as Dian's brow, through cloud descried,
Nigh setting cast a faint beam from the West
  That tinged not lit the wan lake's shallows wide,
Laughing she spake: " Let Dian make a sign:
Its import I—none better—can divine.

" I note long since all meanings of her face ;
  Have seen her startled as the roe that flies ;
Beheld her bend the chalice of her grace
  O'er harvest slopes ; marked her reluctant rise
Like some poor maid ere noontide to be wed ;
Have watched her weep like mourners o'er the dead.

"On a silk scarf blue as her midnight heaven
  My hands those lily flowers she loves shall braid :
My patron she : to her it shall be given
  When crescent next.   If, rising o'er yon glade,
Her brows distempered lour, or softly shine,
I shall know well, and make her answer mine."

Her father laughed :—" To Dian make your vows !
  Good choice !   Your Dian's placable as fair !
She loves true maids ; when true maid turns to spouse
  Scorns not, more late, the young mother's frightened
      prayer,
Lucina then.   Work hard !   Next week we spend,
I and your mother, with our Phrygian friend."

With wrinkling brows much labouring to look wise
  Again he laughed, admiring his own wit :
Thecla laughed too, lifting on his her eyes
  Albeit his meaning she discerned no whit :
Her mother smiled ; "Work, Thecla !   Work—and think !"
She nodded ; and her eyes began to wink and blink.

At morn while sat the maid with flower-like hand
  Braiding white flowers into that mantle blue,
She heard, without, a voice of high command :
  Close to the casement scarf in hand she drew :
She sat no more : there hung she hour by hour
Listening : that kingly voice still swelled in power.

Forward full oft she bent, yet nought could see
  Save wandering crowds clustered with eyes fast fixed
On him who spake—to her invisibly.
  Not far he stood ; but him and her betwixt
A low-roofed fane there rose. The hours rushed by :
Around her feet that scarf lay movelessly.

But though she saw not him, before her passed
  The things whereof he spake, by power benign
Within her phantasy immaculate glassed
  As in nocturnal seas each starry sign :
Single her eye ; her heart was without flaw :
Through strength of faith the things she heard, she saw.

She saw the angel of the Annunciation ;
  She saw that Maid who, startled by his word,
To that all strange yet heavenly Salutation
  Replied, " Behold the Handmaid of the Lord."
She saw that light which clothed her as the sun
Then when she spake the words, " Thy Will be done."

She saw her o'er that hilly region wending ;
　　Saw her beside her time-worn cousin's door ;
She saw the Bethlehem star, the Magians bending
　　Their splendour-smitten heads that Babe before :
She saw that Mother tremble ; then, restored,
Meet with calm front Simeon's predicted sword.

She saw that mount whence He, the Son of Man,
　　Launched o'er the earth His new Beatitudes
Like Seraphs winged ; nor less with flail and fan
　　Lashed back to demon-haunted solitudes
Those glittering Woes, blessings by this world held,
That kept mankind so long in blindness spelled.

She saw that Garden of Gethsemane ;
　　She saw God's angel hold the chalice forth
High in both hands ; she saw those sleepers three ;
　　Saw One Who knelt with forehead nigh the earth ;
With aching heart she saw, the branches through,
Those sacred blood-drops reddening grass and dew.

And ever as those sequent pictures rose
　　And to her spirit's vision clave and clung,
She heard, like torrent flood that seaward flows
　　Through black ravines the cloud-girt woods among,
Still heard that wondrous voice of him, the unseen,
Which told of what must be, and what had been.

It changed. She saw the hosts, of the Forgiven
   That Conqueror entering Hades, rise to greet Him :
From all the multitudinous gates of heaven
   She saw the Sons of God ride forth to meet Him :
She saw the God-Man take the eternal Throne
Cinctured by shining armies of His own.

The great voice ceased : the twilight came : the night :
   Still by that casement stood that listening maid :
The gloom but freshened with a keener light
   Those pictures in her amorous bosom stayed,
Amorous of Truth ; the stillness all night long
Made that strong voice more spiritually strong.

That night, as on her pillow sank her head,
   The moon, betwixt a cedar and a palm
Ascending, bathed in light the virgin's bed :
   That light she marked not : glad she lay and calm :
The sun of Faith full-orbed upon her shone :
The moon-cast fancies from her soul were gone.

So passed three days ; daily the Apostle preached ;
   Daily those silent throngs looked up in awe
Their cheeks now flushed with joy, now conscience-
      bleached ;
   Not once that preacher's face the listener saw ;
Wished not for more : " Faith comes by hearing ; " she
Had Faith, nor cared with bodily eye to see.

On the fourth morn was silence.   Strange it seemed,
   Strange, but not sad.   She stood in silent prayer,
Palm joined to palm.   With glorious memories teeméd
   Her heart full-fed : God, like a river, there
O'erflowed her being : Knowledge, not won from sense,
Knowledge infused, filled her intelligence.

Those Truths which from the unseen one she had heard
   Not barren in her spirit, but fruitful lay ;
They spread like growths sun-quickened and wind-stirred
   That sow their seed till blows the breath of May
And woodland lawns compact of violets lie,
Celestial spaces of an under-sky.

Daily she grew in wisdom and in vision ;
   Daily in heart she gloried and rejoiced :
Then in the midst of all that soul-fruition
   Sudden there fell a change.   Two slaves low-voiced
Conversed ; " They spared his life, but scourged ; next
     morn
They drive him from Iconium forth with scorn."

The other ; " Nay, that prophet 'scaped right well,
   For many a man seduced he to his Faith ;
Of these not few in terror from it fell
   When to the præfect dragged : so rumour saith."
They passed : then Thecla took her veil, and spread
Its dusky tissue twice o'er face and head.

She passed that pagan temple close at hand :
   Those meeting ways beyond baffled her eye :
A beggar craved her alms : she made demand
   Where dwelt that prophet : he replied ; " Close by
With Onesiphorus."   There she found him sitting
On the stone threshold, nets for fishers knitting.

'Twas not her childhood's dream : yet all was well,
   For on his brow greatness was written plain :
Before him on her knees the maiden fell,
   Then spake ; " My boldness I might well arraign ;
But I have heard thy word ; and I believe ;
And baptism at thy hand would fain receive.

" I crave a second boon : this city blind
   Spurns thee ; and forth thou far'st again wayworn :
To me unworthy be a place assigned
   'Mong those by whom thy burdens still are borne.
If women tend thee, let me share their joy :
If men, I too can serve, in garb a boy."

The Apostle fixed on her that beaming eye
   Which neither years nor sufferings could subdue :
" Child ! In your face a destiny I descry :
   God hath a nobler, sweeter task for you.
What seek you, seeking Christ?   You seek His cross !
First bear, then preach it : all beside is dross."

Baptized, her heart with joy within her burned :
   Winged by that joy she sought her home, and found
Her mother, Theodora, late returned
   Her six days' absence ended.   On the ground
Still lay that scarf.   One lily flower, but one,
And that unfinished, 'gainst the purple shone.

With reddening brow her mother thus began ;
   " You sent me missive none : excuse I made :
' On Dian's scarf '—'twas thus my fancy ran—
   ' Doubtless she toils : her duteous fingers braid
All round that votive mantle bud and flower ! '
You flung your bauble from you in an hour.

" No doubt your Dian hid her head in cloud :
   No doubt some amorous trickster spake you fair :
Thamyras may have heard of this : he's proud :
   I seek his house the mischief to repair :
I never said the man was wise or true :
I said he's rich, and good enough for you."

The storm subsided : Thecla by her kneeling
   Humbly yet proudly told her mother all :
That three days' preaching ; all its power heart-healing
   And spirit-strengthening : next she spake of Paul ;
Her baptism, and her vow to cast aside
All things for Christ, His handmaid and His bride.

The storm burst forth : upon her daughter's head,
    Pacing that floor a wildered shape and wild,
She hurled her curse :—next to Thamyras sped :
    Denounced that daughter's crime. The young man
        smiled :
"These be girls' tricks ! I come to-morrow morn :
You'll see your convert laughingly foresworn."

He came. As those who knowing well the face
    Forget all else, thus wondering sat the maid
Thamyras entering ; with her wonted grace
    Then gave him welcome, and his pardon prayed.
Her thoughts had tracked bright regions : men like him
To her were "men like trees"—poor shadows dim.

He urged her first with banter, then with pleas
    Such as the emptiest head can quickliest find :
The Christian new replied as one that sees
    To colour-lectures from the man born blind :
A lover's supplications next he tried :
She answered, "Christ I love ; seek nought beside."

With baleful smile the vanquished man departed :
    His love, self-love disguised, had changed to hate ;
A specious man, yet base and evil-hearted :
    Ere long he reached a soldier-guarded gate :
Three times he paused ; but deep within him sin
That day held carnival : he entered in.

It was Iconium's chiefest Basilic :
    Beyond a pillared nave there hung an arch,
Poised upon porphyry columns dusk and thick :
    Beneath its span a bannered host could march :
Ranged round the apse Iconium's judges sate
Down-gazing, dark as death, and fixed as fate.

Thamyras spake ; " Judges, to this high hall
    Hourly, I note, your lictors with their rods
Hale wretches starved whom late the Apostate, Paul,
    Once Jew, seduced to scoff the Roman Gods ;
Shall nobles 'scape, where slaves unlettered bleed ?
Thecla is Galilean, rite and creed."

Gladly those judges would have closed their ears,
    Devised some cause for doubt or for delay :
They dared not : round them circled scoffs and sneers ;
    Soon, like sea-thunders in some cliff-girt bay,
Uprose the popular tumult, and the cry,
" If Thecla be a Christian let her die ! "

That crowd gave way : before them Thecla stood ;
    Beauteous and basking like a rose new blown,
She smiled on that tumultuous multitude :
    Majestical as queen upon her throne
She spake at last ; glorying, her Christ confessed ;
Bade all who heard adore Him and be blessed.

The judgment followed ;—"To the Lions!" She
  Received that sentence with a quiet smile :
Once more in storm that people's mad decree
  Rolled forth.   Not scared, yet sad, she stood awhile ;
Still on her lip that smile all golden hung ;
" Thou wilt not blame them, Lord ; they mean no wrong."

The noble tale could scarce more fitly end
  Than here ; for what are miracles extern
Compared with gifts interior that descend
  From God on hearts like hers for Him that yearn ?
Not less to Christ's last gift humbly we cleave ;
"These signs shall follow them, my followers, that believe."*

Such signs were then vouchsafed : the old books aver
  That when upon the arena Thecla stood
Within Iconium's amphitheatre,
  The imprisoned beasts beneath ravening for blood,
That lion loosed to rend her dared not meet
The martyr's eye.   He cowered and licked her feet.

A second bounded on that stage : the first
  Fought, her defender ; each by each was slain :
The maid betwixt them stood.   That crew accursed
  Devised for her new torments, but in vain,
The sword, the pyre.   Full many a death she died
In will, not deed : God's shield their rage defied.

* St. Mark xvi. 17.

Then rose Iconium's sons, and thus they said ;
   "She must not die !   Perchance this maid is dear
To Gods Iconium knows not, and, if dead,
   May draw on us their vengeance.   Let her steer
Her little wanton bark what way she will :
The girl's a fool : we meant to fright, not kill."

Next morn they pushed her from their gateway forth :
   Southward huge Taurus heaved his range of snows ;
Rose-red Lycanus slanted t'ward the north :
   The loftier heights, the austerer path, she chose,
And heard next day from Taurian peaks that pæan
Anthemed in thunder from the waves Ægean.

There Thecla made her mountain hermitage ;
   There lived in ecstasies of praise and prayer,
Blithe as a bird that 'scapes its gilded cage
   And houses in green forests.   Everywhere
She saw Creation's God, the All-Good, the All-Wise ;
Saw Him forth-gazing from that Saviour's eyes.

She unamazed could mark the snowy ridges,
   The noontide cloud that o'er them swam or slept,
The rainbow torrent dashed o'er icy ledges,
   The mist that o'er the sighing pinewoods crept :—
These are beginnings : Thecla with one bound
Had passed such things, and sat with contemplation
     crowned.

Total Creation seemed the robe of Him
   The great Creator; and its every fold
Revealed to her, though but in outline dim,
   The God beneath. In faith she laid her hold
Upon "His garment's hem;" and evermore
Virtue divine welled thence her being o'er.

Fair were those peopled vales: in them she dwelt
   As Eremite 'mid Lybian sands, alone:
She lived in God, and all the earth, she felt,
   Formed but one marble footstep for His throne:
Yet flower-like was her heart, sweetness sans sin—
It was God's Eden; yea, He walked therein.

To her close by shone out the things remote:
   For that cause holier seemed the things close by:
Them too the eternal light of Duty smote:
   All service service seemed of One on high:
Worldlings, though seeking God, sleep oft, oft faint:
No man is wholly Theist save the Saint.

No other wholly loves his kind: she dipped
   The blind man's pitcher in the darkling wave:
She cheered the sick-room chill: the vines she clipped
   That made its casement gloomy as the grave:
She stayed the widow's tears: from unknown skies
She flashed new light into the orphan's eyes.

What wonder if the mountain shepherds deemed
　　That guest well worthy hymn and incense rite?
Dian herself, their grateful fancy dreamed,
　　For their wild dells had left her Latmian height!
She preached a greater; else their zeal had crowned
That maid the Queen of all their mountain bound.

The little rock-built mountain villages
　　Raised, each, its banner, near them as she drew;
Children, aye babes, with unashamed caress
　　Welcomed her: that she loved them well they knew:
She looked so like the tidings that she preached,
With spring's delight the old man's heart they reached.

Polemic proof, when boastfullest, proves unstable,
　　Powerless for God-like action, prompt for strife:
Music lives on, a power irrefutable:
　　Religion sets to music mortal life.
Still to His Church, bleeding yet unenslaved,
God added daily such as should be saved.

The days went by, and ever year by year
　　She spread abroad the Name Divine and Mary's,
The blithesomest of Christ's hermit saints austere,
　　The tenderest of His Church's missionaries:
At last to God that mountain land was won:
At last Saint Paul's predicted " task " was done.

Then came to her a longing for the ocean
 Whose harmonies the night winds oft had brought her :
She sought Seleucia ; there with strange emotion
 Paced day by day beside the blue, green water
Wherein the Infinite best is typified :
There happy she abode two years ; then died ;

Seleucia of Cilicia.   Farther East
 Cilician Tarsus, " no mean city," stands,
Where he self-styled " of all the Apostles least "
 Was born, and lived by labour of his hands.
T'ward it each sunset Thecla gazed ; and all
Named her " the eldest daughter of Saint Paul."

Later men gave the maid a name more holy,
 " The Proto-martyr of the woman-race ; "
And o'er her sea-lulled grave, humble and lowly,
 A wearied man new-touched by childhood's grace.
The Emperor of the East, Justinian, reared,
Five centuries passed, a fane by all revered.

Likewise God's Church, which evermore condoles
 With mortal pangs, in that supremest prayer
" The Commendation of Departing Souls,"
 To her concedes a praise none others share :
In that last prayer Thecla hath part : in it
No name beside but names of Holy Writ.

C

" Go forth, O Christian Soul, in the name of Him
    The Father, and the Son, and Holy Spirit,
In the name of Cherubim and Seraphim,
    And Saints of earth that heavenly thrones inherit :
God give thee, Christian Soul, a good release :
God in his Sion stablish thee in peace.

" Deliver him, God, as Thou, in days of yore,
    Deliver'dst Noah, Job, and Abraham,
And Paul and Peter from their anguish sore,
    As Thou deliver'dst Thecla, that sweet name,
From beasts and tyrants' rage, and demon snare ;
Save him, Thou Saviour : Judge all-righteous, spare."

SAINT DIONYSIUS, THE AREOPAGITE.

(DIED A.D. 96.)

ARGUMENT.

St. Dionysius was one of the judges of the Court of Areopagus when St. Paul announced there the Faith. He became one of the few converts made there by the Apostle, and was later created by him bishop at Athens, where he died a Martyr. The night before his death he recalls those things in his past life which led up to that happy end; his early distrust of Athens, much as he loved it; his scorn of its Sophists; his abode in Egypt; the great marvel witnessed there and elsewhere during the Crucifixion; and likewise that vision in which he was permitted to see the Nine Hierarchies of Angels.

THE Athenians ne'er were cruel: from the first
Persuasion as a Goddess they revered,
To Pity gave her temple. They have chosen
For me fair prison: through its window bars
The violet odours of the violet city
Reach me from vale and plain. Reed-loved Ilyssus
Whispers far off; and here and there a harp
Reports of happy listeners round it ranged,

Happy ; the younger doubtless innocent ;
While full before me from the Acropolis
The Parthenon sends forth its snowy gleam.
Minerva Polias, Wingless Victory,
The Propylea—great that thought, to place
The city's fortress near its chief of temples—
Are hid.   I see the Parthenon alone.
The first and holiest court in Greece is this,
Our Areopagus.   At first, men say,
It held its sacred sessions in the dark
Lest aught that moves the sense might warp the award.
'Tis sage in earthly things ; in things of heaven
Some strange judicial blindness on it falls :
It saw in Paul "a preacher of new Gods :"
The noblest man in earlier Athens born
Old Socrates, it slew.   If me it slays
'Twill do injustice to itself, not me :
I never valued life ; in what men value
I struck not root profound.

                Brighter each hour
Yon Parthenon makes answer to the moon,
Pallas to Dian.   These the fablers old
Revered as sisters.   Maiden were they both :
I never gazed upon the Parthenon
Without this thought, what depths, while pure herself,
Clear-sighted Athens saw in purity ;

With what a diverse skill she sang its glories—
A Pallas, strenuous, sage, self-mastering, proud,
A Dian, all too bright, too swift for stain,
A Hebè ; Purity meant childhood there,
An accident ; in Iris 'twas essential,
A spirit was she, spanning a fleshly world ;
The Muse, with her 'twas life all intellect ;
Great Vesta, holy there, and venerable,
Vigil it kept o'er hearths.   What worlds of Thought
Here met until one lily flower of earth
Grew wider than the firmament eterne !
What worlds !   O Greece, when centuries had gone by
The virtue honoured in thy youth was that
By thee in age most trampled.   For that cause
God's truth from thee is hid !
                                        Was it to lure
My heart by beauty of this visible world
From spiritual hopes, they chose for me this prison ?
For still the vision of that purple deep
By me so often from Eleusis watched,
Clipping at once far isles and headlands near
Clings to mine eyes.   I will not think of these :
This earth is not our mother, or our sister :
For some it hath, I fear, the syren's snare.
O what a snare to thee, my Greece, was beauty !
Thy fancy robbed thy heart.   Beauty to thee

Was beauty's ruin.   Truth must needs be beauteous :
Yea, but that smile about her lips for thee
Cancelled the lovelier terrors of her brow,
The ardours of her eyes.   Thou mad'st thy pact
Thus with Religion : " Charm, but scare me not ! "
The shadows of high things were dear to thee ;
Their substance was offence.

                     A subtler snare
Thou found'st in Dialectics.   What was that
Which made me, wild and wayward as I was,
In this unlike thee ?   Was it my mother's prayer
Dead at my birth ?   "The shaft of Artemis
Slew her," men told me weeping on her grave
A six years' orphan.   Many a dangerous friend
In that stern sport was keener thrice than I :
They mixed with youthful pleasures large discourse
Of seers from Solon to the Stagyrite,
Yea, Epicurus.   Most were of his crew,
While many, his in life, in spleen of thought
Walked with the Stoic, or with mincing step
Glided from path to path of Academe
Boasting that freedom.   Others proud of lore
Forgotten by the crowd were large in praise
Of earlier names.   " ' All things from water come,'
Thus taught old Thales.   Anaxamines
Made answer, ' Not from water but from air : '

Heraclitus replied to both, ' from fire.'
Anaximander sware that chaos grew
By force inherent to the world we tread :
Some cried the universe was rife with Gods :
And some that Gods were none.   The Ionian School
And Eleatic strove.   Zenophanes
Warred on the priests ; Parmenides not less :"
Thus babbled those around me.   Mute I sat :
Sudden one day in wrath I rose : I cried,
" Ye men of Greece, your prophets were impostors !
They churned their metaphysic seas of words
As girls a milk-pail, but extracted thence
No food for man or beast.   Your great State-Founders
Were dreamers, basing Polities of Law
On lawless wills : the boast of each was this
In turn, to plant a colony in chaos ! "
Thus I continued ; " Philosophic Systems !
Not for asserting wonders scorn I these :
The Truth, when known, will prove more wondrous
        thrice ;
Nor yet because unproven : the Truth, when ours,
If ever ours, will be its own clear proof,
A sun that tasks our eyes yet lights our world ;
Conquering   through   love,   and   crowned   by   man's
        consent :
As little hurl I scoff at rite or creed

Because rich priests have trafficked in such wares :
Best things are most abused :—for this I scorn them,
Because they nothing brought to heart or spirit
Which helped the helpless.   Plato was my guide :
He gave me much : but this he gave not—rest.
He spake of God : I read with beating heart ;
Yet ofttimes cried, ' Believes he what he speaks ? '
A God !   What means a God ?   To me He means
Some heavenly Bender from some infinite height
Who stoops to raise mankind.   Know this, Athenians,
Ye shall not find such God by Syllogisms.
Either some herald from some land remote
Will bring the news; ' He lives !   That God is ours ! '
Or breaking from His heavens that God will cry,
' Behold I come at last.' "   My friends reproved me :
" Theosophist, and not philosopher
Art thou !   In mystic India seek thy home."
    I passed to Egypt.   Heliopolis,
That priestly city, sacred to the past,
Received me.   There I made abode ten years.
Its inmates loved me well.   I said, " Those priests
Who claim no philosophic lore, nor boast
That from her well their agile wand can lift
Truth by the hair, and fling her in the sun
Naked to common gaze ; who guard Traditions ;
Who from their ancient rites, long brooding, draw

Meaning occult that grows o'er Thought's broad dial
Slowly as obelisk's shade o'er evening sands ;
Those priests hold more of Truth than all our Schools :
They welcomed Orpheus, Homer, Solon, Plato,
And, greater yet, Pythagoras. He had found,
Six centuries since, beneath this visible mask
Of shape and hue of motion and of rest,
The spiritual basis of the universe,
Mathesis awful yet all musical,
Ungrasped by sense, alone by Reason known.
He taught men lore forgotten now ; that earth
With many a planet sweeps around the Sun,
Not he round her, and with her sister orbs
Makes part of heaven." Those Seers Egyptian spake
Ofttimes of Hebrew Prophets. These, I learned,
Discoursed long since on social Polities,
But not like Greeks. They ever made proclaim,
Kingdoms that stand are reared on Righteousness,
Not on man's will ; his pleasure or his pride.

How strange the difference 'twixt the quick Greek mind
And these Contemplatives ! To them each Truth
Was as a thing to rest on—kneel upon,
Die on, content to die. To the Greek a Truth
Meant but a thought. He stept from off it lightly :
'Twas but a stepping-stone athwart a stream :

From stone to stone he stept, and then forgot them.
The Egyptian sage with what he knew of Truth
At least held commerce true.

      To the best of these
One day I put that question mine so oft,
" Who made the worlds ? " He answered thus : " A
  God
Who tells not yet His Name." While thus he spake
Behold a wonder ! Darkness o'er the land
Rushed sudden : dreadful night was over all :
The stars shone through it terrible of face
As though they too had died. Three hours went by :
To him that knelt beside me thus I spake,
Apollophanes, comrade of my youth,
" That God who made the universe hath died
This hour ; and all creation mourns her Lord."
That hour the Lord of all had died indeed :
Far off, on Calvary's height, had died for man :
He died ; and darkness swept o'er all the earth.
"Twas then that Athens, awed, that altar raised,
" Unto the God Unknown."

      The years went by :
At last in Athens Paul, my master, stood :
He marked that altar. Fronting it, men say,
He knelt with hands outstretched in prayer three hours.
By it next day his judges thus he judged,

The self-same court which judges me to-morrow ;
" Ye have an altar to the God Unknown :
Him I declare to you."   With him there strove
The Stoics, and the sect of Epicurus,
While sat the sons of Plato reverence-mute.
Some, when he preached the Resurrection, laughed :
Some said, " More late discourse we on this matter."
Then from that city of the proud he passed
To Corinth of the sinners, and from her
Built up a Church to God.

                 I thank Thee, God,
That 'mid those few our Athens gave Thy Son
I found a place—the lowest.   Humble and glad
Ofttimes I walked, the comrade of Saint Paul
Journeying from Church to Church.   I listened mute,
For even as Moses in the Egyptian lore
Was mighty, such was Paul in lore of Greece.
At times of Greek Philosophy he spake,
Spake kindly, yet with sad rebuke.   He said,
" Philosophy at best is mind's ascent
From earth to heaven, an arrow shot in the air :
Not thus the Faith : 'tis ours but by descent
From heaven to earth, even as Incarnate God
Is ours descending from the Eternal Sire.
That verity mankind can ne'er transcend
On earth, in heaven.   How high soe'er man soars

That Truth—the God-Man—still shall over-soar him ;
That Truth God-given, for that the Martyrs bleed :
For speculative systems no man dies."
At times he touched on lowlier themes :—" The men
Who built in Greece her manifold polities
Were great in mind ; yet, building not on God,
Their polities are dust."   I recognized
The teaching of those Hebrew Prophets old,
" Kingdoms that stand are built on Righteousness,"
And later thus their reasonings harmonized.
Man's social life, not less than personal life,
Is fountained from above.   The stateliest Realm,
What is it but the Household magnified ?
The Household, what but Christ's fair Church foreshown ?
In both each citizen must love his brother ;
In both each subject reverence as from God
His ruler ; while that ruler in himself
Sees this alone, the minister of all,
And with all reverence loves his meanest subject.
Yet oft my musings ended thus ; a life
There is, we know, not human, unlike ours,
A race not body and soul, nor marriage-bred,
All love, yet knowing nought of mortal bonds,
A race that feels not after God through types
But sees Him face to face—the Angelic Race.
Roam they at will the starry worlds ?   To them

What grades are fitted save the grades of Love?
What need of States, or Homes? The Angelic City,
How shows it to the City of the Saints?
Then all that Sacred Scripture tells to man
Of angel ministry in heart I pondered,
And prayed of God to grant me angel lore :
To some that knowledge might be help supreme,
Since less by battling with the attempts of flesh
Flesh is subdued than by forgetting flesh
Through commerce with the skies.

      In thoughts like these
One day upon the Asian coasts I rode
Alone, the year that great Apostle died :
The woods were passed; and lo! great Ephesus
Before me stood; and Dian's sacred fane,
A wonder of the world. Long hours that night,
A rock my seat, I gazed upon that fane
As on the Parthenon now. And I remembered
How when great Socrates at Athens died
That Parthenon had sent no thunders forth,
Nor Dian's temple when within its ken
Paul fought with beasts. Likewise I called to mind
How once, once only, he, the Apostle Paul,
That day he placed me o'er the Athenian Church,
Low-voiced had told me that in years gone by
He, in the body, or apart from body,

Into the heaven of heavens had been upraised,
And looked upon the visions of the Lord,
And voices heard unlawful to repeat.
Also that " Loved Disciple " I recalled
Who saw from Patmos isle the end of earth,
And—o'er the grave of that twelfth Cæsar gazing—
Far off the perfect triumph of the Just.
Of Hermas too I thought, and of his Vision ;
" I saw the Church Triumphant, where it rose,
A mighty tower rock-based 'mid raging seas :
Six Angels of the Lord were building it :
Nor ceased they from their toil."
To me these things remembering, then and there
Vision there came : if palpable that Vision
Or else God-kindled in my subject soul,
God knoweth, not I : each Vision is Divine.

I saw the concourse of the Sons of God,
The Hosts Celestial, passing in their number
Perchance all atoms of all visible worlds ;
Images of God's beauty ; bodily beings
Compared with Him ; spiritual with us compared ;
Fed from His Heart with knowledge and with power
Their everlasting Eucharistic Feast ;
Intuitive in Intellect, with their gaze
Ever on Beatific Vision fixed,

Yet active here below, even as man's soul,
Then most in Reason rests while works his hand.
That Faculty Intuitive, their dower,
Passed on to me through sympathy.   I saw them,
And knew their nature, even as Adam knew,
When at God's will God's creatures passed before him,
The end of each.   Plainly on every grade
Some Attribute divine had pressed its seal,
Its character engraved ;—three Hierarchies,
Three Choirs in each.

             The Angels were the lowest :
Their life was simplest, humblest ministration,
Meek helpers of man's race.   A breath of theirs
Had power to quench the sun ; yet their delight
Was this ; to be the servants of God's Poor.
They could have passed all worlds, swifter than thought ;
Yet hour by hour delightedly they spent
Wiling some child from peril, fire or flood :
They who for ever heard the singing stars
Counted the sick man's sighs.   Their faces shone
In rapture of good will.   They felt for each
What lovers feel for one.   Higher I saw
The Archangels potent o'er the soul of man
As Angels o'er his life extern.   'Tis theirs
To sway the elements of his spiritual being
By inspirations brought man knows not whence

Like winds that round the sunset heap the clouds;
Above those two fair choirs I saw a third,
The Principalities that hold in charge
Nation, and city, and house.   Next these the Powers:
'Tis theirs to urge the planets on their course,
Rebrim the fiery chalice of the sun
With beams not lost though hurled beyond our orb,
Creation's wine that never runs to waste.
Yet these high Energies are rhythmical :
Their storms themselves are order.   As a river
Winds from the hills, its countless water-drops
Confluent in one unchanging course, so these ;
God's Living Laws are they, and for that cause
Nature's not less, since Nature's sacred Laws
Are not like edicts of a king deceased,
Or bound in chains, or driven to banishment,
But of a king rejoicing in his halls,
Whose face gives strength to all.   Above the Powers
The Virtues and the Dominations rise :
Kingship divine o'er earth they hold suspense
Spurn it who lists.   Who hates God's Will, perforce
Speeds it, God's purblind drudge.   The peasant child
Hath with the Dominations' choir a part
Praying, " Thy kingdom come."
                           When first I heard
That choral shout, " The Thrones advance," and saw

Their standards dawning on the Mount of God,
I shook with awe.   Vanished that fear like mist !
Not triumph but submission was their joy :
Their title thence :—they are not Gods but Thrones :
Enthroned on them His Judgments Everlasting,
His dread Decrees, His Counsels hid from men,
Yea, secret as the chambers of the deep,
Make visible way through all His universe :
Their glory is to make these manifest,
Their glory and their strength.   To them His Will
Steadies alone their being which sustains it,
No more a burthen than the Spring to earth,
Spring throned upon a hemisphere of flowers
Their joy, their crown.
                        The eighth celestial choir
Far off I saw—a host innumerable
That knelt upon a sunlit mountain's brow
And eastward gazed as when from ocean cliff
A panting people watch their fleet at dawn
Returning victory-flushed.   Of them that knelt
Some fanned their wings ; some screened therewith their
        eyes ;
All bent t'wards one great Vision.   On their heads
Its glory rested tremulously, and streamed
To the utmost skirt of those far-shining robes
Behind them stretched.   Close by, a voice I heard :

                                        D

" Thou seest the Cherub choir : as thou on them
They on that Beatific Vision gaze
Whereof the feeblest flash would strike thee dead.
The Cherubs these of whom Ezekiel spake
That full they are of eyes—the Spirits of Knowledge
In whom, so far as Knowledge Infinite
Can find a mirror in the finite mind,
God makes His knowledge shine, since never they
Pushed forth base hand to clutch forbidden fruit,
Stealing God's gift reserved."

      As thus I gazed
Behind me at immeasurable distance
I heard the winnowing of innumerous wings,
A universe all music.   Fleet as thought
O'er me they swept.   In swiftness form was lost :
They passed me as a lightning-flash that leaves
Blindness behind.   Again my head I raised :
An instant on that Cherub Band remote
And all the aerial ridge whereon they knelt
That lightning flashed, and vanished.   Then that Voice—
" The Seraphs !   Of the Third great Hierarchy
The loftiest choir and holiest of the nine !
These are the Spirits of Love : their life is Love ;
That God-ward Love wherein all lesser loves
First die ; then live sublimed.   So great their Love
They know not that they seek in God their joy,

Seeking that God alone. Through vacant space
Alike, or bulk of intermediate worlds,
God-ward they fleet and obstacle find none.
That flight is rest: they can no more suspend it
Than can the stone that falleth cease to fall,
Since Love that speeds it still is self-renewed.
The Vision Beatific deepens on them
The nearer they approach His Throne. That Throne
Not in the eternal ages shall they reach :
The Infinite is infinite in distance :—
Is this frustration? Nay, fulfilment best !
The Infinite is infinitely near
Not less, and nearest to the Spirits of Love."
   Again that Voice ; "Think not the Spirits of Love
Are less in knowledge than that Cherub Choir :
Each loftier choir retains, yea, closelier clasps
That special grace which names the choir beneath it,
Retains, and lifts it to a higher heaven :
The Spirits of Love in knowledge far transcend
The Spirits of Knowledge, deeplier knowing this
How worthy of love is God. Cherubs in turn
Surpass in reverence for the Will Divine
The Thrones who on their bosoms throne that Will :
Perchance such reverence for that Will it was
Which made such Knowledge theirs. In all the Choirs
The glories of all virtues co-exist

Diverse in measure.   Such diversity
Not envy breeds in heaven, but Love's increase :
The amplest Spirits possess no gift not held
Implicitly by least.   To choirs beneath
Exulting they transmit it.   Seraphs thus
Fling fires of Love on Cherubs.   These in turn
Redound, subdued to milder lights of wisdom,
Their kinglier knowledge on the Choir of Thrones :
Thence down to humbler choirs.

                  One Virtue thus
Too great, too pure to find a name on earth,—
Its nearest earthly name is Charity—
Sacred and prime there lives that in itself
Blends all the Virtues, even as one great Truth,
Ungraspable, we know, except by God,
The paramount of Truths, conjoins all Truths :
That Virtue not ascends but makes descent
A chain long-linked dropt from the Throne of God,
Through all the Angelic grades ; descends to man
Even as that one great Truth, the Lord of Truths—
It's nearest name on earth is " God made Man "—
Descends, man's heritage, to man's race, the sole
That Spirit conjoins with Flesh."

                  All-glorious Vision
Vouchsafed to me unmeet, how oft, and most
In danger's hour, my spirit hast thou made

Still as the central seas ! When first I saw thee
I prayed that I might see thee in my death :
Never since then hast thou so blessed my heart
As on this night ! Means this that death is near ;
Or comes it casual through the law of thought
For this cause that when first that Vision graced me
The Ephesian Temple stood before mine eyes
As now yon Parthenon ? The moon descends :
Eastward that Temple's shadow slowly creeps :
At dawn the judges meet and speak the award.
But Thou, O God, save Thine Athenian people !
Crown her great gifts with this Thy best, to use
Rightly her lesser. Reason is her boast :
Wed it with Faith ; that those two gifts, made one,
May breed o'er earth a race of Truths divine,
Raising a Christian Athens next to Rome !
Ah me, how little knows or man or nation
How near our hand a possible greatness lies
Beyond all wish, all thought !

THE LEGEND OF SAINT LONGINUS.

ARGUMENT.

The soldier who pierced with his spear the sacred side of our Divine Lord was, according to an ancient tradition, no other than that centurion who afterwards made confession, " This was the Son of God." He fled to Cæsarea, in Cappadocia, where, abiding in penitence, he drew many to the Faith. The persecution under Nero reaching Cæsarea, Saint Longinus again makes confession of Christ. The Roman præfect condemns him to death, and is immediately struck blind ; but Longinus promises to pray for him when with Christ. He keeps that promise, and not only the sinner's bodily eyes are restored to him, but the eyes of his spirit are opened also.

THE legend saith that when on Calvary
   Christ, God and Man, for man's redemption died,
That soldier who transpierced His heart was he
   Who later, conscience-smit, in anguish cried,
When earthquake split the rocks, and o'er the sod
Darkness made way, " This was the Son of God."

It saith that at the instant of his crime
   Blindness from God on that centurion fell ;

That on his knees he sank and knelt long time;
   That cure there came to him by miracle:
That with that blood which stained his spear, in awe
Taught from above, he touched his eyes and saw.

"Sinners shall look on Him they crucified"—
   The legend saith his eyes, thus opened, turned
Straight to that wound purpling the Saviour's side;
   That more than eyes can see his heart discerned;
That, ranged so late with sinners—with the worst—
That soldier made of Christ confession first.

He rose; in wrath he cast that spear away:
   Foot-bare he fled to Cappadocia's shore;
There dwelt at Cæsarea: day by day
   He wept; ere passed a year his head was hoar:
There thirty years he lived, and by his word
And by his life drew many to his Lord.

For evermore he preached to man and maid,
   "Cling to the cross! That cross retrieveth all;
Raised on His cross, Christ for His murderers prayed:
   He prayed for me, the last and least of all."
And still to Christ he sued: "Since Thou for me
Didst pray in death, grant me to die for Thee!"

Nero ruled Rome : for sport that Rome he fired,
  Then from a tower, while up the smoke-wreaths curled,
Sang to his lyre, and feigned himself inspired ;
  Next day, to shield a hated head, he hurled
Abroad that charge, "The Christians' Crime," and dyed
With innocent blood the ruins far and wide.

At last to Cæsarea reached that cry :
  "If any scorn upon our gods to call,
Why cumbereth he earth's pavement?   Let him die !"
  Longinus entered first the judgment hall :
There sat the Roman præfect, robed and crowned ;
Twelve statued gods were ranged that court around.

Thereof the lower half that hour was thronged
  By men in Cæsarea one time great
And wealthy still ; to them her lands belonged,
  And they to Rome, their army, and their state :
Rome had required their presence there that day :
They loved her not, yet dared not disobey.

Lightly that præfect spake : "More serious task
  Than that of scourging fools, good friends, is mine :
Longinus, speak : thou wear'st, I think, no mask,
  Rome's soldier once ; her gods, remain they thine ?"
He answered : "Mine they were that day gone by :
My Christ forgave my sin ; and His am I."

Then fell on all a great astonishment :
　Across that præfect's face there passed a leer ;
Far back upon his gilded throne he leant,
　Then thus : " What further witness need we here ?
Yon man has courage : what he lacks is sense :
Death by the axe ! Ho, Lictors, take him hence ! "

Of various minds that throng till then had stood :
　Most part were zealous for the pagan rites ;
Whilst others shrank from shedding brothers' blood
　For themes which, shrouded on the cloudy heights
Of thought—for so they deemed—had never once
To questioner given oracular response.

But when *her* voice was heard whose voice was one,
　Whose Law o'er-ruled all laws, whose will unflawed
Spake to all lands, " Do this," and it was done,
　There came to them a change : not only awed,
But with a servile rapture filled, aside
They cast all doubts : " Death by the axe ! " they cried.

Sadly the captain of the Lictor band
　Approached to lead the sentenced to his death :
Calmly Longinus drew from out his hand
　The axe ; he spake, yet scarce above his breath :
" I die : 'tis well ; but first I will to show
If these be gods ye worship—ay or no."

Forward he stepp'd ; sudden up-heaved on high,
   Facing that statued Jove, his battle-axe,
And smote.   From each stone idol rang a cry
   Piteous and shrill.   Then, frail as shapes of wax,
Those twelve strong gods fell shivered to the ground,
While all who saw it stared in panic round.

Their panic changed to anger.   Where was now
   That fixed resolve and single, theirs so late,
To stand with Rome close bound by will and vow ?
   A single moment can precipitate
A thousand jarring motions into one :
A thread gives way : their unity is gone.

That anger changed to madness : fury fell
   On those who thronged that hall, both guard and guest :
Each smote at each : that hall seemed changed to hell ;
   Its inmates into men by fiends possessed :
One only in the midst serene and high
Stood up unmoved ; that man condemned to die.

Unmoved he stands ; who is it before him kneels
   Forth lifting, like some drowner in the wave,
Hands ineffectual, agonized appeals,
   To him, the sole, who, if he wills, can save ?
That præfect on the sudden stricken blind !
His victim thus made answer meek and kind :

" I blame thee not ; according to thy light
    Thou madest decree : by law thy word must stand.
Fear nothing ! God will give thee back thy sight ;
    Let two young children take thee by the hand,
And be to thee as eyes, and with soft tread
Conduct thee to my tomb when I am dead.

" There kneel, and register thy vow ; and I,
    If God gives grace, will prop with mine thy prayer ;
For though, ere regioned yet in yonder sky,
    Christians plead well, they plead more strongly there
Where He who grants each prayer that prayer inspires,
The nearer nurslings of His heavenly fires."

Next, turning to that raging host, he raised
    His hand, and made the Venerable Sign :
And straight the tempest ceased.   They stood amazed ;
    Then, drawing to the sentenced, knelt in line ;
And thus he spake, as one who speaks with power :
" Spirits impure, where dwelt ye till this hour ? "

Then came an answer : " There where Christ is not,
    Where no man makes His Sign, or names His Name,
We dwell ; but most in idols deftly wrought :
    In them our palace-fortresses we claim ;
In yon poor wrecks for ages we had rest,
Houseless through thee this hour, and dispossesed."

To whom the conqueror : " Think not that for long
    Ye shall retain man's godlike race your thrall ;
For Christ Who drave you forth so oft is strong,
    And strong the house of them on Him who call."
He spake ; then passed, with lictors girt around,
To that fair hill-side named the " Martyrs' Mound."

Softly it rose, half-girdled by a wood,
    Open elsewhere to every wind that blew,
And violet-scented.   On its summit stood
    A company of grave-stones—some were new—
Grav'n with dear names of those in days gone by
Who died in Christ, rejoicing thus to die.

In those old days the name of " Holy Rest "
    That hill sustained : but when the Roman sword
Went forth 'gainst all who Christ their God confessed,
    The " Martyrs' Mound " they named it, to record
That laureled band which braved an empire's frown :
Of these Longinus wore the earliest crown.

They read the process : he no word thereof
    Noted : in heart he stood on Calvary ;
Looked up again upon that Lord of Love ;
    Followed the Eternal Victim's wandering eye;
Saw it once more upon him fix.   It said :
" Centurion, fear not ; I for thee have prayed."

Ah ! then well knew he that Christ's potent word,
 His prayer, though spoken by the eye alone,
The hour he spake it had in heaven been heard,
 Likewise another, later prayer—his own—
Rushed on his memory back : " Since Thou for me
Didst pray in death, grant me to die for Thee."

They read the sentence : straight there fell such grace
 On that centurion from the Crucified,
Such splendour from the Eternal Father's face,
 That well he knew—the moment ere he died—
Those proud ones, late from demon bond set free
Through prayer of his, Christ's servants soon would be.

When the third morn, brightening the horizon's bound,
 Touched first the snow-white portals of that tomb
New raised upon the holy " Martyrs' Mound,"
 A stately man drew near it.   Twilight gloom
Between him and its bosky bases lay ;
But on its height the grave-stones laughed in day.

Why should a man so stalwart pace so slowly ?
 Why should a port stamped by habitual pride
Sustain the shadow of a grace so lowly ?
 What boys are those his doubtful steps who guide ?
Each clasps a hand—a little lags behind,
Though zealous, shy.   The man they lead is blind.

Is this the man on whom, but three days since,
  All Cæsarea hung for life or death,
In name a præfect, yet in power a prince?
  Whence came the change? Alas, how slight a breath
Can shake the light leaf from the autumnal tree!
When summer flushed his veins how firm was he!

Before that tomb the vanquished Strong One knelt;
  Down on that grave his head discrowned he laid;
With each blind hand its lintels cold he felt;
  He raised his sightless eyes : to God he prayed :
At idol shrines he made that hour no plaint :
To God he prayed; to God and to His Saint.

In heaven God's Saints fix still their eyes on God;
  Yet, as a man beside a lake's clear mirror
Notes well the trees behind him sway and nod
  In that still glass reflected without error
So, in the mirror of God's knowledge high,
His Saints the things of earth in part descry.

Longinus from the haven of his rest
  Descried that suppliant bent and with him prayed
While prayed with both the synod of the Blest;
  Since God, sole source of Love and loving aid,
Wills that His creatures, each to each, should bear
His gifts; and what He gives concedes to prayer;

That so in heaven and here on earth alike
   All creatures may be links in one great chain
Down which His gifts, innocuous lightnings, strike
   From loftiest to the least.   Unmeasured gain
Is this, since thus God's creatures, each and all,
One temple grow through love reciprocal.

A sinful soul is ofttimes not so far
   From God and aid divine as men suppose :
The sea-rim brightens though unrisen the star ;
   In him a star of hope thus gradual rose :
He mused : " The Christian's God may help me yet !
Longinus promised : he will not forget."

Strong in that hope the blind man raised his eyes—
   O wondrous change ! Where lately all was black
Flashed the clear wave and laughed the purple skies :
   The sun had risen : the night, a cloudy wrack,
Fled like some demon host repulsed with scorn ;
And as a pardoned spirit rejoiced the morn.

But he, that man late blind, the child of Rome,
   What heart was his ? That world, his own once more,
Seemed less the earth we tread, our ancient home,
   Than pledge of worlds to be ! That sword, of yore
Barrier 'twixt man and Eden, was withdrawn :
Beyond there lay some new Creation's dawn.

Old songs he heard, sung by his Hebrew nurse :
    " God stands around our Salem like the hills :
His light is Truth : He made the Universe :
    Like the sea-chambers are His oracles :
Who shall ascend His Holy Mountain ? They
Whose eye is single ; undefiled their way."

On that vivific Vision long he gazed ;
    Then, shivering, sank upon his face, with eyes
That sought once more the darkness, splendour-dazed,
    Still as some creature bound for sacrifice.
Wondering those children stood.   He rose at last
And spake : " A Task is mine.   The Past is past."

To Cæsarea straight his steps he turned :
    Near it a throng came forth to greet him ! They
Who sinned like him that sin to expiate burned :
    The madness of a life-time, not a day,
At once had left them.   To themselves restored,
Self they renounced, and found, instead, their Lord.

They stood with countenance glad, yet wonder-stricken,
    Like face of one who some great sight hath seen
And still, with heart whose pulses ever quicken,
    Seeing no more, fronts the remembered sheen.
Silent they stood, their eager eyes wide bent
On him, with hands forth held in wonderment.

With him returned they to their ancient city :
    A light till then unseen upon it shone ;
Christ they confessed : they sought nor praise nor pity :
    Sharp was the conflict ; the reward soon won :
The " Martyrs' Mound " holds still their hallowed dust :
Their spirits abide with Him in Whom they placed their
    trust.

Farewell, Longinus ! Thou one hour didst seem
    Of all mankind, save one, unhappy most,
Yet lived'st, to vanquish fiends, from death redeem
    Not one poor sinner but a sinful host ;
Pray well for men sin-tempted to despair :
Lift up thy spear and chase the fiends their souls that
    scare !

THE LEGEND OF SAINT PANCRATIUS.

(DIED A.D. 287.)

PART I.

ARGUMENT.

Saint Pancratius was born in Phrygia, and after the death of his
parents abode with his grandfather in an ancient house outside
Rome. The Diocletian persecution raging at that time, Pope Cornelius with many of the faithful lay concealed in a catacomb, and
converted to the Faith first the youth, and afterwards his grandfather. Pancratius, then fourteen years of age, was dragged before
Diocletian, who required him to sacrifice to the gods. The youth
scorned that command, denouncing the pagan gods. He died
with great gladness outside the city wall, and Concavilla, the wife
of a Roman senator, interred his body honourably nigh to the
Aurelian Gate, which, having been later dedicated to the Saint, is still
called the Gate of Saint Pancratius.

THE child Pancratius, blithesome as a bird,

    Glorious of countenance and of heart undaunted

Abode in Phrygia. He had never heard

    His ancient race by friend or minstrel vaunted :

How 'scaped he flattery ?—thus : though great at Rome,

His sire had lived since youth remote from home.

That sire, Cledonius, had no heart for things
  Whereof the dull and brainless make their boast,
Huge halls with tapestries hung, the gift of kings,
  The unceasing revel and the menial host :
" Here," said he, " all is base : I seek some clime
By genius graced, or hallowed by old time."

He sailed to Athens ; beauteous as a dream
  Her fortress-steep and temples met his eye,
Ilyssus, and Colonos, Academe :
  Eastward he passed ; great Sunium's sea-cliff nigh,
He hailed that fane world-famous ; from its steep
Saw next its reflex in the violet deep.

In turn he visited the Cyclades ;
  At Delos slumbered 'neath the laurel shade ;
Coasted the Asian shores ; where'er the breeze
  At random wafted him his dwelling made,
Headed the natives both in sports and jars :
Now judged the prize ; now led them in their wars.

His was a soaring yet a careless nature,
  Winged with high impulse, scant in self-control :
Nature he loved. in every form and feature,
  And Art, when Art expressed or strength or soul :
Loved battles most, and still, whate'er betide.
Sustained the juster, spurned the ignobler side.

One morn, sole wandering in a Phrygian wood,
　　He met the loveliest lady of that land
With maidens girt.   At once her grace he sued
　　And from the King, her father, won her hand,
Quelling his foes.   Within that realm in joy
They dwelt; and there she bore her lord a boy.

The years went by, and each endeared yet more
　　The growing youth to those who knew him well;
He joyed to tame the horse, to chase the boar;
　　Foremost he raced o'er Taurus, crag and fell,
Farthest his arrow launched, spoke truth, and clave
Swiftliest, as Iris seaward swept, the wave.

One morn his father took him by the hand:
　　" My son," he said, "should ill befall thy sire,
Weep not o'er-long, but reverence his command:
　　Thy mother guard; with her to Rome retire:
There dwells thy grandsire, now grown old and grey
I owe to him a debt which thou must pay.

I left him though I loved: not anywhere
　　Found I that prize I sought o'er all the earth:
What if I lost it, leaving Rome?   When there
　　Seek it thou too!   In fanes—by home or hearth—
It dwells no more.   Perhaps deep underground
With Rome's old Sibyl it may yet be found!

Rome is thy place of duty : work her good !
    Toil for her future, mindful of her past :
I left her, seeking Truth. O son, I would
    Some God would make it man's ; for Truth will last.
I sought her for her freedom, brightness, beauty :
Perchance they find her best who seek but duty.

I sought her long : not less myself I sought—
    Well, well ! It needs more leisure to repent
Than war-fields grant. Meantime, as parents ought,
    I tag with counsel my last testament :
Fear none : the true man help : the false man fight ;
And keep the old house, not proud, yet weather-tight."

A trumpet-blast rang out : upon his horse
    The brave man vaulted : from a trivial fray
Ere two hours passed they bore him back a corse :
    The wife, the mother, met them on their way :
She raised her hand : they laid him down : wide-eyed
She gazed ; upon his breast she sank, and died.

A month went by ; three miles from Rome, and more,
    A stately mansion shrouded in a wood
Caught on its roofs the sunset. At its door
    Beauteous but weather-worn a stripling stood :
His form showed fourteen years at most : his mien
The bravest was, yet gentlest, ever seen.

A crowd of slaves in raiment rich but old
  Led him through galleries long and many a room
Spacious yet dim with walls of rusty gold
  To where his grandsire sat in twofold gloom,
Within, of velvet hangings stifling sound,
Of ilex woods without, and miles around.

The boy in reverence sank upon his knees
  Craving a blessing.   Soon was told his tale :
The old man listened mute ; by slow degrees
  He brightened like some hillside wan with hail
When sudden sunbeams flash from wintry skies :
And fires of days long dead were in his eyes.

" 'Tis well !   A missive from my son late sent
  Announced your coming.   You are welcome, boy !
I had my wrongs, but now in part repent :
  Your face is like your sire's ; that gives me joy :
He might have lived the chiefest man in Rome :
Here you shall fill his place and find your home.

" I was too silent once in grief; in wrath
  Too loud.   Your Father, boy, and I had words :
I held my own : the young man chose his path :
  He passed o'er seas and lands like passage birds :
I mused in this old chair nor told my pain ;
Yon terrace paced : the footprints still remain."

Next morn the old man called from far and near
    The slaves that served his house or delved his lands
And bade them in that youthful guest revere
    Their future master.   They with lifted hands
Shouted applause; then bowed their necks, and sware
True service to their lord and to his heir.

Day after day his grandsire gladdened more
    Gazing upon that boy : with honest pride
He clothed him in the garb young nobles wore
    When he himself was young, and bade him ride
His stubborn'st steed.   " Who rules his horse," he said,
" Shall find the rule of man an art inbred."

He gave him best instructors, Romans each :
    " Read Varro, boy, read Ennius : these were ours ;
Those gaudy scrolls from Hellas filched but teach
    That fancy-lore which saps the manlier powers :
Our younger nobles scarcely know to speak :
They mar Rome's tongue with babblings from the Greek."

That grandsire to the boy was teacher best,
    For still his speech was not from books, but life,
Life of old days in liveliest pictures dressed,
    Huge dangers, rapturous victories, ceaseless strife :
At times his speech dealt warning, seemed to chide
Some latent weakness in the boy descried.

"A man must choose his friends; not less his foes;
   Welcome rough truths; abhor a flatterer's praise :
He must not sail with every wind that blows,
   Nor, vowed to virtue, walk in fortune's ways;
Nor seek contrarient Good. The knave that sues
God's lesser gifts His greater doth refuse."

Oft of old days he spake : " The Gracchi first
   Let loose dissension's plague; that plague to bind
The Empire rose : it laid a hand accursed
   On high and low, the keen-eyed and the blind.
There History ends : Ixion's wheel rolls round—
So ours." Once more he spake with sigh profound :

" That plague came earlier ! Then when Carthage died
   Her Conqueror, corse on corse, above her fell ;
Scipio * was prophet : loud and oft he cried,
   ' Your rival slain, your vices will rebel;
First pride ; then civil strife ; then sloth and greed :
Compared with such worst foe were friend at need.'

" It proved so ! Till that hour survived that awe
   True patriots feel, which, like the thought of death,
Confirm laws civil by religious law :
   Carthage consumed, Rome breathed the emasculate
     breath

              * Scipio of Nasica.

Of Eastern climes ; Capuan she lived since then :
Cornelia was the last of Roman *men.*

" The Gracchi too were men, scorned all things base,
 Pitied the poor, the slave : they erred through zeal :
In time they might have won the conscript race :
 They to the popular passions made appeal :
They ranged 'gainst Rome the nobles' wrath and
 pride :
The last they might have lured to virtue's side.

" The nobles with Pompeius fell ; with them
 Fell that republic theirs through virtuous might :
The Gods placed next the imperial diadem
 On Cæsar's forehead. I deny their right !
My sentence here is Cato's *—With the Gods,
Albeit religious, here I stand at odds."

Pancratius fixed in silent trance of thought
 Full on his grandsire's face those lustrous eyes
Which beamed as if they ne'er had gazed on aught
 Less splendid than the splendour of clear skies
When throned within them sits the noontide day :
He spake : "The Gods — my grandsire, what are
 they ?"

---

 * Causa victrix Diis placuit : Causa victa Catoni.

His grandsire then : " The old teaching saith that Jove
   Exists, and they, the rest.   Our Cynics new
Flout that old faith, yet never can disprove :
   Our Gods live ill ; not less they may be true :
Till speaks that greater God, the All-Wise, All-Blest,
Let man await His voice, and be at rest."

The old man never from his wood emerged ;
   In his great Roman home refused to dwell ;
Yet oft of Rome he spake, and ever urged
   The boy he loved to learn her annals well.
" All History there," he said, " is summed ; yet all
Her greatness past but aggravates her fall.

" Son, walk in Rome, but wisely choose thy way ;
   Seek first great Vesta's fane by Numa built :
Unnoted pass those trophies of the day,
   Pillar or arch, that fawn on prosperous guilt :
The Augustan and the Adrian Tombs to thee
Be what those upstarts crowned to man shall be.

" Hold thou no commerce with Mount Palatine ;
   Revere the Hill Saturnian's * templed crest ;
Still to Tarpeia's Rock thy brows incline,
   Ambition's latest leap and earliest rest :
Seek last that hallowed spot where regal pride
A second Brutus met, and Cæsar died.

          * The Capitoline Hill.

" Turn from that huge Pantheon's godless boast
  Where all Gods met became, not one, but none ;
That Coliseum by a captive host
  Ill-raised, the ill-omened vaunt of deeds ill-done.
Trample such memories ! To thy bosom fold—
In them high mysteries lurk—our records old.

" Romulus, that Sword of Mars, as warrior reigned ;
  Numa as priest. He served the Unnamed, the Un-
    known :
If lesser Powers he honoured, he ordained
  They should have image none in hue or stone.
He built the ' Fecials' House : ' until they swore
' This Cause is just,' Rome dared not march to war.

" Like Indian sage he lived : his thoughts were tuned—
  His laws—to mystic strains beyond the skies ;
One law was this : ' Vintage of vine unpruned
  Use not, 'twere sacrilege, in sacrifice : '
That meant, Religion shorn of Self-restraint
Insults the God ; not worship, but a feint.

" The great Republic honoured still the Kings :
  Long stood their statues on the Capitol :
From Kings our noblest Houses came : great things
  Thus live though dead, while centuries onward roll.
Boy ! he who for the present spurns the past
Shall reap no future while the world doth last.

"'True men were honoured then, or poor or rich :
    Peace made, the conqueror tilled anew his farm :
Order was friend to Freedom : each in each
    They lived ; and each its rival kept from harm :
Sages gave counsel : heroes held command :—
What now ?   The hard heart, and the silken hand !

"Strong thinkers ruled—not chosen for bribe or boast ;
    Far-seeing, serious men of silent power ;
Those who the Senate's pride denounced the most
    Invoked that Senate still in danger's hour :
They knew the old tree anchors on deepest root ;
Swings safest in the gale ; bears amplest fruit.

" Rome had her poets, too : their work is done :
    Her earlier history lives alone in verse :
The perils gladly braved, the triumphs won,
    The songs alone were worthy to rehearse :
Not much the songs loved *us ;* but them we prized :
In them the people's voice grew harmonized.

"'Those songs were sung the banquet-hall to charm :
    Coriolanus lived once more in them ;
In them Virginius raised that conquering arm ;
    In them King Tarquin's starry diadem
Fell to the earth ; Camillus spurned the Gaul ;
Attilius passed to death at duty's call.

" To these we owe our best.   Livius from these
     Flung fire upon his many-coloured page :
From them, the Aphroditè of new seas,
     Rome's Latian Muse had risen some later age :
Our Civil Wars trampled that hope in blood :
The Empire came, and choked that blood in mud.

" Then Maro piped, and Flaccus : Rome turned Greek :
     Barbaric now she turns, gloom lost in gloom :
My buried Rome if any care to seek,
     Boy ! let him seek it in the Scipios' Tomb !
Enough !   My song is sung, and said my say :—
Numa his best Muse named his ' Tacita.' "

He rose : he gazed on that long cloud which barred,
     Its crest alone still red, that dusking west :
At last he turned ; with breath all thick and hard
     He spake, his white head drooping t'ward his breast,
" 'Twas not her pangs, her shames, that tried me most :
I thought of all Rome might have been, and lost."

That night beside a cabinet he stood
     Musing ; unlocked it next with carefulness ;
Last, from a perfumed box of citron-wood
     Drew slowly forth a lithe and golden tress ;
Slowly he placed it in his grandson's hold :
" Your father's hair—cut off at three years old."

PART II.

PANCRATIUS' grandsire left him ever free :
   " If good the heart," the man was wont to say,
" Feed it with lore, but leave it liberty ;
   The good, wise heart will learn to choose its way :
Virtue means courage : man must dare and do :
Who does the right shall find at last the true."

The boy, though gay, was studious ; swift to learn,
   To him the acquest of knowledge was delight,
For his the sacred instinct to discern
   How high true knowledge wings the spirit's flight.
The youth of Rome no comrades were for him :
Triflers he deemed them, fooled by jest and whim.

Often on that great plain which circles Rome
   He spurred his steed Numidian ; oftener far
In that huge wood which girt his lonely home
   Sat solitary, while the morning star
Levelled along some dewy lawn its beam,
Or flashed remote on Tiber's tremulous stream.

Pacing its glades at times, he seemed to hear
   Music till then unknown, a mystic strain
That sank or swelled alternate on his ear
   Like long, smooth billows of some windless main.
" Is this a dream ? " he mused ; " if not, this wood
Houses some Spirit kind to man and good."

One day he sat there, sad.   The year before
   That self-same day his parents both had died.
" Where are they now ? Upon what distant shore
   Walk they this hour? " For them, not self, he sighed.
" They have not changed to clay ; they live : they must :
But where, and how, I know not.   Let me trust !

" What loyal love maintained they each for each !
   With what bright courage met they peril's hour !
How just their acts, how kind and true their speech !
   They never drave the outcast from their bower :
Some great belief they must have held ! In whom ?
Believe I will ! My altar is their tomb."

Wearied with grief, the orphan sank asleep,
   And, sleeping, dreamed. In dream once more he heard
That mystic music sweeter and more deep
   Than e'er before ; and now and then a word
Reached him, he deemed from shadowy realms beneath :
At times that word was " Life ; " at times 'twas " Death."

Then, o'er the sheddings which the west wind's fan
   Had strewn beneath the pine-woods, he was 'ware
That steps anear him drew ; and lo ! a man
   Beside him stood.   The sunset touched his hair
Snow-white, down-streaming from that reverend head,
And on his staff cross-crowned a splendour shed.

The dream dissolved : upright he sat, awake :
   The Apostolic Sire of Christian Rome
Beside him stood—Cornelius : thus he spake :
   " Fear naught !   I come to lead a wanderer home :
Thou mourn'st thine earthly parents.   They are nigh
More than in life, though throned in yonder sky.

" God's angel brought to each in life's last hour
   That Truth they sought, both for their sake and thine :
They left thee in the flesh : since then in power
   With love once human only, now divine,
Have tracked thy wandering steps : this day, O boy,
Through me they send thee tidings of great joy.

" That God who made the worlds at last hath spoken :
   The shadows melt : the dawn of Truth begins ;
That Saviour God the captive's chain hath broken ;
   Reigns o'er the free : our tyrants were our Sins :
He reigns who rose, that God for man Who died,
Reigns from the Cross, and rules—the Crucified."

He told him all.   As when within the East
  The ascended sun is glassed in seas below
So that high Truth with light that still increased
  Lit in the listener's mind a kindred glow
Because that mind was loving, calm, and pure
With courage to believe and to endure.

In blank astonishment he stood at first,
  By Truth's strong beam though raptured yet half-dazed :
As when upon the eyes of angels burst
  Creation new created, so he gazed :
He questioned ; but his questions all were wise :
Therefore that Truth he sought became his prize.

Later he mused ; then spake : "Whilst yet a child
  Something I heard—my memory is not clear—
Of Christ, and her, His mother undefiled :
  Alas ! it sank no deeper than mine ear.
An old nurse whispered me that tale.   Ere long
She died, some said, for God.   Her heart was strong."

An hour gone by, Pancratius made demand,
  "That heavenly music, came it from above ?"
Cornelius then : " The persecutor's brand
  Rages against us : not from fear but love,
Love of Christ's poor—the weak, the babe—we hide :
If found we die : to seek our death were pride.

                                        F

"Men scoff at us as dwellers 'mid the tombs :
    Beneath your grandsire's woods, till late untrod,
Extends the largest of the Catacombs :
    There dwells the Christian Church, and sings to God :
Our hymns betray us oft.   Descending, thou
One day wilt hear them—When?"   He answered :
        "Now."

That twain in silence passed to where the mouth
    Of those dread caverns yawned ; they stooped beneath ;
Instant upon them fell that heat and drouth
    Which Nubian sands o'er wayworn pilgrims breathe :
Red torches glared the winding ways among ;
To roofs low-arched the lingering anthems clung.

Their latest echo dies : the Lector reads,
    Then speaks : plain, brief, and strong is his discourse :
"Brothers ! each day ye know the martyr bleeds ;
    What then ?   Does any fear that fleshly force
Can slay the soul ?   God lives that soul within,
And God is Life.   Death dwelleth but with sin.

"This day ye heard of David.   Who is he
    That strides o'er earth brass-armed, six cubits high?
And who that shepherd ?   Think you he will flee,
    Unarmed, a boy ?   A brook goes warbling by ;
Its song is glad ; its pebbles laugh : 'twixt whiles
That shepherd eyes his giant foe and smiles.

" He bends above that brook ; a stone he lifts ;
    He fits it on his sling ; he waves it round :
The giant spreads his hands ; he shifts and drifts
    Like drunkards.   Dead, he lies along the ground.
David unwounded triumphed ; sang ; reigned long :
The martyr reigns in death, and deathless is his song."

That eve Pancratius mused : "'Mid yonder vaults
    God holds His court, and love, and peaceful cheer :
Who rules in Rome?   There Vice her crown exalts
    Shameless yet sad ; beside her, Jest and Fear."
That night his dream was of that shepherd boy,
The sling, the stone.   He wakened full of joy.

Then with a solace never his before
    His thoughts reverted to his parents dead ;
" That Truth," he said, "they sought, yet missed, of yore,
    Is theirs this hour : its crown is on their head ;
Its sword within their hand.   That Christ whom we
Discern through mist they in God's glory see.

" Thank Heaven, my grandsire lives !"   Straight to his
      ear
    He brought his tale.   Upon that Roman's brow
Hung thunder-cloud : the things supremely dear
    To him were these, Reverence and Rule ; and now
A boy, a child that daily ate his bread,
Had heaped dishonour on his hoary head.

" Renounce thy madness, boy, or hence this day ! "
    Pancratius answered, with that winning smile
Dear to the sad man's heart, " Not so : I stay !
    There cometh one your anger to beguile ;
I told him you were good : thus answered he,
' Good-will means Faith : the Truth shall set him free.' "

Thus as he spake the mitred Sire of Rome,
    Without disguise, his pastoral staff in hand,
Entered : " I seek, great sir, your ancient home,
    By you unbidden, at this youth's command :
If this molests you, you can have my head :
The law proscribes, the Emperor wills me dead."

Silent the Roman noble sat : anon
    A glance on that strange guest at random thrown
Wrought in him change : then first he looked on one
    Of presence more majestic than his own.
" Cornelius is your name ; unless I err,
Yours is that ancient stock Cornelian, sir.

" Within this mansion I abide recluse ;
    I with the Emperor slight acquaintance boast,
None with his court.   Such things may have their use ;
    They pass us quickly.   As becomes a host
All guests alike I honour, old or new ;
I war on no man, but converse with few.

" Perhaps you come with tidings : if from me
  Aught you require, speak briefly, without art."
Cornelius smiled, then answered placidly,
  " To each the self-same tidings I impart :
Beside your house a gold-mine lurks ; with you
Remains to sink your shaft or miss your due."

Courteous that Roman bowed, yet scarcely listened ;
  Ere long he gave attention : by degrees
The strong, imperious eye now flashed, now glistened ;
  Point after point he seemed in turn to seize.
He proffered question none ; he spake no word,
In mind collected, but in spirit stirred.

Lo ! as some statued form of art antique,
  Solon or Plato, sits with brow hand-propt
And eyes the centre of the earth that seek,
  So sat he, when that strain majestic stopt,
In silence long. He raised his eyes, and then
Spake thus alone : " In three days come again."

Three days went by ; in that dim room once more
  Cornelius spake : inly Pancratius prayed ;
The old man listened mute. His message o'er,
  The Venerable Sign the Pontiff made
Above that low-bent forehead. With it grace
Fell from on high and lit that hoary face.

Then questioned thus that man severe and grave :
  "What was the birthplace of this Creed decried
Which in all lands attracts the meek and brave?"
  To whom the Roman Pontiff thus replied :
"Judah—not Greece!   Fishers, not seers, went forth ;
They preached that Creed, and died to prove its worth."

His host : "This Faith is then at least no dream—
  A dream, albeit perchance of dreams the best
In youth I deemed it, and dismissed the theme :
  Pity 'tis new!   'Tis Time doth Truth attest."
The answer came : "This Faith is old as man :
'The Woman's Seed.'   It ends as it began.

"This is that Faith which over-soars the sage
  Yet condescends to him, the peasant boy :
This is that Hope which brightest shines in age
  All others quenched : this is that Love, that Joy,
Which all retrieves ; to patriots worn that cries
'Thy great, true Country waits thee in yon skies.'"

The Roman next : "The Creeds of ages past
  Lived long ; yet most have died ; the rest wax old :
Yours is the amplest : it will prove the last :
  For he who, having clasped it, slips his hold
Shall find none other.   Of the seas of Time
This is high-water mark, stamped on the cliffs sublime.

" Not less that question, 'Is it true?' recurs.
    What Virtue is, by virtuous life is shown :
She lights the paths she walks on ; no man errs
    Who treads them. Would that Truth might thus be
        known !
Sir, I must ponder these things. Agèd men
Perforce are slow. In ten days come again."

In ten days more that Christian priest returned :
    The Roman noble met him at the door,
But altered. " You are welcome ! I have yearned
    To see your face and hear again your lore.
At times I grasp it tight : but I am old :
Close-clutched it slides like sand from out my hold.

" Mark well yon Sabine and yon Alban ranges !
    The north wind blows ; clear shineth each ravine :
Thus clear stands out your Creed: the north wind changes;
    The clouds rush in, and vapours shroud the scene :
Thus dims more late that Creed. My end draws nigh :
Honest it were Truth's Confessor to die."

Cornelius answered, " Sir, not flesh and blood
    But God's own Finger wrote one sacred word
Upon your heart when by you, first I stood :
    That word was ' Christ.' Brave man ! In this you erred,
Not seeking then and there that conquering light
Which shines, like sunrise, on the baptism rite."

Hour after hour, and far into the morn,
  Those two conversed of God.   That saintly sage
Witnessed, not argued.   "Truth," he said, "is born
  Alike in heart of childhood and of age,
A spirit-birth.   Invoke that Spirit by whom
God become Man hallowed the Virgin's womb."

To all demands he made the same reply :
  Within that old man's breast—by slow degrees
Stirred like Bethesda's waters tremulously—
  God's Truths put on God's splendour. "Men like trees
Walking," in mist at first such seemed they ; then
They trod the earth like angels, not like men.

Sudden that old man rose ; he cried, "I see !
  Thank God !   The scales are fallen from mine eyes !
I see that Infant on His Mother's knee,
  That Saviour on His Cross, man's Sacrifice.
It could not but be thus !   From heaven to earth
That Cross fills all ; all else is nothing worth ! "

At sunrise he received baptismal grace ;
  And ever from that hour its radiance glowed
A better sunrise on his wrinkled face,
  For all his heart with gladness overflowed,
And childhood's innocence returned ; and all
His childhood loved seemed near him at his call.

Once more the aspirations of his youth
　About him played like pinions ; by his side
Now better known than when her nuptial truth
　To him she pledged, beside him walked his bride ;
And to that love he bore his Land returned
That hope, long quenched, wherewith it once had burned

Still as of old his country's past he praised :
　" Numa revered one God ; no idols crowned ;
Two altars—holy were they both—he raised ;
　One was for Terminus who guards the Bound ;
One was for Faithfulness who keeps the Pledge :
These spurned, he taught, all rites are sacrilege.

" A matron wronged dragged down the race of Kings ;
　A virgin wronged hurled forth those Ten from Rome :
Omen and auspice these of greater things ;
　Of Truth reserved to make with her its home.
Man needs that aid ! The proof? Man lives to act ;
And noblest deeds are born of Faith and Fact."

Yet, though before him ever stood the vision
　Of that high Truth which gives the human soul
Of visible things sole mastery and fruition,
　More solid seemed he, and in self-control
More absolute, than of old ; and from his eye
Looked lordlier forth its old sobriety.

In him showed nothing of enthusiasm,
    Of thought erratic wistful for strange ways,
Nothing of phrase fantastic, passion's spasm,
    Or self-applause masking in self-dispraise :
Some things to him once great seemed now but small :
In small things greatness dwelt, and God in all.

Three months gone by, he freed his slaves ; above
    That rock, the portal of that Catacomb,
He raised an altar " To the Eternal Love "
    Inscribed : more low he built his humble tomb :
" Not far," he said, " repose God's martyrs ; I,
Albeit unworthy, near to them would lie."

In one month more serene and glad he died ;
    An hour ere death painless the old man lay,
Those two that loved him watching at his side :
    " In Christ, yet not for Christ," they heard him say ;
" This is the sole of Faiths, for which to bleed
Were wholly sage.   My son had loved this Creed."

The tidings that a noble of the old race
    Had spurned the old rites transpired not till that hour
Which laid him in his woodland burial-place ;
    'Twas Diocletian's day : the Imperial power
Had made decree to trample to the ground
God's Church.   A worthy victim it had found.

For when about the dead the Romans thronged
  Much wondering at the unwonted obsequies
Nor pleased to see their old traditions wronged,
  Pancratius answered, " Christian rites are these ; "
Then made proclaim to all men far and nigh,
" My grandsire died a Christian : such am I."

Two pagan priests to Diocletian sped :—
  " Yon man who died an atheist left an heir ;
Asian he is, a Christian born and bred :
  Shall that new Faith with Jove and Cæsar share ?
Usurp a Roman noble's place and pride ? "
" Bring here that youth," the Emperor replied.

That Emperor looked upon the Gods as those
  Who shared his reign.   In majesty and mirth
They sat enskied above the Olympian snows :
  The Goddess Rome, their last-born, ruled the earth ;
The Roman Emperor was her husband.   He
Partook perforce in their divinity.

The inferior Gods of barbarous realms scarce known
  Rome's latest conquests in the utmost East,
Revered the Roman Gods.   One God alone
  Refused with them to traffic, share their feast ;
His votaries served Him only ; Gods beside
They banned as Idol-Gods, and Rome defied.

That Emperor was not cruel; from the height
  Of that imagined greatness gazing down
To rule he deemed his duty as his right;
  The world his kingdom was, and Rome its crown:
Who spurned that crown he deemed as sense-bereaven,
Rebel 'gainst earth, and blasphemous 'gainst heaven.

Next day at noon within his judgment court
  He sat, by all his pomp of majesty
Compassed and guarded; lion-like his port;
  Then whispered man to man: " That terrible eye
Without yon Lictors' axes or their rods,
Will drive the renegade to his country's Gods."

Pancratius entered—entered with a smile;
  Bowed to the Emperor; next to those around
First East, then West.   The Emperor gazed awhile
  On that bright countenance; knew its import; frowned:
" A malefactor known !   Yet there you stand !
Young boy, be wise in time.   Hold forth your hand !

" Yon censer mark !   It comes from Jove's chief fane;
  See next yon vase cinctured with flower-attire :
Lift from that vase its smallest incense-grain;
  Commit it softly to yon censer's fire :
Your father, boy, was well with me; and I
Would rather serve his son than bid him die."

Pancratius mused a moment, then began :
  " Emperor, 'tis true I am a boy ; no more :
But One within me changes boy to man,
  Christ, God and Man, that Lord the just adore.
A pictured lion hangs above thy head :
Say, can a picture touch man's heart with dread ?

" Thou, too, great Emperor, art but pictured life :
  He only lives who quickened life in all :
Men are but shadows : in a futile strife
  They chase each other on a sun-bright wall.
Shadows are they the hosts that round thee throng ;
Shadows their swords that vindicate this wrong.

" What Gods are those thou bidst me serve and praise ?
  Adulterers, murderers, Gods of fraud and theft.
If slave of thine walked faithful in their ways
  What were his sentence ? Eyes of light bereft ;
The scourge, the rope ! Our God is Good. His Name
Paints on His servants' face no flush of shame.

" Exteriorly, 'tis true, thy Gods are great,
  They and their sort : this hour they rule the lands :
Ay, but, expectant at an unbarred gate,
  A greatness of a different order stands,
The Babe of Bethlehem's. He thy Gods shall slay
Though small His hand, and rend earth's chain away."

The Emperor shook : as one demon-possessed
    He glared upon that youth ; his wan cheek burned :
With wonder dumb panted his struggling breast :
    Silent to that Prætorian Guard he turned ;
He pointed to Pancratius.   " Let him die ! "
Pancratius stood, and pointed to the sky.

That night a corse beside the Aurelian Way
    Lay as in sleep.   Hard by, two maidens fair
Now knelt and lifted high their hands to pray,
    Now bent and kissed his cheek and smoothed his hair :
Two daughters of a Roman matron these :
A grove not far shook, moonlit, in the breeze.

O fair young love—for when could love show fairer ?
    O maids, should earthly love e'er house with you,
With love thus heavenly may that love be sharer ;
    Like this be cleansing, hallowing, self-less, true !
Thou too, O boy, love's guerdon hast not missed
Though young, by lips so pure so kindly kissed.

A youth he lay of fourteen years in seeming ;
    A lily by the tempest bent, not broken :
Round the lashed lids a smile divine was gleaming ;
    And if that mouth, so placid, could have spoken
Plainly its speech had been : " Thank Heaven, 'tis past !
The secret of the skies is mine at last."

Softly those maidens with their mother bore
    Pancratius to that grove, and made his grave :
O'er his light limbs the radiant scarfs they wore
    Softly they spread.   Such wreaths as grace the brave
On him they strewed next morn, and buds of balm ;
And by that grave planted the martyr's palm.

Near it the Roman Walls ascend, and Gate
    Aurelian called of old, Pancratian now,
Honouring that youth who smiling met his fate
    So soon, so gladly kept his baptism vow.
King Numa's " Faithfulness " in him was found ;
Therefore old " Terminus " guards still that bound.

Some say that when that Gate to him was given
    A mystery therein was signified :
Earth hath her " Holy City ; " but in heaven
    A holier waits us : one that aye shall bide :
Twelve gates it hath : each boasts high trust and fief :
The Gate of Martyrdom of these is chief.

Yea, and the Martyr is himself a gate,
    Since through the fiery ether of his prayer
Which Vision blest kindles and doth dilate
    Who strives for heaven finds help to enter there.
O Martyr young, by Death made glad and free,
In Death's dread hour pray well for mine and me !

THE LEGEND OF SAINT DOROTHEA.

(DIED A.D. 287.)

ARGUMENT.

Saint Dorothea on the death of her parents is reared a Christian by her nurse, near Cæsarea. Fabricius, its Prefect, desires to marry her ; but she has vowed to belong wholly to Christ. The Prefect throws her into prison as a despiser of the Gods. He sends to her there two sisters, beautiful but of evil life, who in their youth had abandoned the Faith, and promises them much gold if they can induce her to apostatize. They are themselves won back by Dorothea, and die martyrs. She is then sentenced to death. On her way to the place of execution, a certain youth derides her, promising to become a Christian if on entering heaven she sends him flowers and fruits, the ground being then covered with snow. She sends them. The youth keeps his word, and dies for Christ.

In Cappadocia, close to Cæsarea
   A babe was born beneath a star benign,
A star whose light was laughter, Dorothea,
   The last, best offspring of an ancient line :
That name her parents gave her, for they said,
" She is God's gift : God's pathways she shall tread."

As spreads some water-lily on a river,
  Whitening the dark wave in some shady nook,
So grew that babe in beauty, winning ever
  A grace more winsome and more beaming look :
The Pagans as they passed her stood and gazed :
The Christians blessed her, and her Maker praised.

At three years old a spirit of peace and gladness
  She moved : whoever passed her, all that day
Forgot all fretful spleen or wayward sadness :
  Shy creatures shunned not her : the birds, men say,
Would perch, as in greenwood she took her stand,
One on her shoulder, one upon her hand.

Her parents gloried in her more and more :
  Prosperous for years, their cup was brimmed at last—
Frail lot of man ! A sudden storm of war
  Broke on the land. Domestic traitors massed
With alien hordes resistless made the wrong :
Dire was the conflict ; but it dured not long.

Brave hearts and true ! While hope remained, they fought ;
  When treason triumphed they nor wept nor sighed :
They said, " The worst is come ; and worst is nought :"—
  They faced the desert : fever-struck they died :
Where Plantains shadow Melas' watery bed
Her nurse concealed their orphan's shining head.

That nurse had saved a casket jewel-laden :
    It kept the twain from hunger.   Day by day
She bound with pearls the dark hair of the maiden,
    Then bade her join that region's babes at play.
Ere long the pearls were sold : all debts were paid :
That old nurse treasured still the crimson braid.

She told her nursling of her parents' greatness
    Mindful that childhood's memories soon depart ;
Their strength, their state, in danger their sedateness,
    In peace their help to all and generous heart :
" Be sure that thousands weep, this day, their fall !
Likeliest the men who wrought it most of all."

She told her of their palace in the mountains,
    Their stag-hunts, and their bugles on the wind,
Their gardens flushed with flowers and dinned with
        fountains,
    Their galleries long with page and menial lined :
Pages and menials to the girl were nought ;
Each name of garden flower, and fruit she sought.

But other themes, and loftier far than these,
    That nurse discoursed on. " Kneel, my child, and pray !
What music, think'st thou, were those lullabies
    Thy mother sang above thy cot ?   Each day
While sinks the sun the self-same songs are sung
In yon low church those Plantains old among."

Thenceforth to that low church in woodlands hidden
  The child went oft through skirting willows grey
On Melas' bank. Fearless, though guest unbidden,
  She knelt; prayed well, though taught by none to pray :
The prayer came to her as to birds their song :
Soon learned she more from Nuns who dwelt those trees
    among.

Things wondrous most to Dorothea seemed
  Easiest of Faith. That God should be All-Wise,
All-Good, All-Great, such Truth upon her beamed
  With rapture always ; never with surprise ;
The pettiness of life, man's hate, his pride—
These things surprised her : 'twas for these she sighed.

Whate'er held in it nought of fair and true
  Like wind passed by her. Lovely things and fair
That once had found her never bade adieu :
  Far down into her heart they made repair,
And there, awaiting wings, in trance of bliss
Kept sleeping watch like silk-sheathed chrysalis.

At times some act in woodland beast or bird
  Thus sealed within her bosom, sudden waking,
Would flash a gleam upon the Preacher's word
  As when the dawn through cleft of cloud-land breaking
Illumes a distant stream. Half thought, half sense,
Some new Truth then fired her intelligence.

Shapes outward thus to heavenly meanings mated,
  The world became to her, now maiden grown,
A world transformed, and transubstantiated :
  A Mountain of Transfiguration shone
Around her, wide as earth ; and far and near
Still heard she, " It is good to tarry here."

None knew how wise she was ; for still with her
  Each Truth, when mastered, changed from Thought
    to Love
By alchemy divine.   An atmosphere
  Of loving Faith thus wrapped her from above :
All helpful tasks her hands enjoyed as much
As though a lute responded to their touch.

Those holy Nuns in their Scriptorium small
  Treasured some sacred scrolls : of these was one
Most prized, most honoured, most beloved of all,
  The Tidings Good and Letters of Saint John :
Upon that scroll by day the maiden fed :
And when the moonbeams lit her pallet bed.

Trial came soon.   Within the neighbouring city
  Fabricius dwelt, its Præfect.   Impious love
He felt for her ; a love that knew not pity :
  His vows she deemed but jest : later he strove
To win her for a wife, yet strove in vain :
One time she answered—'twas not in disdain—

" I am a Prince's Bride.   In heaven—unseen—
 He dwells : I join Him but through gates of death :
Yet happier am I than earth's proudest queen,
 Since exiles too may serve that Prince ; each breath,
Each thought, each act of spirit, or heart, or hand
Be bride's obedience to her Lord's command."

Frowning the Præfect spoke : " A dreamer ! fie !
 A Nympholept subdued by magic spell !
That Bridegroom-Prince you boast beyond the sky
 Exists not : there our great Olympians dwell."
She smiled : ' " Each morning from His gardens He
Three apples sends to me, and roses three."

Some say she spake as children speak that glory
 To toss in sunshine words but used in jest :
Some say she taught mysteries in allegory,
 Banquets of Souls and triumphs of the Blest ;
Some think she told a simple truth, nor knew
'Twas wondrous more than that the heavens are blue.

Not far, as gaily thus that bright one spake,
 There stood a youth, Theophilus by name,
Who lived but tales to tell and jests to make :
 Some swore he earned his dinner by the same :
Yet others thought him sad, and that he went
To feasts to drown dark thoughts in merriment.

" Lady," he said, " I grant that flower and fruit
　　Beseems such beauty : yet, if guess were mine,
I deem that, sweetened more, by lyre or lute,
　　Such gifts are likelier laid upon such shrine
By some pale youth that haunts yon Plantain grove
Than winged from heaven by cloud-compelling Jove."

The smile had vanished from her young, fair face :
　　There reigned, instead, great sadness—nought beside—
No touch of anger.　Mute she stood a space ;
　　Then, looking at him sweetly, thus replied ;
" You scoff : when died your mother long ago
You wept : more noble are you than you know."

That year the Decian Persecution raged
　　Against God's Church.　To attest at Rome his zeal
Fiercelier than all beside Fabricius waged
　　That war : ere long, wounded self-love to heal,
He sent, in vengeance for rejected vows,
To dungeon vaults whom late he sought for spouse.

Next day two sisters, beauteous but ill-famed,
　　Who, years before, had left the Christian fold,
Christea and Calista they were named,
　　He sped to her.　" Rich jewels and much gold
Shall be your meed ; but first yon proud one draw
To serve our Gods, and spurn her Christian Law."

They went : she welcomed them : with speeches fair
  They praised the vanities of earthly life,
Its pleasures and its pomps ; and bade her spare
  Her youth, unfit to meet the ensanguined knife,
The rack, the flame. She sat in silence long ;
Then rose like one inspired advanced and flung

Round them her arms. At last with many a tear
  Showering the chaplets on each festive head
She spake : " Ah me, sisters unknown, yet dear !
  Are ye not orphans ? Are your parents dead ?
Remains no friend to help you ? None to say,
' Repent the past ! Rejoice some future day ! '

" O by the memory of your spotless youth,
  You said 'twas Christian ; by those happy years
When strong ye walked in simpleness and truth
  Perhaps the wonder of your gamesome peers,
By all the tears shed o'er some first, small sin—
'Tis not too late—your better life begin !

" Perhaps they brought you up in ways too soft
  And, sorely tried, you feared for Christ to die :
And yet for you He died ! He lives ! Full oft,
  Chiefly in saddest hours, He standeth nigh :
He woos you to that peace whereof bereft
Ye pine. Ye left Him : you He never left."

Heart-pierced those sinners stood in mute amaze,
   For they heart-sore full many a wasted year
Had walked in flattered sin's forlornest ways
   Yet never loving voice had reached their ear :
A love from interest free, unsmirched by sense,
Was strange.   They knew not what it was nor whence.

Again she spake : remembrance of a time
   In which the spirit watched, the body slept,
Came back to them ; when, tender yet sublime
   A breeze from heaven through all their being swept :
Again it blew, for Love that conquers death
Had wakened Hope.   By both awakened, Faith

New-born from dark emerged like sun from ocean
   In climes where Day treads close on skirts of Night :
Torn was each heart with wildly mixed emotion :
   That sun was red and threatening, yet 'twas bright :
The Saint a cross drew slowly from her breast :
They kissed it ; with her wept ; and were at rest.

In two weeks more misgiving had departed :
   Old truths, now learned anew, they learned to feel :
Then came what comes alone to those deep-hearted,
   That high and glad " revenge " of loving zeal :
They sought their judge : that Faith by them denied
In girlhood they confessed, and martyrs died.

Next day the Præfect sentenced to the sword
    That maid who to their royal Shepherd, Christ,
Those wanderers from His sheepfold had restored ;
    What Christians name " restored " he named " enticed."
Silent she heard : serene to death she passed :
Throngs girt her round, some weeping, all aghast.

Then many a time neighbour to neighbour spake,
    " Is not this maid the same whom, two weeks since,
Our Præfect bound with chains her will to break
    And wrest her, recreant, from her heavenly Prince ?
I stood close by when thus Fabricius said,
' A cell the darkest ; and your blackest bread.'

" Yet not like face of faster is her face,
    But like some bride radiant with gladsome life ;
And o'er the ways snow-cumbered she doth pace
    Like youths to fields of honourable strife
Where victory waits their country ! Mark that eye !
What sees it regioned in yon cheerless sky ?"

Half-way between the prison and place of doom
    The Præfect's palace frowned. Beside its door
Theophilus stood. No touch of pity or gloom
    That rueful day his mobile countenance bore.
" Lady, 'twas June when last we met—Remember !
'Tis now your frosty feast in late December.

"That June I said your flowers and fruits were sent
  Not by a heavenly but a human lover,
Not one that thunders in the firmament
  But one who pipes in yonder Plantain cover :
He'll send you none this day : for leagues the snow
Cumbers the earth : for months no bud will blow.

"Doubtless a God even now from heaven might send
    them :
  If sent, those amorous trophies speed to me !
What Christians call good fortune will attend them :
  Thenceforth your Master's follower I will be ! "
She passed ; looked back ; stood mute ; then smiling still
That smile he knew, nodded, and said, " I will."

She reached the spot.   Lo, where in snowy vest
  Stands the pure victim, modest, shy, yet still,
While two old crones from throat to vestal breast
  Draw its warm fold that so with practised skill
The headsman grey, though failing now in sight,
May note his mark and plant his stroke aright.

Then came, the Legend saith, from heaven a Sign :
  For, while the raised sword flashed before her eyes,
O'er her an Angel hung, a Child divine
  On purple wings starred like the midnight skies—
" From Him thou lovest, these."   She answered thus ;
" Not mine ! I sought them for Theophilus."

That moment at the Præfect's festal board
    That mocker sat, and in his airiest mood,
When lo, between him and the banquet's lord
    A beauteous Child lifting a casket stood.
Sweet-voiced he spake—yet they that heard him feared—
" From Dorothea these," and disappeared.

Theophilus clasped that casket, ill at ease,
    The Præfect opened. Lo, three apples golden
That waxed in radiance till by slow degrees
    The unnumbered torches round the board high-hoiden
Were lost therein. The great hall shone more bright
Than heaven when August's sun has scaled its height.

Next from that casket forth he drew three roses :
    The scent thereof that palace filled as when
The dawn-mist raised, some blossoming vale discloses
    A world of flowers ; and all the wind-swept glen
Grows satiate with the sweets that o'er it stream
Seaward, dissolving in the matin beam.

Long time that night through alley, court, and street
    The Præfect's guard that Child all-beauteous sought
Despite the wildering snow and wounding sleet ;
    Sought him to slay him : when they found him not,
The courtiers swore that marvel was but fancy ;
The priests, imposture mixed with necromancy.

Again the revellers revelled; all save one,
  The last in whom till then or friend or foe
Had looked for serious thought or deed well done:
  Propping on steadfast hand a head bent low
Theophilus mused.   Still in his heart he said,
" How knew she that I loved my mother dead?

" I hid my grief."   At dawn o'er snow-plains frore
  He saw that Plantain grove and narrow field,
And slowly t'ward them moved, like one in war
  Wounded nigh death and yet not wholly healed,
And found, half hid in trees, a chapel low:
Its altar-lights gold-barred the frozen snow.

Its door stood open:—lo! a choir of Nuns,
  'Twas Christmas morn, around a cradle kneeling
Wherein an imaged Infant lay, at once
  To woman-instinct and to Faith appealing,
The Bethlehem Babe.   Low-voiced they sang a hymn;
Then sought their convent nigh through vapours dim.

The young man followed—questions many made
  Of her by them so loved; so lately dead:
They wept; they smiled; that slender crimson braid
  Kept by her nurse, which wound the young child's head,
They showed; and showed on Melas' bank that stone
Whereon each morn the maid had knelt alone.

Somewhat they told him of her later days ;
   But early and late were now alike gone by,
And dear things kenned through memory's farthest haze
   To them seemed dearer yet than dear things nigh :
"All she became she was," they said, " even then,
A Saint to Angels whilst a child to men.

" O what a charity was hers ! All night
   Last June for one a moment seen she prayed
On yonder stone ! She said, ' his words were light ;
   Yet sinners worse have oft, with God to aid,
Made happy deaths.' Farewell, sir ; we must go:"
He sought that stone : no more his steps were slow.

There as he mused, drew near an aged Sire
   Who served that chapel from his cell hard by
With peril to his life and not for hire :
   He to that questioning youth made kind reply,
And showed him what that is in Christian faith
Which, sweetening life, more deeply sweetens death.

Feeble that old man looked ; depressed his head
   Save when he spake : then tall he grew once more;
It seemed as though his body long since dead
   Lived through his spirit's life, like those of yore,
Salem's old Saints who, when the Saviour died,
From graves close-sealed arose and prophesied.

When stared that youth as one who stares through mist,
    Seeking lost paths, he added ; " Love can see :
'Tis wondrous less the All-Wondrous should exist
    Than that, without Him, man should live, or tree.
If God be Love, that God for man should bleed
Is natural as that flowers should come of seed.

" Three steps suffice ; from Nature first to God ;
    From God to Love ; from Love to Calvary's Cross :
The bird that builds, the beast that crops the sod,
    Know all which not to know were deadly loss
To their small being.   Think'st thou God hath left
His noblest work of needfullest light bereft ?

" Live thou no more in thraldom !   Rome was great :
    Her Virtue made her great : Greatness can die :
Virtue's reward brings Pride ; and Pride brings Fate :
    A maniac that declines to idiotcy
Is Rome this day.   Her blessing spurn : her ban !
To be a Christian learn to be a man ! "

Faith came at last.   That mocker long abused
    By tricksome follies cast that bond aside :
The better genius in his spirit was loosed :
    He kept his pledge : martyr for Christ he died :
And still when Dorothea's Feast its grace
Bestows, Theophilus with her hath place.

I.

CONSTANTINE IN THRACE.

(A.D. 324.)

ARGUMENT.

The Emperor Constantine, the day before he reaches Byzantium, projects the building of Constantinople upon its site, esteeming that site the fittest for the metropolis of a Christian Empire, or, more properly, of a Christian Caliphate, one and universal, to be created by him. He resolves, that task completed, to be baptized ; but not till then.

HA, Pagan City ! hast thou heard the tidings,
Rome, the world's mistress, whom I never loved !
Whilst yet a boy I read of thy renown,
Thy Kings, Thy Consuls, and thine Emperors,
Thy triumphs, slow but certain, in all lands,
Yet never yearned to see thy face.   Thy heart
Was as my heart—averse, recalcitrant.

I left my charge ; I clave that British sea ;
I crossed the snowy Alps ; I burst thy chain ;
I drowned thy tyrant in the Tiber's wave,
Maxentius, him whose foot was on thy neck :
I sat lip-worshipp'd on thy Palatine Hill ;

But well I knew that to that heart of thine
Nero's black memory was a welcomer thing
Than all my glories.   Hast thou heard the tidings?
The Cross of Christ is found!   By whom?   Not thee!
Thou grop'st and grovel'st in the gold-stream's bed
Not there where lies the Cross!   I, Constantine
The Unbaptized, am cleaner thrice than thou—
I found it through my mother!   The Cross is found!

    I left thee: I had heard a mighty voice:
Eastward it called me : there Licinius reigned,
Ill-crowned compeer and of my rivals last,
Who made the inviolate Empire twain, not one :
One crown suffices earth.   Licinius fell :
I saw him kneeling at his conqueror's feet :
I saw him seated at his conqueror's board :
I spared him, but dethroned.   New tumults rose :
Men said they rose through him.   Licinius died;
"Twas rumoured, by my hand : I never loved him :
The truth came out at last :   I let it be.

    He died : that day the Empire stood uncloven,
One as in great Augustus' regal prime,
One as when Trajan reigned and Adrian reigned—
Great kings, though somewhat flecked with Christian
     blood :—
Whom basest Emperors spared the best trod down ;
I judge them not for that : not yet had dawned

That day when Faith could be the base of Empire.
The Antonines came later, trivial stock,
Philosophers enthroned.   Philosophers!
I never loved them : Life to me was teacher :
That great Cæsarian Empire is gone by :
'Twas but the old Republic in a mask
With Consul, Tribune, Pontiff rolled in one :
A great man wrought its ruin, Diocletian :
The greatest save those three who built it up :
He split his realm in four.   Amid the wreck
What basis now subsists for permanent empire ?
Religion.   Of Religions one remains :
The rest are dead Traditions, not Religion.
The old gods stand in ivory, stone, and gold
Dozing above the dust-heaps round their feet :
The Flamen dozes on the altar-step :
The People doze within the colonnades :
The Augurs pass each other with a smile :
The Faith that lives is Christ's.   Three hundred years
The strong ones and the wise ones trod it down :
Red flames but washed it clean—I noted that :
This day the Christian Empire claims its own.
The Christian Empire—stranger things have been ;
Christ called His Church a Kingdom.   Such it is :
The mystery of its strength is in that oneness
Which heals its wounds, and keeps it self-renewed.

It rises fair with order and degree,
And brooks division none.   That realm shall stand ;
I blend therewith my Empire ; warp and woof
These twain I intertwine.   Like organism
Shall raise in each a hierarchy of powers
Ascending gradual to a single head,
The Empire's head crowned in the Empire's Church.
The West dreamed never of that realm twin-dowered
With spiritual sway and temporal : the East,
I think, was never long without such dream,
Yet shaped not dream to substance.   Persia failed :
Earlier, the Assyrian and the Babylonian ;
Colossal structures these, but scarcely noble :
The Alexandrian Empire later came
And more deserved to live.   A better fault
Was hers, a bodiless fragment shaped of cloud :
The Conqueror lacked material ; he had naught
To work on save the dialectics keen
And Amphionic song of ancient Greece.
His dream was this—an Empire based on Mind,
The large Greek Mind.   Mind makes a base unstable :
Large minds have ever skill to change their mind :
Then comes the fabric down.   He died a youth,
A stripling ; ay, but had his scheme been sound
'Tis likely he had lived.   Religion lives.
Perhaps a true Faith only could sustain

A permanent Empire's burthen. Mine is true :
If any speaks against it he shall die :
'Tis known long since I brook not bootless battles.
   The Church had met in synod, for a man
Had made division in that "seamless robe"
Regal this day. Arius schismatic stood
For what? A doctrine! Fool! and knew he not
The essence of Religion is a Law?
Doctrine is but the standard o'er it flying
To daunt, to cheer; daunt foes, and cheer the friend.
What was that Hebrew Church? A sceptred Law
Set up in Saul, and, when that strong man died,
Less aptly in the Shepherd with the harp.
The Church had met in synod at Nicæa,
Nicæa near Byzantium. There was I :
The Church in synod sat and I within it.
Flocking from every land her bishops came ;
They sat and I in the midst, albeit in Rome
My title stood, "Pontifex Maximus."
They came at my command, by me conveyed.
A man astonished long I sat ; I claimed
To sit "a bishop for the things without."
Amid those bishops some were Confessors
Maimed by the fire or brand. I kissed their wounds :
None said, " What dost thou 'mid the Prophet Race ? "
They saw I honoured God, and honoured me.

Day after day went on the great debate,
And gradual in me knowledge grew.   'Twas strange !
I, neither priest nor layman ; I, that ne'er
Had knelt a Catechumen in the porch,
I, patron of the Church, yet not her son,
Her Emperor, yet an Emperor unbaptized,
I sat in the synod.   At the gates stood guards :
Not all were Christian : two, the best, were bold :
One from Danubius winked at me ; and one
From Rhenus smiled at me.   The weeks went by,
And in me daily swelled some spirit new :
I know it now ; it was the imperial spirit.
The imperial spirit—ay !   I at the first
Had willed the question should be trivial deemed,
And license given, " think, each man, what he will."
The fires had burned too deep for that : I changed :
I sided with the strong, and kept the peace :
Rulers must take my course, or stand o'er-ruled.

   That was my triumph's hour : then came the fall.
I made return to Rome.   Twelve years gone by
My sword had riven the Western tyrant's chain :
Since then the tyrant of the East had perished :
The world was echoing with my name.   I reached
The gate Flaminian and the Palatine ;
I looked for welcome such as brides accord
Their lords new-laurelled.   Rome, a bride malign,

Held forth her welcome in a poisoned cup :
Mine Asian garb, my ceremonious court,
Its trappings, titles, and heraldic gear,
To her were hateful.   Centuries of bonds
Had left her swollen with Freedom's vacant name :
A buskined greatness trampled still her stage :
By law the gods reigned still.   The senate sat
In Jove's old temple on the Capitol :
My fame Nicæan edged their hate.   The priest
Shouldering through grinning crowds to sacrifice
Cast on me glance oblique.   Fabii and Claudii
Whose lives hung powerless on their Emperor's nod
Eyed me as he who says, " This man is new."
One festal morning to some pagan fane
The whole Equestrian Order rode—their wont—
In toga red.   I saw, and laughing cried,
" Better their worship than their horsemanship ! "
That noon the rabble pressed me in the streets
With wrong premeditate ; hissed me ; spat at me :
That eve they brake my statues.   Choice was none
Save this, to drown the Roman streets in blood
Or feign indifference.   Scorn, twelve years of scorn—
Changed suddenly to hate.   A fevered night
Went by, and morning dawned.
                                        My council met ;
Then came that fateful hour, my wreck and ruin.

Fausta, my wife, hated her rival's son,
Mine eldest born, my Crispus ; hated her
The glory and the gladness of my youth
By me for Empire's sake repudiated,
The sweetness of whose eyes looked forth from his.
She lived but in one thought—to crown her sons,
My second brood, portioning betwixt those three
My realm when I was dead.
My brothers holp her plot.   She watched her time :
She waited till the eclipse which falls at seasons
Black on our House was dealing with my soul ;
Then in that council-hall her minions rose ;
They spake ; they called their witnesses suborned,
Amongst them of my counsellors some the best ;
They brought their letters forged and spurious parch-
        ments,
And showed it plainer thrice than sun and moon
That he it was, my Crispus, Portia's child,
Who, whilst his sire was absent at Nicæa,
Month after month had plotted 'gainst him, made
His parricidal covenant with Rome :
The father was to fall in civil broil,
The son to reign.   Their league the day gone by
Had made its first assay.
                    That hour the Fates
Around me spread their net : that hour the chains

Of Œdipus were tangled round my feet :
I stood among them blind.

                    The noontide flamed :
I, in full council sitting—I since youth
A man of marble nerve and iron will,
A man in whom mad fancy's dreams alike
And fleshly lusts had held no part, subdued
By that Religion grave, a great Ambition ;
I self-controlled, continent in hate itself,
Deliberate and foreseeing—I that hour
Down on that judgment-parchment pressed my seal :
That was my crime, the greatest earth has known ;
My life's one crime.   I never wrought another.

   'Twas rage pent up 'gainst her I could not strike,
Rome, hated Rome !   I smote her through my son,
Her hope, the partner of her guilt.   That night
My purpose I repented.   'Twas too late :
The ship had sailed for Pola.   Tempest dire,
By demons raised, brake forth : pursuit was futile.
Within his Istrian dungeon Crispus died.
I willed that he, but not his fame, should perish ;
Therefore that deed was hid.   With brow sun-bright,
Hell in my heart, I took my place at feasts :
At last the deed was blabbed.

                    My mother loved—
My mother, Helena, the earth's revered one,

Cybéle of the Christians termed by Greeks—
Loved well my Crispus for his mother's sake,
Wronged, like herself, by royal nuptials new,
And hated Fausta with her younger brood.
She brake upon my presence like a storm :
With dreadful eyes and hands upraised she banned me :
She came once more, that time with manifest proof
Of Fausta's guilt.   The courtiers had confessed it ;
My brothers later ; last the Accursed herself.
Two days I sat in darkness : on the third
I sent to judgment Fausta and her crew :
That act I deem the elect of all my acts.
They died : at eve I rose from the earth and ate.

   But fifteen months before, I at Nicæa
Had sat a god below !   No more of that !
'Twas false, the rumour that by night, disguised,
I knelt before a pagan shrine, and sought
Pagan lustration from a pagan priest,
And gat for answer that for crime like mine
Earth held lustration none.

                               I built great fanes,
Temples which all the ages shall revere :
Saint Peter's huge Basilica ; Saint John's ;
I roamed from each to each, like him who sought
A place for penitence, and found it not ;
Then from that city doomed—O ! to what heights

I, loving not, had raised her !—forth I fared,
Never thenceforth to see her. Rome has reigned :
She had her thousand years. Unless some greatness
Hidden from man remains for man, her doom
Approaches—dust and ashes.

                   I went forth :
I deemed the God I served had cast me off :
The Pagan world I knew my foe : the Christian
Thundered against me from a thousand shores :
There was a dreadful purpose in my soul :
It was my mother saved me ! She, keen-eyed,
Discerned the crisis ; kenned the sole solution.
In expiation of my crime she sped
A holy pilgrim to the Holy Land :
She spread her hands above the sacred spot
As when the Mother-Beast updrags to light
The prey earth-hidden for her famished young :
Instinct had led her to it : she dug and dug ;
She found the world's one treasure, lost till then,
That Cross which saved the world. With lightning
    speed
The tidings went abroad : I marched : last night
I raised mine eyes to heaven. I ne'er was one
Of spirit religious, though my life was pure,
Austerely pure amid an age corrupt :
I never was a man athirst for wonders ;

My fifty years have witnessed three alone :
The first was this—while yet Maxentius lived,
My army nearing Rome, I marked in her,
Though bondslave long, a majesty divine ;
She seemed earth's sum of greatness closed in one :
Some help divine I needed to confront her :
That help was given : I looked aloft : I saw
In heaven the God-Man on His Cross, thenceforth
My battle-sign, " Labarum."   Yesternight
Once more I saw it !   He that hung thereon
Spake thus : " Work on, and fear not."

                        Those two Visions,
The first, the third, shine on me still as one :
The second was of alien race and breed.
New-throned in Rome I doubted oft her future :
One night I watched upon Mount Palatine,
My seat a half-wrought column.   It had lain
For centuries seven rejected, none knew why,
By earlier builders : in more recent times
Ill-omened it was deemed, yet unremoved.
The murmur from the City far beneath
Had closed my eyelids.   Sudden by me stood
A queenly Form, the Genius of great Rome ;
Regal her face ; her brow, though crowned, was ploughed
With plaits of age.   She spake : " Attend my steps."
Ere long I marked her footing the great sea

Eastward : I followed close.   Then came a change :
Seven hills before me glittered in her light :
Save these the world was dark.   I looked again :
On one of these she stood.   Immortal youth
Shone splendid from her face no long furrowed ;
And all her form was martial.   On her head
She bore a helm, and in her hand a spear
High-raised.   She plunged that spear into the soil,
And spake : " Build here my City and my Throne ;"
Then vanished from my sight.   High up I heard
The winnowing of great wings.   The self-same sound
Had reached me while that Goddess trod the sea :
'Twas Victory following that bright crest for aye.
Morn broke : I knew that site ; it was Byzantium ;
So be it !   There shall stand the second Rome,
Not on the plain far-famed that once was Troy,
A dream of mine in youth.

Byzantium !   Ay !

The site is there : there meet the double seas
Of East and West.   The Empire rooted there
Shall stand the wide earth's centre, clasping in one—
That earlier Rome was only Rome rehearsed—
The Alexandrian and Cæsarean worlds :
Atlas and Calpé are our western bound ;
Ganges shall guard our Eastern.   To the North
Not Rhenus, not Danubius—that is past—

But Vistula and far Boristhenes;
Tanais comes next.   Those Antonines, poor dreamers,
Boasted their sageness, limiting their realm :
They spared Rome's hand to freeze her head and heart :
An Empire's growth surceased, its death begins :
Long death is shame prolonged.   Let Persia tremble !
Rome's sole of Rivals !   Distance shields her now :
My Rome shall fix on her that eye which slays :
She like a gourd shall wither.   O my son,
That task had been for thee !

                         Ha, Roman Nobles !
Your judgment-time approaches !   Shadows ye !
Shadows since then are ye !   Those shades shall flit :
My city shall be substance, not a shadow.
Ye slew the Gracchi ; they shall rise and plague you :
Ye clutched the Italian lands ; stocked them with slaves ;
Then ceased the honest wars : your reign shall cease :
Again, as when Fabricius left his farm
To scourge his country's foes, Italian hands
The hands of Latium, Umbria, and Etruria,
In honourable households bred, made strong
By labour on their native fields, shall fence
Their mother-land from insult.   Mercenaries !
Who made our Roman armies mercenary ?
Slave-lords that drave the free men from the soil !
Your mercenaries bought and sold the realm !

In sport or spleen they chose Rome's Emperors !
The British hosts chose me.   I, barbarous styled,
I Constantine decree that in the ranks
Of Rome the Roman blood, once more supreme,
Shall leave scant place for hirelings ill to trust :
The army to the Emperor shall belong,
Not he to it, henceforth,

                 On these seven hills—
The seven of Rome, with them compared, are pigmies—
I build earth's Empire City.   They shall lift
High up the temples of the Christian Law
Gold-domed, descried far off by homeward fleets,
Cross-crowned in record of my victory.
To it shall flock those senators of Rome
Their Roman brag surceased.   Their gods shall stand,
Grateful for incense doles diminishing daily,
If so they please, thronging the lower streets,
These, and the abjects of the Emperors dead ;
Ay, but from those seven hills to heaven shall rise
The Apostolic Statues, and mine own,
Making that race beneath ridiculous,
Above the Empire which that city crowns,
Above its Midland, Euxine, Caspian seas,
Above its Syrian Paradises lulled
By soft Orontes' and Euphrates' murmurs,
Above its Persian gardens, and the rush

Of those five Indian rivers o'er whose merge
The Man of Macedon sadly fixed his eastward eyes,
Above all these God's Angels keeping watch
From East to West shall sweep, for aye sustaining
My Standard, my " Labarum " !

       It shall last,
That Empire, till the world herself decays,
Since all the old Empires each from each devolved
It blends, and marries to a Law Divine.
Its throne shall rest on Right Hereditary,
Not will of splenetic legions or the crowd ;
Its Sovereigns be the elect of God, not man :
Its nobles round their lord shall stand, sun-clad
In light from him reflected ; stand in grades
Hierarchal, and impersonating, each,
Office and function, not the dangerous boast
Of mythic deeds and lineage. Age by age
Let those my Emperors that wear not names
Of Cæsar or Augustus, but my name,
Walk in my steps, honouring the Church aright :
The Empire and the Church must dwell together
The one within the other. Which in which ?
The Empire clasps the world ; clasps then the Church :
To shield that Church must rule her. Hers the gain :
I, who was never son of hers, enriched her
Making the ends o' the earth her heritage :

I ever knew 'tis poverty not wealth
That kindles knave to fanatic: silken saints
Like him of Nicomedia, my Eusebius,
Mate best with Empire's needs. When death draws nigh,
I, that was ever jealous lest the Font
Might give the Church of Christ advantage o'er me,
Will humbly sue for baptism, doffing then
My royal for my chrysome robe. Let those
Who through the far millenniums fill my throne
In this from me take pattern. Wise men choose
For wisest acts wise season.
                              Hark that trump !
The army wakens from its noontide rest :
Ere sunset fires its walls I reach Byzantium.

II..

CONSTANTINE AT CON-STANTINOPLE.

(A.D. 337.)

ARGUMENT.

The Emperor Constantine at Constantinople, a few days before his death, revolves his past life and the failure of his design for the creation of an Imperial Church under the Emperor's sway. He calls to mind several of the causes which have forced him with his own hand to break up the boasted unity of his Empire: but he suspects also the existence of some higher and hidden cause. His career he declares to be finished ; yet he suddenly decrees a new military expedition.

A MISSIVE from the Persian King! Those kings!
Their prayers and flatteries are more rankly base
Than those of humbler flatterers. I'll not read it :
Place it, Euphorbos, on my desk. 'Tis well :
The sea-wind curls its page but wafts me not
Its perfumed fetor. Leave me.

                  From the seas,
The streets, the Forum, from the Hippodrome,
From circus, bath, and columned portico,

But chiefly from the base of that huge pillar
Whereon Apollo's statue stood, now mine,
Its eastern-bending head rayed round with gold—
Say, dost thou grudge thy gift, Helopolis?—
The multitudinous murmur spreads and grows.
Wherefore? Because a life compact of pangs
Boasts now its four-and-sixtieth year, and last.
Give me that year when first I fought with beasts
In Nicomedia's amphitheatre;
Gallerius sent me there in hope to slay me:
Not less he laughed to see that panther die;
Laughed louder when I charged him with the crime.
Give me that year when first my wife—not Fausta—
That year when launching from the British shore
I ceased not till my standard, my Labarum,
Waved from the walls of Rome. When Troy had fallen
That brave and pious exile-prince, Æneas,
Presaged the site of Rome: great Romulus
Laid the first stone: Augustus laid the second:
I laid the last: 'twas mine to crown their work:
From her she flung me and her latest chance:
Eastward I turned.

         Three empires to the ground
I trod. My warrant? Unauthentic they:
Their ruling was misrule. Huge, barbarous hosts
I hurled successive back o'er frozen floods:

Yet these, the labours of my sword, were naught :
The brain it was that laboured.   I have written
The laws that bind a province in one night :
Such tasks have their revenge.   O for a draught
Brimmed from the beaming beaker of my youth
Though all Medea's poisons drugged its wave,
And all the sighs by sad Cocytus heard
O'er-swept its purple margin !   Give me youth !
At times I feel as if this total being
That once o'er-strode the subject world of man,
This body and soul insensibly had shrunk
As shrinks the sculptor's model of wet clay
In sunshine, unobserved by him who shaped it,
Till some chance-comer laughs—
I touch once more dead times : their touch is chill :
My hand is chill, my heart.

                        I thought and wrought.
No dreamer I.   I never fought for fame :
I strove for definite ends ; for personal ends :
Ends helpful to mankind.   Sacred Religion
I honoured not for mysteries occult
Hid 'neath her veil, as Alexandria boasts
Faithful to speculative Greece, its mother ;
I honoured her because with both her hands
She stamps the broad seal of the Moral Law,
Red with God's Blood, upon the heart of man,

Teaching self-rule through rule of Law, and thus
Rendering the civil rule, the politic rule
A feasible emprise.   My Empire made,
At once I sheathed my sword.   For fifteen years
I, warrior-bred, maintained the world at peace
There following, 'gainst my wont, the counsel cleric.
What came thereof?   Fret of interior sores,
A realm's heart-sickness and soul-weariness,
The schism of classes warring each on each
And all to ruin tending, spite of cramps
Bound daily round the out-swelling wall.   'Twas vain !
Some Power there was that counter-worked my work
With hand too swift for sight, which, crossing mine,
Set warp 'gainst woof and ever with my dawn
Inwove its night.   What hand was that I know not :
Perchance it was the Demon's of my House ;
Perchance a Hand Divine.

   I had two worlds to shape and blend in one,
The Pagan and the Christian, glorious both,
One past her day, one nascent.   Thus I mused—
Old Pagan Rome vanquished ignobler lands,
Then won them to herself through healing laws :
Thus Christian Rome must vanquish Pagan Rome,
The barbarous races next : both victories won,
Thus draw them to her, vanquishing their hearts
Through Law divine.   What followed?   Pagan Rome

Hates Christian Rome for my sake daily more ;
Gnashes her teeth at me. "Who was it," she cries,
" That laid the old Roman Legion prone in dust
Cancelling that law which freed it from taxation ?
Who quelled the honest vices of the host
By laws that maimed all military pride ?
Who hurled to the earth the nobles of old race
And o'er them set his titular nobles new
And courtier prelates freed from tax and toll ?
Who ground our merchants as they grind their corn ? "
False charges all ; they know them to be false :
The Roman legion ere my birth was dead :
Those other scandals were in substance old ;
My laws were needfullest efforts to abate them.
They failed : when once the vital powers are spent
Best medicines turn to poisons. "God," 'tis writ,
" Made curable the nations :" Pagan Rome
Had with a two-edged dagger slain herself ;
Who cures the dead ? To her own level Rome
By equal laws had raised the conquered nations ;
Thus far was well. Ay, but by vices worse
Than theirs, the spawn of sensual sloth and pride,
Below their level Rome had sunk herself ;
The hordes she lifted knew it and despised her :
I came too late : the last, sole possible cure
Hastened, I grant, the judgment.

Pagan Rome
Deserved her doom and met it.   Christian Rome—
'Twas there my scheme imperial struck its root;
Earliest there too it withered.   Christians cold
Cheat both themselves and others.   I to such
Preferred at first the ardent for my friends :
Betimes I learned a lesson.   Zealous Christians
Have passion that outbraves imperial threats,
Outbids imperial bribes.   To such a man
Earth's total sphere appears a petty spot
Too small for sage ambitions.   Hope is his
To mount a heavenly, not an earthly throne,
And mount it treading paths of humbleness.
Such men I honoured ; such men, soon I found,
Honoured not emperors.   Christians of their sort,
Though loyal, eyed us with a beamless eye
Remembering Rome's red hand, remembering too
This, that the barbarous race is foe to Rome
And friendly oft to Christ.   To Him they rush
Sudden, like herds that change their haunts at spring
Taught from above.   At Rome the Christians gain
A noble here, a peasant there.   Those Christians,
I note them, lean away from empires ; mark
Egypt in each or Babel.   I from these
Turned to their brethren of the colder mould,
But found them false, though friendly ; found besides

That, lacking honour 'mid the authentic Faithful,
Small power was theirs to aid me.   Diocletian
Affirmed that Christians, whether true or false,
At best were aliens in his scheme of empire,
At worst were hostile.   Oft and loud he sware
That only on the old virtues, old traditions,
The patriot manliness of days gone by,
The fierce and fixed belief in temporal good
And earthly recompense for earthly merit,
Rome's Empire could find base.   That Emperor erred
In what he saw not.   What he saw was true.
I saw the old Rome was ended.   What if I,
Like him, have missed some Truth the Christians see ?
Men call the Race Baptized the illuminated.

      The Race Baptized : To me it gave small aid !
That sin was doubly fatal.   It amerced
My growing empire of Faith's centre firm
Round which a universe might have hung self-poised :
Likewise the on-streaming flood of my resolve
It froze in 'mid career.   The cleric counsel
Was evermore for peace.   The Barbarous Race
For that cause lies beyond my hand this day
Likelier perchance to absorb, more late, my empire
Than be in it absorbed.
I missed my spring : no second chance was given :
I failed ; none know it : I have known it long.

What were the lesser causes of that failure?
The sophists and seditious thus reply ;
" The Emperor caught the old imperial lust ;
He bound his realm in chains." They lie, and know it :
The People, not their Emperor, forged their chains :
Rich nobles had expelled the free-born poor :
Slaves filled their place ; these gladdened in their bondage ;
It gave them life inert and vacant mind
Unburdened by the weight of liberty.
Slaves tilled the fields. What followed next ? Ere long
Stigma was cast on wholesome Industry.
The slave worked ill ; the master sought no more
His wealth from grateful glebe, and honest hand
But tribute-plagued the world. The Italians bought
Exemption from a tax world-wide. What next ?
Through the whole Roman world, thus doubly mulct,
The o'er-weighted tax crumbled ; brought no return :
Then dropped the strong hands baffled. Slowly, surely
The weed became the inheritor of all :
The tribute withered : offices of state
Were starved : and from the gold crown to her feet
Beneath her golden robe the Empire shrank :
Fair was the face ; the rest was skeleton ;
Dead breast ; miscarrying womb. A hand not mine
Had counterworked my work.
　　　　　　　　　" The slave," they say,

" Finds lot more kindly in a Christian State :"
That saying lacks not truth.   What followed ?   This,
That freemen daily valued freedom less
Chiefly the Pagan freemen, slaves within.
Slavery with us was complicate in malice :
From rank to rank half-bondage crept and crept
Yearly more high and bound the class late free,
Their burdens waxing as their incomes waned.
Sorrowing I marked the deadly change ; heart-sore
I learned my edicts were in part its cause :
The tribute lost, perforce I had replaced it
With net-work fine of taxes nearer home,
Small but vexatious imposts.   Rose the cry,
" No Roman now can move or hand or foot
Save as some law prescribes."   The Citizen
Deserted like the soldier.   Streets, like farms,
Became a desolation.   Edicts new
Hurled back the fugitive to city or glebe,
Henceforth a serf ascript.   In rage of shame
Or seeking humblest peace at vilest cost,
There were that voluntary changed to slaves !
A priest made oath to me, " There's many a man
Sir, in your realm, who gladly, while I speak,
Would doff his human pride and hope immortal,
And run a careless leveret of the woods
Contented ne'er to see his Maker's Face

Here or in worlds to come." Death-pale he sware it !
What help ? I worked with tools : my best were rotten,
Some Strong One worked against me.
    Let me compare my present with my past.
My courtier bishops helped me once : this day
The spiritual power hath passed to men their foes.
Of late I made my youngest son a Cæsar :
I craved for him the blessing of God's Church :
I sought it not from prelates of my court :
I cast from me away the imperial pride :
I sent an embassage of princes twelve
In long procession o'er the Egyptian sands
To where within his lion-cinctured cave
Sits Anthony the Hermit. Thus he answered :
" Well dost thou, Emperor, in adoring Christ :
Attend. Regard no more the things that pass :
Revere what lasts, God's judgment and thy soul :
Serve God, and help His poor." His words meant this :
" That work thou wouldst complete is unbegun ;
Begin it Infant crowned."
                Three years of toil
With all earth's fleets and armies in my hand
Raised up this sovereign city. Mountains cleft
Sheer to the sea, and isles now sea-submerged,
Surrendered all their marbles and their pines ;
And river-beds dried up yielded their gold

To flame along the roofs of palace halls
And basilics more palatial.   Syrian wastes
Gave up their gems ; her porphyries Egypt sent ;
Athens and Rome their Phidian shapes eterne :
The Cross stood high o'er all.   That work was dream !
That city should have been an Empire's centre :
That Empire had existence, but not life :
The child it was of Rome's decrepitude,
Imbecile as its sire.   No youth-tide swelled
Its breast, or nerved its arm, or lit its eye :
Its sins themselves had naught of youth within them.
On Rome the shadow of great times was stayed ;
The shadow and the substance here alike
Were absent ; and the grandeur of the site
But signalized its lack.   To the end Rome nursed
Some rock-flower virtues sown in years of freedom :
Music of Virgil thrilled the Palatine :
Great Arts lived on ; great thoughts.   Pagan was Rome :
Ay, but the Catacombs were under Rome
With all their Christian dead.

                       That Rome was mine.
I left it for some future man ;—for whom ?
Old Sabine Numa can he come again
To list Egeria's whisper ; or those priests
White-robed that, throned on Alba Longa's height,
Discoursed of peace to mortals ?   Romulus ?

Augustus? These have left their Rome for ever:
With me they left it. Till some deluge sweeps
Her seven-hilled basis life is hers no more:
Haply some barbarous race may prove that wave:
Haply, that wave back-driven or re-engulfed
Within some infinite ocean's breast unknown,
From the cleansed soil a stem may yet ascend;
A tree o'er-shade the earth.

      That Rome I left:
I willed to raise a city great like Rome,
And yet in spirit Rome's great opposite,
His city, His, the Man she Crucified.
What see I? Masking in the name of Christ
A city like to Rome but worse than Rome;
A Rome with blunted sword and hollow heart,
And brain that came to her at second-hand,
Weak, thin, worn out by one who had it first,
And, having it, abused. I vowed to lift
Religion's lordliest fane and amplest shrine:
My work will prove a Pagan reliquary
With Christian incrustations froz'n around.
It moulders. To corruption it hath said,
"My sister;" to the wormy grave, "My home."
 Not less that city for a thousand years
May keep its mummied mockery of rule
 Like forms that sleep 'neath Egypt's Pyramids

Swathed round in balm and unguent, with blind eyes.
That were of dooms the worst.

                My hope it was
That that high mercy of the Christian Law
Tempering the justice of the Roman Law,
Might make a single Law, and bless the world :
But Law is for the free man, not the slave :
I look abroad o'er all the earth : what see I ?
One bondage, and self-willed.

                 I never sinned
As David sinned—except in blood—in blood :
Was this my sin, that not like him I loved ?
Or this, that, sworn to raise o'er all the earth
Christ's realm, I drew not to His Church's font ?—
The Church's son could ne'er have shaped her course.
   Again I mete the present with the past.
Central I sat in council at Nicæa :
In honour next to mine there stood a man—
I never loved that man—with piercing eye
And wingèd foot whene'er he moved ; till then
Immovable as statue carved from rock ;
That man was Athanasius.   Late last year
A second sacred council sat at Tyre :
It lifted Arius from Nicæa's ban :
From Alexandria's Apostolic throne
Her Patriarch, Athanasius, it deposed :

Her priesthood and her people sued his pardon;
He was seditious, and I exiled him:
That was my last of spiritual acts.
Was it well done? Arius since then hath died:
Since then God's Church is cloven.

       Since then, since then
My Empire too is cloven, and cloven in five.
No choice remained. I never was the man
To close my eyes against unwelcome truth.
My sons, my nephews, these are each and all
Alike ambitious men and ineffectual:
Since childhood left them I have loved them not,
And late have learned that they conspire against me.
No zeal parental warps my life's resolve
To leave my Empire one and only one:
Once more a net is round me. To bequeath
To one among those rivals five that Empire
Were with the sceptre's self to slay that Empire,
To raise the war-cry o'er my funeral feast,
And, ere the snapt wand lay upon my grave,
To utter from that grave my race's doom
And yield the labour of my life a prey
To Vandal and to Goth.

       Conviction came:
It comes to all; slowliest to him who knows
That Hope must flee before its face for ever:

It came at first a shadow, not a shape;
It came again, a body iron-handed:
It took me by the hand from plausive hosts;
It took me by the hand from senate halls;
It took me by the hand from basilic shrines;
It dragged me to the peak ice-cold; to depths
Caverned above earth's centre.   From that depth
I kenned no star; chanted no " De Profundis."
One night, the revel past, I sat alone
Musing on things to come.   In sleep I heard
The billow breaking 'gainst the huge sea-wall,
Then backward dragged, o'erspent. For hours I mused:
" The life of man is Action and Frustration
Alternate.   Both exhausted, what remains?
Endurance.   Night is near its term.   The morn
Will see my last of Acts, a parchment writ,
A parchment signed and sealed."   Sudden I heard
Advancing as from all the ends of earth
Tramp of huge armies to the city walls:
Then silence fell.   Anon my palace courts
Were thronged by warring hosts from every land
Headed by those disastrous rivals five,
My sons, my nephews.   Long that strife rang out :
First in the courts, then nearer shrieks I heard :
Amid the orange-scented colonnades
And inmost alabaster chambers dim;

And all the marble pavements gasped in blood,
And all the combatants at last lay dead :
Then o'er the dead without and dead within
A woman rode ; one hand, far-stretched, sustained
A portent—what I guessed—beneath a veil :
She dropped it at my feet : it was a Head.
She spake : " The deed was thine : take back thine own !
Bid Crispus bind in one thy broken Empire !
Thy first-born : his should be the heritage,
Son of that earlier wife—the wife well-loved."
Then fires burst forth as though all earth were flame,
And thunders rolled abroad of falling domes,
And tower, and temple, and a shout o'er all,
" The Goth, the Vandal ! "   'Twas not these that roused
    me ;
It was a voice well-loved, for years unheard,
" Father, grieve not !   That deed was never thine ! "
Standing I woke, and in my hand my sword.
This was no vision ; 'twas a dream ; no more :
Next day at twelve I wrote my testament,
Designed, and partly writ, the day before.
I wrote that testament in my heart's best blood :
That Empire, vaster far than in the old time,
That Empire sundered long, at last by me
Consolidated, and by Christian Law
Lifted to heights that touch on heaven, that Empire

This hand that hour divided into five.
This hand it was which wrote that testament;
This hand which pressed thereon the imperial seal:
Then too I heard those shouting crowds.   Poor fools!
They knew not that the labour of my life
Before me stood that hour, a grinning mask
Disfleshed by death.   Later they'll swear I blundered:
'Tis false!   What man could work to save my Empire
I wrought.   It willed not to be saved.   So be it!
When in the Apostles' church entombed I lie
Five kinglings shall divide my realm.   That act,
Like Diocletian's last, was abdication:
How oft at his I scoffed!

                They scoff not less
The ripples of yon glittering sea! they too
Shoot out their lips against me!   They recall
That second crisis in my vanished years,
When from this seat, Byzantium then, forth fled
Vanquished Licinius.   There, from yonder rock,
Once more I see my fleet steer up full-sailed,
Glassing its standards in the Hellespont,
Triumphant; see the Apostate's navy load
The Asian shore with wrecks.   He too beheld it:
Amazed he fled; and all the East was mine.
It was my Crispus ruled my fleet that hour!
That victory I saw was his, not mine:

His was the heroic strength that awes mankind,
The grace that wins, the majesty that rules them :
No vile competitor had he to fear.
Had he but lived !   Well spake my dying sister
Wedded to that Licinius whom I slew,
" God for thy sins will part from thee thy realm."
I heard that whisper as my city's walls
Ascended, daily.   Night by night I heard
The tread of Remus by his brother slain
Circling the walls half-raised of Rome.

'Tis past !

My Empire's dead : alone my city lives :
My portion in that city is yon church
Named of the Apostles : there I built my tomb :
In that alone my foresight stands approved :—
Around it rise twelve kingly cenotaphs
In honour of the Twelve Apostles raised ;
These are my guards against the Powers unblest :
Within that circle I shall sleep secure :
Thou Hermit of the Egyptian cave, be still !—
Regret I then my life, my birth ?   Not so !
To seek great ends is worthy of a man :
To mourn that one more life has failed, unworthy.
But be ye mute, O mocking throngs far off !
Be mute, sweet song and adulating hymn !—
What scroll is that wind-curled ?   Ha ! Persia's missive !

K

I ever scorned that Persia!   I reject
Her mendicant hand, stretched from her bed of roses;
She that of Cyrus made of old her boast,
That tamed the steed, and spake the truth; even now
The one sole possible rival of my Rome;
One from the Caspian to the Persian Gulf,
The Tigris to the Ganges; she that raised
In part that Empire I designed but wrought not,
That raised an Empire throned o'er Idols quelled,
An Empire based on God and on His Law,
A mighty line of kings hereditary,
Each "the Great King," sole lord of half the world,
And, raising, proved my work was feasible!
This day she whines and fawns; one day she dragged
A Roman Emperor through her realm in chains,
By name Valerian.   Roman none forgives her!
Dotard at last, she wastes her crazy wits
On mystic lore and Manichean dreams:
I ll send no answer; yet I'll read her missive.

"The Great King thus to Constantine of Rome:
Galerius stole from Persia, while she slept,
Five provinces Caucasian.   Yield them back!
If not, we launch our armies on thy coasts
And drag thee chained o'er that rough road and long
Trod by Valerian."   Let me read once more:

Writ by his hand, and by his sigil sealed !
So be it !   My boyhood's vision stands fulfilled !
Great Alexander's vow accomplished :— Earth
From Ganges' mouths to Calpé's Rock one realm !
Insolent boy !   Well knows he I am old :
I was : I am not : youth is mine once more :
To-morrow in my army's van I ride.
Euphorbos !   Sleep'st thou ?   Send me heralds forth !
Summon my captains !   Bid these mummers cease !—
The error of my life lies plain before me,
That fifteen years of peace.

NOTE.—The next day Constantine set out on his Persian expedition ; he fell sick at Hellenopolis, a city erected by him in honour of his mother, the Empress Helena.   He demanded Baptism, and died soon after he had received it.

THE LEGEND OF SAINT ALEXIS.

(DIED A.D. 398.)

PART I.

ARGUMENT.

Eupheumian, the descendant of a great Roman stock, is a Christian, as is Aglaë, his wife; and each day they have three tables set forth—one for orphans, one for widows, and one for pilgrims. After many years a son is granted to their prayers. While yet a child, he is esteemed by all Christian Rome to be a saint. In time, his parents contract the youth to a Greek maiden. On the day of his marriage, there is sent to Alexis one of those wondrous mandates from on high, whereof men read in the sacred Scriptures; and he at once leaves all, and abides at Edessa, among the pilgrims who kneel in the porches of its chief church. After many years, a second divine mandate requires him to return to his father's house, and abide there unknown till death. There he is known to none, and lies ever in a little cell under a marble staircase, being unable to rise through great pains. After many years, when death draws nigh, he commands that paper and ink should be brought; and he writes down his history and dies alone. As soon as that scroll is read there is great lamentation in the house; but God turns that sorrow into joy, and Alexis is followed to his grave by all the great ones of Rome; and the house of his fathers' is changed into a church, which remains to this day.

In Rome long since upon Mount Aventine
There stood a marble palace vast and fai

'Mid gardens rich in mulberry and vine,
  With columned atrium and Parian stair,
Statued by godlike forms at either side,
Ancestral chiefs, a Roman noble's pride.

That stock was ancient when great Cæsar fell;
  Ancient when Hannibal with gloomy brow
From Zama rode, till then invincible;
  Ancient when Cincinnatus left his plough;
Ancient when Liberty in crimson dyed
Leaped forth, re-virgined, from a virgin's side—

Virginia's bleeding 'neath her father's knife;
  Ancient when Rome in civil conflict reeled
By rapine torn or fratricidal strife
  Ill fruit of that Licinian Law repealed,
And free-born peasants, famed in peace and war,
Gave place to slaves, base scum from realms afar.

Then too the Euphemian race held high its head
  Above the custom new and mist of error;
The native husbandmen with freedom's tread
  Walked still its fields; in gladness not in terror
Their young, fair daughters, rising from the board,
Greeted the entrance of an unfeared lord.

He came not only when the flocks were shorn
   To claim his half; when corn-clad slopes grew fat;
When russet sheaves to golden barns were borne;
   When olives bled, or grapes made red the vat:
He stood among them when the son was wed;
He followed to his grave the grandsire dead.

Centuries went by; they brought the great reward:
   That Senate-Order of a later day,
Fooled by their flatterers, by their slaves abhorred,
   Reaped as they sowed, each upstart anarch's prey
Successively proscribed.   'Mid seas of blood
The Empire by the dead Republic stood.

In time that Empire tottered to its fall;
   Awhile the princely hand of Constantine
Sustained it.   Faithful to a heavenly call
   He linked its glories with that Conquering Sign
Inscribed, "Through me is Victory."   But, within,
Still lurked that empire-murdering poison—Sin.

The Christian Truth, held truly, had sufficed
   Even then to save that Empire: naught availed
The name invoked but not the Faith of Christ,
   Or Faith that made its boast in words, but failed
To rear on Pagan wrecks of sense and pride
The Christian throne of greatness sanctified.

The imperial sceptre to the East transferred
    Left prouder still the West.   More high each day
The pomp up-swelled of Rome's great Houses, stirred
    By legendary lore and servile lay,
And hungry crowds contented long to wait
The bread-piled basket at the palace-gate.

" My Lord receives his clients."   In they throng,
    Freedman and slave, Greek cook and Syrian priest,
Wizard and mime, adepts in dance or song ;
    The perfumed patron, recent from the feast
Or drunken slumbers reddening still his eyes,
Enters ; and plausive shouts insult the skies,

Startling a score of scriveners, forms grotesque
    That bend lean foreheads, seamed by fevered veins,
Across the ledger broad or mouldering desk ;
    For then each Roman noble held domains
By Rhenus, Rhodanus, and every shore
That hears or viol's sigh or panther's roar.

Those nobles seldom rode to battle-fields ;
    They steered to distant ports no ships broad-sailed :
But well they knew that gain which usury yields ;
    Or, borrowing oft, when tricksome fortune failed
Pawned their best plate and many a gem beside,
Knee-crooked to soothe some upstart lender's pride.

The gilded barge is launched : a score of slaves
    Drag back the flashing oars ; a second score
With incense charge each wind that curls the waves,
    Or harmonize blue Baiæ's watery floor
With strains that charmed Calypso's halls erewhile,
Or lured Ulysses t'ward the Siren's isle.

They trod the marbles of the Thermæ vast
    Their skirts aflame with legend-broideries ;
Bull-born, Europa here the Bosphorus passed,
    The Idean shepherd there adjudged the prize ;
Or Venus, fisher turned, with bending rod
Landed a wet-winged Cupid on the sod.

Their litters borne by sweating slaves, they clomb
    On August noons Soracte's steepest ridge ;
Or, pinnace-cradled, pushed the creamy foam
    Onward through dusk Avernus' waving sedge ;
They turned not there great Maro's page, yet oft
Alike the Poet and his Sibyl scoffed.

Temples and shrines adorned their palaces ;
    Syrian the rite once Roman, later Greek :
Old libraries remained : they sought them less
    For song heroic than for tale lubrique ;
Here sophists warred in turn on body and soul ;
There dust lay thick on Plato's godlike scroll.

Travelling, a troop Numidian cleared their way;
　　Their carrucæ were silver, gold-embossed;
In festal barge they coasted Cumæ's bay:
　　If there a keener gust the ripple crossed
They shook like some sick child that sees in dream
Ixion's doom or rage of Polypheme.

Harp, lyre, and lute for ever dinned their bowers;
　　But witless, loud, or shrill was every strain:
They feared the incense-breath of innocent flowers
　　Yet quaffed their wine-cups near the uncovered drain;
Feared omens more than wrath divine, and fled
The fevered child, the parent's dying bed.

The poison root of those base ways was this:
　　Self-love had slain or fouled each household tie:
The wedded seldom loved, or loved amiss:
　　Child-birth was tribute paid to ancestry;
Rottenness reigned: the World, grown old, stripped bare,
More ruled than when the Witch was young and fair.

Need was there that the Lord of Love should burst
Once more on man as in man's prime estate,
And, teaching that the " First Command " is first
　　The "Second" second only, vindicate
For human loves that greatness theirs alone
When Love's far source and heavenly end are known.

Ages of Sin had heaped on high a debt
    Heroic Virtue could alone defray :
The limb ill-joined could never be reset
    Till broken ; Love, till cleansed, resume its sway.
Conventual cells that seemed to spurn the earth,
And hermit caves, built up the Christian Hearth.

Fire-scorched Thebais, lion-tenanted !
    'Twas in thy lion's abdicated lair
Ascetic Virtue laid its infant head :
    The heart, dried up, found waters only there :
That Faith burnt in upon it from above
By pain, sent up at last Faith's offspring—Love.

Rome caught the sacred flame. Brave men, and those
    Infected least by wealth and popular praise
Could walk in strength, in dignity repose,
    In part were faithful to the old Roman ways :
Matrons there were on whom Cornelia's eye
Might rest ; and youths well pleased like Regulus to die.

Pagan were these ofttimes, but less revered
    Venus than Pallas, Plutus less than Pan :
The gods " Pandemian " they nor loved nor feared :
    In nobler gods the noblest thoughts of man
Looked down, so deemed they, from the Olympian throne,
Or types or delegates of that God Unknown.

Others, incensed at priestly conjuring trick,
    Reluctant bade the fane profaned adieu,
But with the Sophist's godless rhetoric
    Their own hearts wronged not. Far as truth they knew
They lived it ; wrought for man, and peace ensued
Branding the Bad, and cleaving to the Good.

An exhalation of celestial grace
    Moved o'er the Empire from the Martyrs' tombs :
Christians, oft slaves, were found in every place ;
    Their words, their looks, brightened the heathen glooms :
Such gleams still hallow Antoninus' page,
The saintly Pagan and Imperial Sage.

Prescient of fate the old worship lay in swoon,
    Helpless though huge, dying and all but dead ;
The young Faith clasped it as the keen new moon,
    A silver crescent risen o'er ocean's bed,
Clasps that sad orb whose light from earth is won :—
Its youthful conqueror parleys with the sun.

The Poor came first, and reaped the chief reward ;
    Old Houses next : Truth loves Humility :
Humility is humblest when most hard
    To reach—the lowliness of high degree :
Such bowed to Christ : in turn He gave to them
The stars of Truth's whole heaven for diadem.

The thought of greatness in them long had dwelt:
    The difference 'twixt the greatness counterfeit
And genuine greatness plainly now they felt:
    Eyes had they; and they saw it.   Henceforth sweet
Was every sacrifice that Vision brought:
No wish had these to purchase heaven for naught.

They knew 'twas sense and valour, not the hand
    In unguents drenched, that won the world for Rome:
Sublimer ends sublimer pains demand:
A spiritual kingship, country, hope, and home
Shone out and hailed them from the far-off shore—
" To sea, though tempests rage and breakers roar !"

Piercing remorse was theirs whene'er they mused
    On all which God to Rome in trust had given;
The majesties profaned, the rights abused:
    What help to earth, what reverence to heaven,
Had these bequeathed? What *meant* her realm world-
    wide ?
Injustice throned, and Falsehood deified !

Through all that boundless realm from East to West
    Had Virtue flowered? Had Wisdom come to fruit?
Had Freedom raised to heaven a lordlier crest?
    Had household Peace pushed down a deeper root?
More true were wives, were maids more pure that day
Than Portia, Clelia, or Nausicaa?

Behold, the flowering was of vices new ;
  The fruitage fruits of hate and self-disgust ;
Knowledge had bathed her roots in lethal dew :
  If higher now her branching head she thrust
The Upas shade spread wider than of old ;
And wealth had bound man's heart in chains of gold.

The Christian noble spurned the old Roman pride ;
  Whate'er the Christian prized the Pagan hated,
And clasped, his zeal by wrath intensified,
  Rome's meanest boasts with passion unabated :
Their homes stood near : for that cause further still
The inmates were estranged in thought and will.

The Christian ofttimes sold his all, and gave
  The poor its price ; another kept his lands
But spent their increase freeing serf and slave,
  Himself sustained by labour of his hands :
Thus each renounced himself, for others wrought
Yet found that personal good he had not sought.

Wedded were some, and reverently to Christ
  Upreared a race to Him obedient.   Some
For His sake hearth and household sacrificed ;
  Others, in that fresh dawn of Christendom,
Though spoused lived on in vestal singleness,
Young chastity's severe yet sweet excess.

Of Christian homes the noblest and the first
  Was that huge palace on Mount Aventine :
Fortune and Pagan spite had done their worst :
  They maimed it, yet not marred.   The time's decline
Made it but holier seem.   The Christian Truth
Shone, starlike, from its breast in endless youth.

Three hundred freemen served there as of yore,
  Bondsmen whilom.   The clients of old time
Walked there as children, parasites no more ;
  Mastery and service, like recurrent rhyme,
Kissed with pure lip ; for one great reverence swayed
Alike their hearts who ruled and who obeyed.

The beast that drew the water from the well
  In nearer stream had earlier quenched his thirst,
Nor laboured over-burdened : placable
  Was each man : vengeance there was held accursed :
Before one altar knelt the high, the low ;
Heard the same prayer : it rose for friend and foe.

Euphemian was the name far-known of him
  The lord of all those columned porticoes,
Those gardens vast with ilex alleys dim,
  Those courts enriched with orange and with rose :
Happy in youth ; thrice happier since his bride,
Aglaë, paced those halls her lord beside.

She was a being beautiful as day,
   Tender and pliant to her husband's will
As to the wind that flower each breath can sway
   While branch and leaf and blade close by are still,
And therefore " wind-flower " named.   On her Christ's
     Poor
Looked ever with moist eyes and trust secure.

One thing alone was wanting to this pair—
   The sound of children's feet patting the floor,
The ring of children's laughter on the air,
   Their clamorous joy at opening of a door
To see, to clasp their parents newly come
Once more from Tibur or from Tusculum.

The Poor pray well : at last the prayer was heard
   From countless hearths ascending eve and morn ;
From countless hearts.   The joy so long deferred
   Was sent at last ; the longed-for boy was born.
That day all Rome kept festival ; that night
Each casement shone, and every face was bright.

The months went swiftly by : the Seven-Hilled City
   Well loved that Babe ; the poor man's boast was he,
The theme of neighbour's tale and minstrel's ditty :
   Maiden and matron clasped him on her knee :
And many a saintly mother said—and smiled—
" Christ died a Man : but came to earth a Child ! "

Once as he slept his mother near him knelt :
    She prayed as never she had prayed before,
And, praying, such an inspiration felt
    As though some breeze of hope o'er ocean's floor
Missioned from Bethlehem's star-loved crib, came flying
O'er her and him in that small cradle lying.

It passed : then in her memory rose that word
    Simeon to Blessed Mary spake erewhile,
" Also through thine own soul shall pierce the sword ; "
    She mused, like those who weep at once and smile,
" The Mother of a Saint, how great soe'er
Her joy, in Mary's sacred grief must share ! "

Years passed : a Monk, that child at vespers singing
    " Salve Regina," while a tear down stole,
Spake thus, that anthem through the rafters ringing,
    " That voice is music of a singing Soul !
That child shall live on earth as lives a Spirit ;
When dead, some crown seraphic shall inherit ! "

The child became the boy, but never lost
    That charm which beautified his childhood's ways :
Skilful the most of those the quoit who tossed
    Or chased the boar, he nothing did for praise,
Nor e'er in feast or revel sought a part ;
Rome was to him pure as a forest's heart.

Raptured he read her legends of old time—
  The Father-Judge who doomed his sons to die ;
The Wife that, sentencing another's crime,
  Pierced her own heart, then sank without a sigh.
Great acts to him were all : not then he knew
That oft Endurance wins a crown more true.

Later, for him the Meditative wore
  Greatness more great than Action's, and more dear :
The weight of Thought with neck unbowed he bore
  As Saints their aureole crowns.   All objects near
Were lost in lights of sunset or sunrise :
His one sole passion was Self-Sacrifice.

His guides in Christian as in Classic lore
  Boasted untired the youth's intelligence :
Ere long he marked these twain were still at war,
  The prophets one of Spirit, one of Sense :
" I will not serve two masters ;" thus he cried,
And pushed the flower-decked pagan scroll aside.

Was it that sacred moment shaped his life,
  Keeping it flawless ?   Thousands safeliest pace
Faith's lower road, dusty and dinned with strife ;
  Not so the man elect to loftier place,
For sins in others small are great in him
Whose grace is large—that grace least stains bedim.

L

Thenceforth his "eye was single." Loss was gain
  To him, since Suffering had the world redeemed;
For that cause still he sought the haunts of pain;
  Still on the sufferer's couch like morn he beamed,
And in his father's house with wine and bread
Served still God's Poor, or with them sat and fed.

He lived a life all musical, for still
  Discords of earth by faith grew harmonized;
He lived in a great silence, spirit and will
  Hushed in his God.   Because naught else he prized
Loud as that first, great world-creating word,
God's "small, still voice" within him, still he heard.

Nothing in him was sad, nothing morose;
  The serious face still tended to a smile;
In him sorrow and joy still harboured close,
  Like eve and dawn met in some boreal isle.
Bad actions named, sad looked he and surprised;
But seldom strove, rebuked, or criticised.

There were who marvelled at his piercing thought;
  There were who marvelled at his simpleness:
High Truths, and Inspirations rapture-fraught
  Came to his mind like angels: not the less
Where fools walk well at times his footstep erred:
He heard the singing spheres, or nothing heard.

His father loved the boy with love and pride ;
  There, and there only, pride regained a part;
He who had spurned the world, its scorn defied,
  Now gladdened that his son had won its heart.
He smiled when kinsmen said : " This boy shall raise
Waste places of thy House in later days ! "

" All that is mine Alexis must inherit,"
  He answered.   Then the mother, " Who is she
Worthy by race, by beauty, and by merit
  To be to him true wife as I to thee ? "
Such maid they sought long time ; when hope was o'er
They found her—found on earth's most famous shore.

Her race had dwelt in Athens ere it wrestled
  With Sparta for the foremost place in Greece ;
Earlier, in Colchian vales, less known had nestled
  Ere Jason thence had filched the Golden Fleece.
Thus to his mates on wintry nights her sire
Boasted—true Greek—beside the fir-cone fire.

Euphemian and that sire were ancient friends
  So far as Greek and Roman friends might be,
Friends in their youth ; but though unlikeness blends
  Natures cognate with finer sympathy,
So diverse these, men said 'twas memory's tie,
Not love's, that held them still, through severance, nigh.

Not less, ere died the Greek, that friend of old
   Had sought him out, and, standing by his bed,
Had vowed to nurture in his own fair fold
   His daughter, lonely left.   Her father dead,
And sacred mourning days expired, the twain
Spread sail for Rome across the wine-dark main.

At sea, to please the maid, her guardian took
   The sweet and venerable name of Sire ;
Her winsome grace, her wit, her every look—
   But few could witness such and not admire ;
Gravely Euphemian marked them, sadly smiled,
Yet loved her as a father loves his child.

Likewise, as up and down his musings swayed,
   A thought recurred : " The girl is light of wing !
What then ?   Alexis is too grave and staid :
   Christian she is ; to each the years must bring
Fit aid by friendly difference best supplied :
Ere three months more Zoe shall be his bride."

Zoe, the loveliest of Athenian girls,
   Was prouder thrice to bear the Athenian name
Than if the East had rained its gems and pearls
   Knee-deep about her path.   To Rome she came
Curious, yet spleenful more.   The world's chief site
To her meant sceptred dulness, brainless might.

The ship that bore her thither smiled to waft
   Creature so bright ; smooth seas revered their charge :
Cythera's uplands, as she neared them, laughed :
   The Ætnean heights, Trinacria's wave-washed marge,
Gladdened ; they sang, " Our Proserpine again
Is come to gather flowers on Enna's plain ! "

She, when they reached the soft Campanian coast
   Where Pestum's roses redden twice a year,
Reddened for joy—its valleys seemed almost
   As Tempé soft, its streams as Dircé clear—
But frowned on tawny Tiber with raised fist
Mocking, half-Mænad and half-Exorcist.

When Zoe entered Rome, she turned, heart-sick,
   From arch and column flattering regal pride,
From cliff-like walls up-piled of sun-burned brick
   Beneath whose shade men lion-torn had died,
From alien obelisks hieroglyph-o'ergraven,
For centuries glassed in Egypt's stillest haven.

That mood went by : sudden the cloud she spurned
   And, shaking from lashed lids an angry tear,
To that mute man beside her, laughing, turned
   And spake : " The trophies of all lands are here !
Rome conquered earth : but why ? Too dull her brain
For better tasks, the victories which remain !

"They boast their Heroes : but they love them not !
    Lo, there !   An Emperor stands yon column's crown !
What Greek would strain his eyes to scan a spot
    Jet-black in sun-bright skies?   No Attic clown !
There Trajan towers, and, eastward, Antonine :
O brains Beotian, fatter than your kine !"

Lightly thus spake that beaming creature hard,
    Nor noted that, as one in still disdain,
Her comrade silent rode.   A fixed regard
    He bent upon a cross-surmounted fane :
A Grecian temple near it stood : his eye
Saw but that small, low church, that sunset sky.

He answered late : " Your Grecian pride of Art,
    Daughter, and Rome's old pagan pride of arms,
Alike stand sentenced here.   For Christian heart
    No greatness save of heavenly birth hath charms.
In Rome the Faith found martyrs three long ages :
She won but audience from the Athenian sages!"

The beauteous one looked up; her sensitive lip
    And tender cheek asked leave, it seemed, to smile ;
Then, as a bud that frosts of April nip,
    That smile, discouraged, died.   Pensive awhile
She rode; her palfrey nearer drew to his :
She raised his hand, and pressed thereon a kiss.

"Forgive," she said, "the petulance of youth !
    Wisdom serene, and Virtue proved by years,
Note not ——" She wept ; but soon her cheek in sooth
    Like leaves rain-washed beamed brighter for her tears,
And livelier than before her critic tongue
This way and that its shafts of satire flung.

At times the unbending Roman smiled perforce ;
    At times the patriot stern essayed to frown :
She noted either mood ; and her discourse
    Accordant winged its light way up or down
Like those white-pinioned birds that sink then soar
O'er high-necked waves breasting a sandy shore.

The sun had set ; they clomb Mount Aventine,
    That Augur-haunted height. They paused : she saw
Old Tiber, lately bright, in sanguine line
    Wind darkening t'wards the sea. A sudden awe
Chilled her. She felt once more that evening breeze
Which waves that yew-grove of the Eumenides

Where Athens fronts Colonos. There of old
    Sat Destiny's blind mark, King Œdipus ;
And, oft as she had passed it, shudderings cold
    Ran through her fibred frame, made tremulous
As the jarred sounding-board of lyre or harp :
So thrilled the girl that hour with shiverings sharp.

"I know it!   This is Rome's Oracular Hill !
    Dreadful it looks ; a western Calvary !
A sacrificial aspect dark and still
    It wears, that saith, 'Prepare, O man, to die !'
Father ! you house not on this mount of Fate ?"
Thus as she spake they reached his palace gate.

There stood, still fair—tenderer than when more young—
    She who had made her husband's youth so bright :
Long to her neck the Athenian Exile clung
    Wearied and sad.   Not less that festal night
The gladsomest of the radiant throng was she,
Centre and soul of Roman revelry.

PART II.

" ALL hail to Rome !   She lords it o'er the world
    From Ganges' flood to Atlas' snowy crown :
Heavenward from cape and coast her praise is hurled :
    She lifts the nations up and casts them down :
Like some great mountain city-thronged she stands
Her shade far cast eclipsing seas and lands.

" She flings that shade across the tracts of Time
    Not less than o'er the unmeasured fields of space ;
Processional the Empires paced sublime ;
    Her heralds these ; they walked before her face :
Assyrian, Persian, Grecian—what were they ?
Poor matin streaks, yet preludes of the day !

" The Pyramids that vault Egyptian kings
    When near her legions drew bowed low their heads ;
Indus and Oxus from their mountain springs
    Whispered, ' She cometh.'   Dried-up river-beds
From Dacian plains to British cried aghast,
' This way but now the Roman Eagles passed ! '

" She fells the forest, and the valley spans
    With arch o'er arch : the mountain-crests she carves
With roads, till Nature's portents yield to Man's :
    Wolf-like the race that mocks her bleeds or starves ;
Alike they lived their lives, they had their day :
Her laws abide ; men hear them and obey.

" Beyond the far sea-limit of old Tyre
    Her gold fleets waft earth's harvest through the storm ;
Carthage, Tyre's daughter, crossed her path : the fire
    Went o'er her walls ; in blackening heaps deform
Her league-long ruins ridge the desert grey ;
Above them pard and tiger chase their prey.

" All hail to Rome !   Her mighty heart serene
    Houses at will all nations and their gods
Content to know herself of all the Queen.
    Who spake that word ; 'The old Religion nods?'
Ah fools ! at times, but gathering heat, the levin
Sleeps in Jove's hand.   Yet Jove reigns on in heaven."

Such was the song that from beyond that wall
    Girdling the palace pleasaunce swelled what time
Zoe awoke, till then sleep's lovely thrall,
    And marked the splendours of the dewy prime
Brightening the arras nymphs beyond her bed ;
Upright she sat, and propped a listening head.

She listened as the choral echo rang
    Lessening from stem to stem, from stone to stone ;
Then rose, and, tossing wide the casement, sang
    In briefer note a challenge of her own :
" Ye honour still the old Faith—when dead condole it—
That Faith was Greek, my masters !   Rome but stole it !"

That Faith was hers in childhood ; threads thereof
    Still gleamed 'mid all those golden tissues woven
Which decked her fancy's world of thought and love :
    Her conscience clung to Truths revealed, heart-proven :
Her fancy struck no root into the true,
A rock-flower fed on ether and on dew.

She had a pagan nurse and Christian mother :
    That mother taught her girl the Christian Creed ;
She learned it, she believed : Yet scarce could smother
    Memories first hers of heathen race and breed
Which, claiming to be legend only, won
Perchance more credence as exacting none.

When girt by pagans, she their rites derided :
    The Christian Faith, that only, she revered ;
Yet oft at Christian hearths with sceptics sided :
    Sacred Religion less she loved than feared,
Still muttering sadly; " Easy 'tis, I wean,
To dread the Unknown, but hard to love the Unseen."

Stronger she was in intellect than spirit ;
    In intellect's self less strong than keen and swift :
Immeasurable in beauty, interest, merit
    To her was Nature's sphere ; but hers no gift
To roam through boundless empires of the Soul :
She craved the definite path—not distant goal.

Seldom the girl's unlovelier moods looked forth
    When first she housed in that Euphemian home
So rich in loftiest reverence, lowliest worth :
    There the great ways of Apostolic Rome
Confronted her, and steadied and upraised :
A part of heaven she saw where'er she gazed.

And deeplier yet her better spirit was moved
   When, by Aglaë led, she trod those spots
Where bled the martyrs.   Oft, torch-lit, they roved
   Those dusky ways like sea-wrought caves and grots
Rome's subterranean city of the tombs,
This hour her noblest boast—the Catacombs.

The soundless floors with blood-stains still were red :
   Still lay the martyr in sepulchral cell
The ensanguined vial close beside his head,
   " In pacé " at his feet.   Ineffable
That peace around : the pictured walls confessed
Its source divine in symbols ever blessed.

Here the " Good Shepherd " on His shoulder bare
   The sheep long lost.   The all-wondrous Eucharist
Was emblemed near.   Close-bound in grave-clothes, there
   Lazarus stood still fixed by the eye of Christ :
Below his gourd the Prophet bowed his head,
Prophet unweeting of the Three-days-Dead.

Among the Roman martyrs two there were
   Whom most the Greek in wonder venerated,
Cecilia and her spouse, that wedded pair
   Who lived their short, glad life like spirits mated
And hand in hand passed to the Crucified :
" Oh, how unlike Aspasia ! "—Zoe cried.

Yet to her heart dearer Saint Agnes was,
  That lamb immaculate of the Roman fold,
So happy to her Lord, so young to pass,
  By Him so fenced from stain ! Ah ! meek as bold,
With fleece of lambs before thine altar blessed
The shepherds of God's flock this day are dressed !

One morn, from these returned, Agläe spake ;
  " Husband, bestow this maiden on thy son !
She loves our martyrs : that high love will make
  Their marriage blest and holy ! " It was done :
By parents at that time were bridals made
In Rome. Alexis heard them and obeyed.

Zoe at first felt angry : thus she mused :
  " Unsued, and scarce consulted, to be wed ! "
She mused again ; this marriage, wisely used,
  May lift once more my country's fallen head :
That was my dream since childhood : till I die
That stands my purpose : now the means are nigh."

Such was the leaning of her deeper nature ;
  To some she seemed a Muse : to sterner eyes
A Siren to be dreaded : but the creature
  Beneath her sallies gay and bright disguise
Was inly brave and serious, strong and proud :
A child of Greece, to that sad mother vowed.

Betrothed they were what time the earlier snows
   Whitening Soracte's scalp were caked with frost :
The marriage was postponed till April's close,
   Then later till the Feast of Pentecost.
Meantime they met not oft.   The youth had still
High tasks—he loved all duties—to fulfil.

Zoe thenceforth was welcomed more and more
   In all the Roman houses of old fame,
Welcomed by pagans most : they set great store
   Upon her thoughtful wit and Attic name,
And learned with help from her to read with ease
The songs of Sappho and Simonides.

Among them ranged a dame right eloquent
   On all the classic myths of ancient days :
In each she found unrecognized intent
   Occult, and oft her jetty brows would raise
Much wondering how a child of Academe
Could slight Greek wisdom for a Hebrew dream.

Her spouse had been a Flamen sleek and soft,
   Rome's chief of heathen priests.   "His prison-bars
Are burst at last !" that widow clamoured oft :
   "Released, that great one walks among the stars !"
Light-fingered thus, the well-trained Sophists stole
From Truth a part ;—assailed therewith the whole.

With her the Athenian strove that perilous season,
  Most confident belike when certain least.
A perilous staff, for such, is boastful reason;
  On that whene'er she leaned her doubts increased;
The Catacombs propped best a faith unstable:
She said, "Those dear ones died not for a fable."

A help beside 'gainst unbelieving sin
  Illumed her pathway. 'Twas the heaven-lit face
Of him, her destined husband. None therein
  Might gaze ungladdened by a healing grace;
Round him he breathed Faith's sweet yet strengthening
    clime,
Like sea-winds sent o'er hills of rock and thyme.

He spake: the Grecian girl with instinct keen
  Felt that he told of things to him well known,
And for an hour through God's high worlds unseen
  Advanced as one who sees. But when alone
Faith lacked what Love Divine alone can lend her:
Her nature, though impassioned, was not tender.

Her mental powers were wide and far of gaze;
  Ardent her heart, profound, but yet confined:
Her sympathies trod firm on solid ways
  But cast no answering pinions on the wind,
Felt not the gravitation from above:
The depths they knew, but not the heights of love.

Large powers of human love in her had dwelt
    Unknown, long checked like tarns on hillsides stayed
By bars of virgin ice not quick to melt:
    In vain her country's sons their court had paid:
She spurned them: Greece lay bound, a spoil, a jest;
They in her degradation acquiesced!

Her Roman suitors she had spurned yet more
    Save one: she saw in each her country's foe:
That one, strange nurseling of a mystic lore,
    Was brave as wise, and just to high and low:
The ice had burst: the torrent took its way:
" How slowly comes," she thought, " this marriage-day ! "

She loved Alexis well: he loved her better;
    Better, not more.   She loved with all her heart;
He with a portion, for he brooked no fetter
    That bound his spirit to earth.   To her a part
He gave in his large being—not the whole;
'Tis thus they love whose love is of the soul.

Ofttimes when most she loved she scorned to show it,
    Deeming her love repaid by his but half:
Ofttimes she wept; but, fearing he should know it,
    Drank down her tears, or praised with petulant laugh
What least he loved; or curtsied in her spleen
Passing the fane, still thronged, of beauty's Queen.

Sometimes, approaching Constantine's huge piles
  That lifted o'er vast courts their shadowing span
As o'er dusk waters frown Egean isles,
  The Lateran Mother-Church, or Vatican,
She seemed to see them not; but stooped and raised
A violet from the grass, and kissed and praised.

He judged her not, yet mused in boding thought:
  "This marriage—will it help this orphan maid?"
The answer followed plain: "I never sought
  The tie.   My parents willed it: I obeyed:
If they have erred, in time a hand more high
Will point my way.   Till then no choice have I."

More seldom still they met: but when they met
  Airs as from heaven played on her spirit's chords;
And seldom if he spake, with eyes tear-wet
  She sighed; "A man is he of deeds not words!"
Poor child!   She guessed not 'twas her wayward will
Slighting the themes he loved that held him silent still.

She knew him not; his parents but in part:
  They wist not this, that, though to seats divine
Great Love at times can lift the earthly heart,
  On hearts enskied as oft it works decline.
Their course was well-nigh run, their heaven nigh gained;
One sole temptation—and its cure—remained.

The marriage morn had come.   At faith's high call
  Ere sunrise yet the dewy groves had dried
The youth was praying in a chapel small
  That stood retired by Tiber's streaming tide;
Though dull the morn, the boats with flags were gay:
A pagan Feast they kept—Rome's natal day.

Returning from that church, the youth observed
  That 'mid these boats white-winged, and by the bank
A bark lay moored where Tiber seaward curved;
  It bore no flag; its sails were black and dank—
A stern sea-stranger seemed it, sad, alone;
A raven 'mid bright birds of dulcet tone.

Down from that sable bark there moved a man
  With sunburnt brow, worn cheek, and mournful eyes:
He to the youth made way, and straight began:
  "A sailor I, and live by merchandise:
I seek Laodicea: from her shore
Edessa may be reached in three days more.

"There, in her church who bore the Lord of all
  Abides for aye that 'Venerable Face'
Which, like those shadows Apostolical
  That healed the sick, fill all that land with grace.
Thou know'st not of that mystery.   Give ear!
Elect are they who hold that picture dear.

" When Christ, Who died for Man, by slow degrees
  Bearing His Cross ascended Calvary,
O'er-spent at last He sank upon His knees :
  Then of the Holy Women clustering nigh
One forward stept. Above that Face, bedewed
With blood, she pressed her veil, and weeping stood.

" Since then abides upon that Veil all-blest
  The Sacred Image of that Face Divine
Thereon that hour by miracle impressed :
  Some see it not. Who see it never pine
Thenceforth for earthly goods. True merchant he
Who all things sells for one. This night embark with me !"

" This is my wedding-day," the youth replied :
  Then round them closed seafarers loud of cheer
And severed was that Stranger from his side :
  Through all their din thenceforth he seemed to hear
Sad memory's iteration wearisome,
" Wedded am I : therefore I cannot come."

Entering his ancient home in troubled thought
  Once more he heard, " He who great wealth hath won
Let that man live as pilgrims who have naught ;
  The wedded man as he who wife hath none "—
Words heard at Mass the morning of that Feast
Whereon that bride had landed from the East.

He raised his eyes : changed was his Father's house :
    Euphemian thus had sworn : "For one day more
Let vanished times return ; the frank carouse ;
    The harps and dances of our Rome of yore.
Rome reverenced marriage once : this marriage long
Shall record boast in Roman tale and song."

Where was it now, that rust which long had covered
    The mail of Consuls famed in days that were ?
Banners as old as Cannæ swung and hovered
    Shifting with gusts of laughter-shaken air ;
And on the walls hung faded tapestries old
Still Greek in thought though dimmed by moth and
    mould.

Here shone the Huntress Maid the crescent gleam
    Brightening her brow : that Radiance disarrayed
Whitened with imaged shape the forest stream :
    There Galatea with sea-monsters played ;
The self-same breeze that landward o'er the rocks
Waved the dark pine blew back her refluent locks.

Not far stood Pallas wrought in stone.   That eye
    Levelled beneath strong brows and helmèd crest
Though stern looked forth in wisdom clear and high :
    The Gorgon Mask lay moveless on a breast
That ne'er had heaved with love or shook with fear ;
High up her hand sustained that steadying spear.

The art was Christian oft. The Martyr Boy
   Blessed Sebastian, pierced by arrows, stood
In maid-like and immaculate beauty. Joy
   Illumed his front, though dying, unsubdued :
And well those lifted eyes discerned in heaven
That Face Divine His Martyr hailed—Saint Stephen.

Tables there were of sandal-wood carved quaintly
   By fingers lean of cedar-shaded Ind,
Embossed with emblems, shapes grotesque yet saintly ;
   And gods Egyptian, taloned, winged or finned ;
And ivory cabinets with ebon barred,
Musk-scented, pale with pearl, and opal-starred.

Here glittered caskets, gifts of Afric kings ;
   Gold goblets, pledge from satraps of the East ;
Huge incense-burning lamps on demon wings
   Suspense, for rites of funeral or feast ;
And shells for music strung and bows for war,
Fantastic toys, tribute from regions far.

Mosaic pavements glistened, deftly studded
   With Sphinx, or Zodiac-Beast, or Hieroglyph,
As oft with Lotos blossom. Leaned, new-budded
   The April Almond from his shaggy cliff,
Or rained red flakes on Ocean's blameless daughters
Oaring their placid way o'er purple waters.

The nuptial rite was brief, the banquet long
　　For many a gray-haired noble told his tale
And many a youthful minstrel sang his song ;
　　Some marked a trembling in the bride's white veil,
But on her long-lashed lids there hung no tear ;
Flushed was her cheek ; her voice was firm and clear.

Within a tent upon that bowery level
　　Whose tallest palm-grove crowned Mount Aventine,
Hour after hour rang out that ardent revel,
　　While flashed above it many a starry sign ;
Untired that Bride danced on ; beneath the shade
The night-bird sang to listening youth and maid.

Alexis moved amid the throng, heart-sore,
　　Yet welcoming friend or guest.   Pastimes like these
His eyes had never looked upon before ;
　　Now seeing, he misliked them.   Ill at ease,
One voice he heard 'mid all that buzz and hum ;
" I have a Wife ; therefore I cannot come."

Far down, where Tiber caught the white moonshine,
　　He heard, though faint, that hymn at morning sung,
More near, the opprobrious verses Fescennine
　　Trolled by boy pagans as their nuts they flung :
He sought the house, passed to its farthest room,
Lit by one lamp that scarcely pierced the gloom.

Within that room was one sole occupant;
    He stood beneath that lamp; its downward shade
Clasped the slight form, and on him seemed to plant
    A dusky cowl or crown; as one dismayed
The youth gazed on him.   Recognized at last
The Stranger seen that morning near him passed.

Alexis stood as stands a man in trance :—
    Then dawned on him a vision sad, sublime :
No more the marriage pomp, the feast, the dance,
    No more that sable bark and matin prime :
Centuries rolled back; there hung before his eye
The Saviour, crowned with thorn, and Calvary.

That Saviour looked on him and spake.   In heart
    That Bridegroom heard : " Edessa—meet Me there;
There bide with Me alone; and thence depart
    When I that sow, homeward My sheaves shall bear.
Those three thou lov'dst on earth in days of old
Shall then be thine—and Mine—in love tenfold."

The Vision faded; lightest steps he heard,
    And wreathed with rose the Bride before him stood
Warm from the dance, and blithesome as a bird.
    He spake: "Fear naught! What God decrees is good."
Within her hand he placed a ring, and said :
" Farewell ! Wear this till many years are fled.

"Farewell!   Live thou in Faith and Innocence :
  Farewell !   God calls me to a far-off land ;
But He will lead me back Who bids me hence,
  And draw us near ; and yet between us stand.
Farewell, poor child !"   He passed into the night,
And soon was hidden wholly from her sight.

When the next morn had changed dark skies to grey
  They found her with wide eyes and lips apart
Standing, a statue wreathed, in white array ;
  One wedded hand was pressed against her heart ;
One clasped a ring.   "'Tis time to sleep," she said ;
" Lay the poor Bride—'tis late—upon her bed."

PART III.

Not far from where Euphrates, that great river,
  From heights of Taurus seaward winds in flood
Its mighty youth replenishing for ever,
  In days of yore a royal city stood :
Two lesser streams embraced it like two arms
That clasp some bright one in her bridal charms.

Around it gleamed Plane-tree and Poplar shivering
  In Syrian gales tempered by mountain snows,
And gardens green traversed by runnels quivering
  And Palms at each side set in columned rows :
High in the midst a church of ancient fame
There rose.   Edessa was that city's name.

Before that church there stood five porches fair
  Wherein the maimed and crippled sued for alms ;
Likewise God's penitents, admitted there
  As men beloved, might hear the hymns and psalms
Until, their penance past, once more the shrine
Received them, and they fed on food divine.

Within that fivefold narthex one there knelt
  Of race unknown, and humbler than the rest,
His garment hair-cloth 'neath a leathern belt ;
  He deemed himself unmeet to stand as guest
Within that hallowed precinct whose embrace
Cherished the Veil all-blest and "Sacred Face."

For that cause year by year he dwelt without
  Although in spirit kneeling still within ;
And neither civic pomp nor popular shout
  Made way to him.   Propping a haggard chin
On haggard hand he sat with low-bent brows
Absorbed in heavenly thoughts, unearthly vows.

Meantime o'er all the world's circumference
   Euphemian sent wise men to seek his son :
Some to Laodicea sailed, and thence
   Their way like others to Edessa won ;
Near him they drew ; upon him turned their eye ;
They knew him not ; yet passed him with a sigh.

There were who turned again, and, instinct-taught,
   Lodged on those fingers worn a piece of bread ;
And he with gladness ate it, for his thought
   Grew humbler daily ; breaking it, he said
" Thank God that I have eaten of their hand
Whom once I fed and held at my command ! "

So thus by patience and long-suffering first,
   And next through heart self-emptied to its core,
The inmost of Christ's Teaching on him burst ;
   And " Blessed they who mourn," " Blessed the poor,"
Lived on his lips, as he in them with awe
The shrouded Vision of God's greatness saw.

He saw the things men see not.   In a glass
   Nearer to God than Nature's best, in Man
He saw that God Who ever is and was :
   In those whom this world lays beneath her ban
The halt, the stricken, saw their Maker most :
The saved he saw in those the fool deems lost.

Now when those years were past, within the church
  One day, as vespers ceased, was heard a Voice,
" Bring in My Son who kneeleth in the porch :
  The same shall see My Countenance and rejoice."
Then forth God's people rushed, both old and young,
And haled the man to where that picture hung.

Instant that Pilgrim fixed his eyes thereon,
  And saw that Countenance through its mist of blood
Which some see not : and still, ere set of sun,
  A change miraculous swifter than a flood
O'erswept it.   Grief and shame far off were driven :
It shone as shines the Saviour's Face in heaven.

And still he said : " Behold, these Faces twain
  Reveal the portions twain to man allowed ;
For one of these is earth and Holy Pain,
  And one is heavenly Glory, when the cloud
Of time dissolves."   And still his prayer he made
For those far off : " Aid them, Thou Saviour, aid ! "

'Twas needed sore.   The day Alexis fled
  His mother sat in ashes on the ground,
And thenceforth day by day ; and still she said,
  " Lo, thus I sit until the Lost is found ! "
And night by night murmured the one-day bride,
" His wife I am : faithful I will abide.

" I will not muse, as once, in groves of Greece,
　　Nor dance, as once, in palace halls of Rome ;
Until this wedded widowhood shall cease,
　　Here with his parents I will make my home :
I must be patient now, though proud of yore :
He called me 'Child !'　He said, ' We meet once more.' "

While sinks the sun nighing his watery bed
　　The shadow reacheth soon the valley's breast ;
More late it climbeth to the mountain's head—
　　His loved one gone, Euphemian hoped the best :
Not yet the shade had reached him.　Every morn
He said : " Ere night Alexis may return !

" The day my Son was born—the self-same hour—
　　I shook the dust from many a treasured scroll
Precious with that which time would fain devour,
　　The great deeds of our House.　In one fair whole
To blend those annals was my task for years :
They bled full oft : they cannot end in tears."

But when his messengers from all the lands
　　Returning, early some, and others late,
From Gaul, Iberia, Thrace, from Syrian sands,
　　Red Libyan coasts, and Calpé's golden gate,
Brought back the self-same tidings as the first,
That grief which reached him last was grief the worst.

Silent he mused : " Were these our prayers of old ?
   Sent was our child, that late-conceded boy,
To be the lamb unblemished of our fold,
   Then vanish, and to by-word change our joy ?
Had he but won the martyr's crown and fame !
But now God's Church shall never hear his name.

" O ancient House, revered in days of yore,
   House blind yet just, I deemed that years to be
Fourfold to thee, now Christian, would restore
   What time or heathen hate had reft from thee,
And of thy greatness make a boon for all—
That dream is over !   Let the roof-tree fall ! "

Thus as his father mourned Alexis knelt
   One day before that picture-hallowed shrine,
When suddenly he heard at once and felt
   A voice oracular, awful yet benign :
" This day in prayer be mighty for those Three,
Since what to them I grant I grant through thee."

Then prayed the Saint as Saints alone can pray ;
   And on that far-off Three, they knew not why,
There fell a calm undreamed of till that day,
   As when some great storm ceases from the sky
Sudden, and into harbour sweeps the bark,
And green hills laugh, and singing mounts the lark.

Thenceforth for things gone by they hungered less,
   And of the joy to come had oftener vision ;
Thenceforth self-will inflamed not heart-distress,
   Nor pride that draws from pain perverse fruition :
The parents saw their son once more a child ;
The wife, as when he saw her first, and smiled.

Two years passed by : once more within his heart
   That son received an answer from his God :
" Go to the great sea down, and thence depart
   To Tarsus, where My servant, Paul, abode ;
For I will show thee there by tokens true
The things which thou must suffer and must do."

The man of God arose, and gat him down
   To where Laodicea's mast-thronged bay
Mirrored that queenly city's towery crown,
   And found a ship for Tarsus bound that day,
And sailed till o'er the morn-touched deep arose
Her walls, and hills beyond her white with snows.

Then from those hills a storm rushed forth, as when
   An eagle from high cliffs has kenned its quarry ;
And the black ship before it raced like men
   Who flee the uplifted sword they dare not parry
With necks low bent.   So fled that ship : each sail
Split ; and the masts low leaned like willows in the gale.

Amid the slanted rain of falling spars
   And roar of winds and billows far and near
Astonished stood those sea-worn mariners
   Yet mute, since none his neighbour's voice might hear :
Then heard God's Saint : " For all this company
Fear nought ; for thine they are and none shall die.

" Fear not for thine own self : this storm is Mine,
   And it shall lay thee by thy father's door :
There shall the last storm greet thee—storm benign,
   For what I take, that fourfold I restore."
Next morn they entered Tiber's mouth : at Rome
He stood ere noon, and saw his father's home,

Saw it far off whilst yet upon his way
   To earth's cathedral metropolitan,
" Mother and Head of Churches," there to pray
   That what to him remained of life's brief span
Might, through God's help, accomplish God's decree,
And praise His name for all eternity.

Entering, he knelt before that crypt cross-crowned
   Where in a subterranean chapel small
Reposed, awaiting God's Last Trumpet's sound,
   The sacred bones of Peter and of Paul :
A child he oft had knelt its gates before ;
There learned that hour what God had yet for him in
   store.

Evening drew nigh : he left the Lateran :
   Anon, as slow he paced Rome's stateliest street, .
From Cæsar's palace issued forth a man
   Though bent, majestic, with attendance meet.
That man Alexis knew.   With steadfast eye
The sire drew near the son ; and passed him by.

Then cried that son with anguished voice and face
   "Servant of God, revered and loved of all,
Within thy house yield me a little place
   That I may daily eat the crumbs that fall
Down from thy table."   And his sire replied :
" So be it, Pilgrim : walk thou by my side."

Through lonely ways dimmed by the day's decline
   That sire and son made way, and neither spake
Till, step by step climbing Mount Aventine
   They reached that well-known mansion.   Flake by flake
The snows were falling.   'Twas not like the day
Of that fair bridal in that far-off May.

Alexis spake : " A stripling, sir, I saw
   Ofttime thy house ; memory thereof I keep :
Beneath the great stair—on a bed of straw—
   Slept then a mastiff : there I fain would sleep."
And answered thus Euphemian : " Let it be !
Long since he died : his place remains for thee."

Once more the son : " Footsore and weak am I :
 .'Tis time to sleep : my pilgrimage is made :
The mastiff died : the Pilgrim soon will die."
    Then down upon the straw his limbs he laid,
And sank asleep.   For hours, as there he slept
Two women by his couch their vigil kept.

Down from the head of one, silk-soft, snow-white,
    Rolled waves of hair : the younger kept her bloom
Though worn.   They sat beside him till twilight
    At last was lost in evening's deepening gloom,
And longed that he might wake and eat ; and spread
Their silks and velvets closelier on his bed.

At morn he woke.   Sickness and crippling pain
    Fixed each its eye thenceforth on that sole man ;
And like to dead men on the battle-plain
    Silent he lay.   In pain his day began,
In pain worked on till daylight's last had fled,
As though great nails had fixed him to his bed.

And ever by his couch they ministered
    Who loved that sufferer well yet knew him not :
For at the first note of the wakening bird
    That mother came who o'er her infant's cot
Ere break of day so oft had peered ; at noon
His sire drew nigh : and when the rising moon

N

Flung o'er the marble floor a beam as bright
  As that long path wherewith it paves the sea
Softly she came upon whose bridal night
  So black a shade had fallen so suddenly;
And on his bed sat in the white moonshine
Like one that inly says: " This place is mine."

Some deem they knew him not because so long
  Fierce Syrian suns that sweet face had imbrowned;
And some because at God's command there clung
  A mist illusive still their eyes around;
While some are sure that mist, those long sad years,
Was unmiraculous, and a mist of tears.

Yet one avers that, gazing evermore
  Year after year upon that Sacred Face,
Its semblance spread that Pilgrim's countenance o'er,
  Its anguish fixed, its gleams of heavenly grace,
So that who saw the living face, beneath
Its veil saw, too, the Face of Christ in death.

Men say that at that hour when Jesus died
  That Pilgrim watched the Darkness move o'er earth;
And at that hour when rose the Crucified
  He saw God's Universe in angel mirth
Flash forth, created new, and heard that song
The Immaculate sing the singing spheres among.

And Thrones he saw in Heaven; and, 'mid those
    Thrones,
  Three, for those Three he loved in glory set:
His father's was the loftiest, for his groans
    Had risen from crypts of grief profounder yet
Than theirs, the others;—saw a fourth, low down,
Smaller; and o'er it hung a lowlier crown.

But when his parents at high festivals
    Serving the mighty Rite were absent long
A slave, not Christian, reared in those great halls
    Of him had charge.   At times he did him wrong;
Then cried—that wrong rebuked by no complaint—
"A fool he is!   Not less the fool's a Saint!"

And oft to that low couch a man there came
    Old ere his time, with haught yet pleading eye,
Who spake: "My sires to me an ancient name
    Bequeathed.   When I am dead, that name shall die."
And he made answer: "Household none on earth
Can last, save Christ's.   The rest are nothing worth."

And oft a woman sat beside that bed
    Meek-eyed, with soft white hair: "A child had I:
The twentieth winter now is past and fled:
    That child returns not.   O that I might die!"
And he replied: "Have courage, and endure;
Pray well; and find thy children in God's Poor."

And many a time low-bent beneath the rod
    One proud of old, still fair as fair may be,
Though bright no more, spake thus : "Pray, man of God,
    That, living yet, my husband I may see
A living man !"   And thus he made reply :
"Yea, thou shalt see thy husband ere thou die !"

And ever when those Three were set at meat
    Euphemian sent him viands, flesh and wine,
But he of barley crusts alone would eat :
    And still, he spake to them of things divine ;
And still, when back he sank and ceased from speech
Musing they sat, or staring each on each.

For others spake of great things through the ear
    Divulged to faith : he spake of great things seen
That flash as stars descried through ether clear,
    Clearer for frosty skies and north wind keen :
The Martyr means the Witness : such was he,
Martyr, not slain, of selfless charity,

Which, loving well, not self, but Man our brother,
    For that cause loves its God better by far
Than Man ; nor suffers mortal loves to smother
    The immortal Love with lawless loves at war.
Such men here lived of old : such man was he,
Bondsman of Love, thence setting many free.

At times the old passion in their bosoms burned ;
  At times the wound half-healed welled forth anew ;
Then to that man of woes those strong ones turned,
  Child-like ; and thus he gave them solace true :
"God yearns to grant you peace, yet waits until
Your wills are one with His all-loving Will."

And when they said, "Weary we grow of prayer
  Because God hath not given us that we sought,"
He answered : "Love in God, and work, and bear ;
  Let no man say, 'Serve they their God for nought?'
Pray for great Rome ; for him your Lost One pray,
That he be faithful till his dying day."

Suns rose and set ; the seasons circled slow ;
  Upon that house settled a gradual peace
Breathed from that spot obscure and pallet low ;
  Yea, as the dews of midnight drench a fleece
So drenched was every heart with that strange calm,
And wounds long festered felt the healing balm.

Now when the years decreed had all gone by
  There came from God an answer to His Saint :
"Rejoice ! Thy work is worked, and thou shalt die : "
  Then gave he thanks in happy tone though faint,
And, turning to that slave with quiet smile,
Demanded parchment scroll and writing-style.

Straightway he wrote the story of his life
　　And God's Command in love that spares not, given ;
And ended thus : " O Parents, and O Wife !
　　We meet ere long : no partings are in heaven.
I loved you well.　Strangely my faith God proved :
Yet know that few are loved as ye were loved.

" Farewell !　God sent you trials great below
　　Because for you He keeps great thrones on high :
Likewise by you God willeth to bestow
　　New gifts on man.　Each dear domestic tie
Whereof so many a year ye stood amerced
Shall yet rule earth—but raised and hallowed first.

" Because ye loved your God as few men love
　　He called you forth His witnesses to be
That Love there is all human loves above,
　　A Love all-gracious in its jealousy
That, all exacting, all suffices too ;
The world must learn this lesson, and from you."

When all was writ he crossed upon his breast
　　His arms, and in his right hand clasped that scroll :
And as the Roman monks arose from rest
　　Nocturns to chant, behold, that dauntless soul
Cleansed here on earth by fire expiatory
When none was near went hence into the glory :

At noontide, in the Lateran basilic,
   Blessed Pope Innocent who, throned that day
High in Saint Peter's world-wide bishopric,
   O'er all the churches of the world held sway,
Had sung at Mass that text, though dread, benign,
" Unless a man leave all he is not Mine."

That moment from the Holy Place a Voice
   Went forth : " All ye who labour, come to Me : "
And yet again : " All ye that weep, rejoice ! "
   At once that mighty concourse sank on knee
And each man laid his forehead near the ground :
Then, close to each, those pillared aisles around

Distinct and clear thus heard they, word by word :
   " Seek out My Saint, and bid him pray for Rome :
Yea, if he pray, his pleading shall be heard ;
   That lighter thus My Judgments may become,
For now the things concerning Rome have end.
Seek in Euphemian's house My Servant and My Friend."

That hour uprising in procession went
   The Roman people.   With them paced that day
The Emperors twain, and holy Innocent
   Between them, higher by the head than they.
Their crowns Arcadius and Honorius wore,
His mitre Blessed Peter's successor.

Arrived, they questioned if beneath that roof
　　There dwelt a Saint. The Christians said : " Not here ; "
Then rose a pagan slave that sat aloof,
　　He who had watched the sick man all that year :
He spake : " A Saint is here ; I did him wrong,
Yet never heard from him upbraiding tongue."

Straight to that marble stair Euphemian ran
　　And passed beneath its central arch ; and lo !
Dead on his small straw pallet lay the man ;
　　And on that face, so long a face of woe,
Strange joy there lived and mystical content ;
And o'er him with wide wings an Angel bent.

Aloud Euphemian cried : they flocked around
　　And saw and knelt.   But some that stood espied
That parchment in the dead hand clasped and wound,
　　And strove to loose it   To that pallet's side
The brother Emperors drew, and each was fain
To win it from his hold, but strove in vain.

Lastly Pope Innocent approached, and spread
　　Softly upon the dead man's hand his own ;
And lo, that parchment dropped upon the bed :
　　Long, standing by that sacred head alone,
The Pontiff eyed that scroll—at last he raised ;
While each man, rising, nearer drew and gazed.

He spread it wide : he read : the listeners trembled ;
    Each heart beat slow, and every cheek grew pale,
And strong men wept with passion undissembled ;
    For short, and plain, and simple was that tale :
No praise it sued ; no censure seemed to shun :
Record austere of great things borne and done.

Now when Euphemian saw these things, and heard,
    Motionless stood the man like shape of stone ;
Ere long he fell a-shivering without word ;
    And lastly dropped upon the pavement prone :
But, when kind arms had raised him, on the dead
He fixed unseeing eyes, and nothing said.

Next through that concourse rushed the Mother, wailing,
    " Let be !   Shall I not see the babe I bore ? "
And reached the dead ; and then, her forces failing,
    Sank to her knees, and eyed him, weeping sore ;
And as a poplar sways in stormy air
So swayed she ; and back streamed her long white hair.

A change—she stood.   She who, her whole life long,
    Had lived the soft and silent life of flowers
Pleased with the beam, patient of rain and wrong,
    Had held, unconscious, all those years and hours,
A fire within hidden 'neath ashes frore :
It rose—to speak but once, and spake no more.

It spake reproach : " Ah me ! thy Sire and I
  Sought thee while near thou lay'st, but vainly sought.
Likewise a houschold slave right ruthlessly
  Smote thee at seasons : thou didst answer nought :
Thou didst not stanch our tears !   O Son, O Son !
Make answer from the dead, was this well done ? "

Last, with firm foot drew near the one-day Wife,
  And looked on him, and said : " I know that face !
Dead is the hope that cheered the widow's life :
  'Tis time the Wife her Husband should embrace ! "
She spake, and sank in swoon upon his breast,
And in that swoon her heart—then first—had rest.

But by the Dead still stood Pope Innocent ;
  His deacons placed the mitre on his head ;
And on his pastoral staff the old man leant :
  Upon that throng his eye he fixed, and said,
" Henceforth I interdict all tears.   A Saint
Lies here.   Insult not such with grief or plaint.

" This man was God's Elect ; for from a child
  He walked God's prophet in an age impure :
Ye knew him, sirs : harmless and undefiled
  He nothing preached.   To act and to endure,
To live in God's light hid, unknown to die—
This task was his.   He wrought it faithfully.

" This man a great work wrought : its greatness fills
　　True measure since *His* Work Who still divides
To each man severally as He wills ;
　　He common souls in common courses guides :
To some he points strange paths till then untrod :
This thing had been ill-done had it not come from God.

" Behold ! He spreads the smooth and level way
　　And blesses those that walk there pure and lowly :
Behold ! He calls, ' Ascend My hill, and pray,
　　And holy be ye, for your God is holy :
Let each man hear My Voice and heed My Call ;
For what I give to each I give for all.' "

He spake, and ceased.　Then lo ! an angel strain
　　At first breathed softly round that straw-laid bed
Swelled through those halls : and with it mingled plain
　　That voice so loved of him so lately dead
Then when, a child, he poured that vesper hymn
" Salve, Regina," through the twilight dim.

Again and yet again that strain ascended ;
　　And in it, sweeter each time than before,
The child-voice with the angelic met and blended ;
　　The courts, the garden bowers were flooded o'er,
Till sorrow seemed to all some time-worn fable,
As when, to lull sick babes, old nurses babble.

It ceased.　The Emperors gave command, and straight
　　Men stretched the Dead upon a golden bier
For kings ordained ; and passed the palace gate ;
　　And laid him in a church to all men dear ;
And lo ! that night blind men who near him prayed
Made whole, gave thanks, departing without aid.

But in that palace where their Saint was born
　　Till death his parents, sad no more, abode ;
And, yearly as recurred her marriage morn,
　　His wife put on her wedding-dress, and showed
A paler, tenderer reflex, many said,
Of what she looked the morning she was wed.

Serving their God—all lame half-service past—
　　Serving their God, and, in their God, His poor,
They lived ; and God, Whose best gift is His last,
　　Suffered not these that anguish to endure
Worn patriots feel watching their land's decay :
Ere Rome had fall'n they died—on the same day.

Alaric, " the Scourge of God," but two years after
　　To Rome his Gothic host barbaric led :
Down from her wall they laughed a dreadful laughter
　　As sank an ominous sun through skies blood-red
Nighing a stormy sea.　At twelve that night
Men whispered each to each with lips death-white.

The carnage o'er, they passed to farthest shores,
  Exiles or slaves, maiden to matron bound,
Noble to knight, and hoary senators :
  Yet through God's saints who slept in Roman ground
God spared most part ; and scathless towered o'er all
The basilics three of Peter, John, and Paul.

Euphemian's latest act had given command
  To raise where stood his Fathers' house in pride
A church to God. This day that church doth stand
  Honouring the spot whereon his dearest died :
Of that huge house remains that stony stair
Alone, which roofed the dying lion's lair.

The Romans bring their infants to that spot ;
  Young children peer therein, then shrink away
Between those columned ranges twain that blot
  With evening shades the glistening pavements grey ;
And oft the latest lingerer drops a tear
For those so sternly tried, and yet so dear.

But ever while the bells salute that morn
  When from the darksome womb of mortal life
Their Saint into the heavenly realm was born,
  Old Aventine with bannered throngs is rife ;
They mount o'er ruins where the great courts stood :
They mark old Tiber, now a shipless flood.

They reach the church.   Star-bright the Altar stands
  The Benediction Hymns ascend once more :
Nearer they gather : Apostolic hands
  Uplift the Eternal Victim : all adore.
The world without is nought : within that fane
Abide the things that live and that remain.

There still thou livest, Alexis ! livest for ever
  There and in heaven, rooted in endless peace—
Thou, and those Three—like trees beside a river
  That clothe each year their boughs with fresh increase
Of flower and fruit embalming airs divine :
In that high realm forget not me and mine !

SAINT AGATHA.

(DIED A.D. 251.)

I.

Dark as ministers of Hell,
  The gaolers strode the Maid beside :
Light from heaven upon her fell
  As she raised her face, and cried
"Lo, my Jesus, all I am
  Give I freely unto thee :
Guard from harm thy little lamb :
  Quell the demon brood through me."

2.

Dark the Præter sat, his hand
  Pointing to the statued gods :
Round his throne the lictor band
  Reared their axes and their rods.

"Sacrifice!" the concourse cried ;
  "Sacrifice, and thou art free :'
"Christ I serve," the Maid replied ;
  "That is Life and Liberty."

3.

They led her to the haunts of shame :
  Sin was shamed ; and Satan fled :
They stretched her on a couch of flame :
  'Twas to her a rose-strewn bed.
Blissful martyr ! loud she cried,
  "Glory be, my Christ, to thee !
Teach Thou well Thy little bride
  Patience, Love, and Purity."

4.

It was midnight, and the Maid
  Robed from breast to foot in blood
Stood with hands outstretched, and prayed :—
  One she saw not near her stood.
Fell the Apostolic Light
  Where had fallen the Pagan sword :
Beams of healing smote with might
  Her bleeding bosom, and restored.

5.

Blest Palermo ! Lullabied
   Was the babe by thy blue sea !
Catana more blest ! she died
   Dowered with palm and crown in thee !
Share with us your double boast
   Happy land, for poor are we :
Plead, among the heavenly host,
   Agatha, for mine and me.

SAINT LUCY.

(DIED A.D. 304.)

I.

"O LIGHT divine, those outward eyes
   That languish, nothing seeing
Save thine inferior suns and skies,
   Blot wholly from my being;
But grant me one short hour to see
   What Anna saw, and Stephen—
The Babe upon His Mother's knee;
   The Saviour crowned in heaven.

2.

"O heavenly, uncreated Word,
   That took'st our mortal nature,
And, still on high as God adored,
   Didst die on earth, a Creature;

We die because we may not die :—
  Each act, word, thought, betrays thee :
But thy good Martyrs in the sky
  And where they suffered, praise thee !"

3.

Thus sang Saint Lucy, bright like day,
  Where others hoped not, hoping ;
To thy worn tomb, O Agatha,
  A mother's footsteps propping.
She knelt and prayed the Martyr's aid—
  "My mother ! help her, shield her !"
"Why ask my aid?" the Martyr Maid
  Replied ; "Thy prayers have healed her.'

4.

She rose : her country's gods defied ;
  Idol and altar spurning :
To death adjudged, with tenderest pride
  Her cheek, late pale, was burning :—
A thousand men their strength put forth :
  Nor man nor beast might move her !
The hand that made the heavens and earth
  Lay strong that hour above her.

5.

Round her they piled the wood : the fires
  Forth flashed, and fiercely mounted ;
She, like a bird 'mid golden wires,
  The praise of God recounted.
" The Empire falls : the Church is free ! "—
  So rang her song, and ended
" O Agatha ! for Sicily
  Henceforth our prayers are blended."

6.

Sicilian sisters fair and brave
  In bonds of God close-plighted,
That, like two lilies on one wave,
  Float, evermore united ;
Upheaved upon the Church's breast
  In aspiration endless
Plead from the bosom of your rest
  For exiled souls and friendless !

SAINT ANASTASIA AT AQUILEIA.

(DIED A.D. 304.)

I.

OCEAN, anew creating
　Old harmonies;
Ether, star-germinating
　While daylight dies;
Sunset, but lately firing
　The city towers, and still
In crimson flames expiring
　On yonder snow-capped hill:
Far peaks, and cliffs that shiver
　In golden mist;—henceforth
O lure no more forever
　My spirit back to earth!

2.

Moored is at last our galley :
  Our pilgrimage is o'er :
But not for us yon valley ;
  And not for us that shore !
The cymbals from the city
  Shake the water like a breath—
Chant we in turn one ditty,
  O Martyr Maids, ere death !
O people, who can teach thee
  That joy to earth unknown ?
O Saviour, who can preach thee ?—
  Not words, but death alone !

3.

Mother !   Ah, twice, my mother,
  Thou gav'st me Christ !   This day
I thank thee, and that other
  My childhood's staff and stay.
How oft when trial pressed me
  And earthly hope was none,
That more than father blessed me
  And said, " Poor child, strive on. "
He prayed for me ; he cherished :
  He gained me strength to win :
Through him the tyrant perished
  That tempted me to sin.

4.

Like a Seraph in its fleetness
   My life above me flew:
Its sorrow past, its sweetness
   Falls back on me as dew.
Again I tread the prison ;
   I bring the Christians bread :
They have raised their heads : they listen :
   Sweet souls, ye know my tread !
The children hide their faces
   In an unmaternal breast :
And, warmed in my embraces,
   Young mothers, too, find rest.

5.

Once more, the Forum pacing
   Its temples I behold,
As they stand the sun outfacing
   With their marble and their gold :
I scorn them :—I am taken :—
   I am judged to death once more :
Half-famished I awaken
   On the cold dark dungeon floor.
Chrysogonus ! thou hast taught me
   Once more to kiss my chain :
Theodora ! thou hast brought me
   Celestial food again !

6.

'Tis past.   The dream is over,
  And the life that does but seem :
They are past ; and I discover
  The World too is a dream.
Its meaning, its consistence
  From a higher world is caught ;
Thy Will is its subsistence ;
  Its order is Thy Thought.
Thou hast made it : it arrays Thee :
  Yet it cannot fill man's heart :—
For what Thou art I praise Thee :
  And I praise Thee that Thou art.

7.

Entering his own creation
  True God true Man became.
Who wrought the world's salvation ?
  " Redeemer " is His Name.
For each man death he tasted :
  He died that Death might die :
Three days entombed He rested :
  He rose into the sky.
Ne'er watched I spring flower waking
  From its grave beneath the sod
But I saw that tombstone breaking,
  And that Form ascend to God.

8.

How oft in youthful slumber
  I saw all worlds ascend :
Unmeasured, without number,
  Still up they seemed to tend !
Like angels interwoven
  Up passed the shining choir
Through the black vault o'er them cloven :
  And higher rose and higher.
Creation seemed a fountain
  Sun-changed to heavenward mist :
But I knew the parent mountain
  Was God; the sun was Christ.

9.

As one that, gold refining,
  Bends o'er the metal base
Till, purged by fire, and shining
  It reflects at last his face,
So God oft saw I clearing
  By pain man's race from sin
Till, the perfect mirror sphering,
  He, imaged, shone therein.—
The city stays its revels :
  The minstrel bands retire :
No sound o'er the sea-levels :
  No light, save yonder pyre !

10.

O wind, once more that playest
   With the palm-grove near the bay
Low words to us thou sayest
   Of palms that live for aye.
That veil the ocean dimming
   Brings the world of stars more near :
And the anthem they are hymning
   In my spirit I can hear.
They sing, "Of dust partaker
   Our wondrous world must die :
But our Master and our Maker
   Lives on eternally."

THE FEAST OF ST. PETER'S CHAINS.

(A.D. 438.)

1.

HER crown is bright with many a gem ;
    But costlier far each tear that glides
Down that pale cheek.   Jerusalem !
    She weeps as up thy steep she rides.
Before their empress,* gifts they shower :
    One only to her heart is pressed :
An iron chain.   In Herod's hour
    It bound the Apostle ever blest !

2.

The beauteous vision melts in gloom—
    What lights are those that pierce yon shade ?
One walks, the mitred sire of Rome :
    Beside him moves a crownèd maid.†

  * The Empress Eudocia.
  † Eudoxia, daughter of the Empress Eudocia,

Mamurtine prison ! In Nero's reign
  O'er Peter's head that shade was thrown :—
They kneel ; and, kneeling, kiss the chain
  That bound him to his couch of stone.

3.

That Roman, that Judean bond
  United then, dispart no more—
Pierce through the veil : the rind beyond
  Lies hid the legend's deeper lore.
Therein the mystery lies expressed
  Of Power transferred, yet ever one ;
Of Rome—the Salem of the West—
  Of Sion built o'er Babylon.

4.

A city set upon a hill
  Whoe'er has eyes may turn and see :
Through thee the Church is visible ;
  Made visible by unity !
The " Pillar and the Ground of Truth "—
  Through thee she speaks what all may hear :
Peter ! to hear and hearken, both
  Were hard indeed wert thou not near.

5.

Through thee her Mysteries high and sweet
  The Church with History weds, and Fact ;
Through thee the strife of Time can meet ;
  Through thee can witness, and can act.
Bind round the Church thy sacred Chains !—
  The electric life that feeds her heart
Flashing through them, her iron veins,
  Makes thus the whole sustain the part.

6.

Droop but a branch, to natural blight
  Subjected, or the storms of men,
Through thee, sent forth like life and light,
  Health flows into that branch again.
Through thee that strength the world hath missed
  The Church renews while ages flee :
Her inward Unity is Christ ;
  Her outward, Christ set forth in thee.

SAINT PERPETUA.

(DIED A.D. 203.)

SILENCE, ye crowds ! how dare ye thus make start
An infant feeding at its mother's breast,
Feeding on sacred food and sacred rest?
Vain are your cries, your pity vain.   Depart !
But ye, dread masters in death's fatal art,
Torturers ! remain : and try, though shame-opprest,
Once more your skill ; fulfil the dread behest :
Her head ye shall not bow nor shake her heart.
The Lady's eyes alternately were bent
On Heaven and on her child ; a grave, sweet smile
Tenderly circling her pale lips the while ;
Until at last the infant was content :
Then drooped her lids, and sighing o'er his sigh
The mother's spirit sought its native sky.

SAINTS VALERIAN AND CECILIA.

(DIED A.D. 230.)

THE eyes that loved me were upon me staying :
The eyes that loved me, and the eyes that won :
Guardian or guide celestial saw I none ;
But the unseen chaplets on her temples weighing
Breathed heaven around ! A golden smile was playing
O'er the full lips. Meekly her countenance shone,
And beamed, a lamp of peace 'mid shadows dun—
Round her lit form the ambrosial locks were swaying.
Fair Spirit ! Angel of delight new-born
And love, unchanging love and infinite,
Aurorean planet of the eternal morn !
That gaze I caught ; and, standing in that light,
My soul, from Pagan bonds released by thee,
Upsoared, and hailed its immortality.

SAINT EMMELIA.

I.

Her Convents on the Iris in Pontus.

Not for thy snowy peaks, thy woods that wave
Where rolls thine Iris on in swift career;
Not for thy mountain floods that downward rave,
Thy river-breadths shattered o'er ledges sheer;
Not for the gems thy myriad streams that pave;
Not for roe-haunted glade or shadowed mere;
Not for green lawn, blue gorge, or ivied cave;
'Tis not for these that Christians hold thee dear,
Thou Pontic Paradise!   In Pagan days
Beauty was thrall to Pleasure or to Pride:
Earth's beauty here Emmelia sanctified
Teaching wild wastes to sing their Maker's praise;
Here first *her* Basil taught his Rule austere;
Asia's monastic life was rooted here.

II.

Her domestic life by the Halys in Cappadocia.

The Halys to the Iris whispers low :
"Thy Saint—Emmelia—came to me a Bride ;
Each morn, my waving lily beds beside,
Knelt with her lord, then strayed with footsteps slow :
Amid my flowers I saw her flowers up-grow—
Her babes—I bathed them in my crystal tide,
I that through flowery meads delight to glide
Though born, like thee, among the thrones of snow."
Then Iris answers : "Yea, and Saint not less
Was my Emmelia when she walked with thee
Than cloistered in my mountains.   Saintliness,
Ascending, mounts by order and degree ;
From thee and me alike our Saint is passed :—
In thee the flower, in me the star was glassed."

P

THE ALEXANDRIAN VERSION OF THE SCRIPTURES.

BESIDE a little humble Oratory
There sat a noble lady all alone :
Over her knees a parchment lay, whereon
Her slender fingers traced the Gospel story.
Old Nile flowed noiseless by : through vapours dun
A low-hung moon let forth its last faint glory
On all the dark green flats, and temples hoary,
That grey and ghostly through the morning shone.
Thecla ! Mankind will ne'er forget that zeal
Which, ere the night-bird stays her melody,
Raises thee daily to the Church's needs :
No doubts, no fears hast thou—thou dost not feel
The cold, damp winds of morning as they sigh,
Murmuring forlorn through leagues of murmuring reeds !

SAINT LEO THE GREAT.

(ATTILA BEFORE ROME, A.D. 452.)

LEAGUERING doomed walls—as when on some wild coast
The high-ridged deep, storm-driven from afar,
Makes way in thunder, whitening reef and bar—
Leaguering great Rome, the old world's shame yet boast,
Comes up at last that dread Barbarian host :
To meet them, placid as that morning star
Whose rising quells the elemental war
Forth moves, his hands upon his bosom crossed,
That Puissance new, the Church's mitred Sire !
His eye is fixed : as reeds before the breeze
Bending, that host sinks down on suppliant knees :
The standards droop : the trumpet blasts expire :
The Man of Fate in heaven his sentence sees ;
The embattled Gentiles tremble and retire.

EUSTOCHIUM, OR SAINT JEROME'S LETTER.

(A.D. 382).

ARGUMENT.

Saint Jerome, after his earlier sojourn in the desert of Chalcis and the Holy Land, made abode at Rome, where many enemies waged war against him by reason of the zeal with which he denounced abuses. Notwithstanding, Pope Damasus honoured him, and made him the spiritual director of certain noble Roman ladies, such as Marcella, who had changed her palace into a convent, Paula a young widow, her daughters Eustochium and Blesilla, and others who ennobled yet more the greatest families of ancient Rome by their heroic exercise of the Christian virtues. The Saint had written to Eustochium, then a young girl, his celebrated letter concerning Christian perfection. In return the girl sent to him three lines and three presents.

A MAN so great to one so slight, so small !
Mother ! this letter 'twixt my hands high held—
I dreamed of it all night ; I dreamed a star
Shone ever on the scroll—this precious letter
Is full of wisdom as the spring of flowers ;
Full as your eyes are full of beams and tears

At times, upon me gazing ; as your lips
Are full of sweetness closing upon mine.
How gently bends this seer to teach a child !
I grow to something better. Once I wept
When from the Catacombs they fetched triumphant
Some new-found vial red with Martyr's blood :
This day I fain would share such death ! What wonder ?
Ere speech was mine you vowed for me a vow
That never sin should stain that chrisom-robe
Which pledged your babe to Christ. Maidens each night
Wear garb as white !—you see how glitters mine
Touched by the rising sun. The vow you made
Each morning I renew. That anchoret grave
Was bound by sterner rule.

      His hair is grey ;
His forehead seamed and weather-worn ; his hand
Rough as that desert's tawniest tract ; and yet
How tenderly it writes ! "She sold her gems,
And gave the poor their price. Her festal robes
She changed for cloak of penitential brown :
One narrow cell to her was paradise :
At night she glided to the Martyrs' tombs ;
There knelt in prayer till morning. In that mien
Severity was blithesome, blithesomeness
A thing severe. Where else save in that face
Was sweetness e'er so sad, so beauteous grief ?

Its paleness meant detachment from this world,
Converse with heaven.   Her speech was soft as silence ;
Her silence sweet as music."   Thus he ends :
" Let her not see this letter : praise disturbs her !
Show it to Pagans."

                  Sternly he writes of these :
" Shun thou those Pagan maids who, serpent-like,
Shoot out from creviced chinks of rock a crest
That shines out to betray ; and shun not less
Those worldlings that usurp the Christian name
Yet, Pagans still at heart, stretch fearless forth
A full-fed, gem-lit, sacrilegious hand
Even to the sacred chalice !   Shun those widows
Shrill-voiced because some Consul of their kin
Rode up triumphant to the Capitol
Dragged by the snow-white steeds.   Predestinate race !
That golden-gated Capitol is void !
Trembles the seven-hilled city !   Suppliant throngs
Rush on by vacant temples of the gods
Rush to the Martyrs' graves."

                  Forgive me, mother '
Back blew the casement, and rose-scented airs
Ruffled the pages.   Thus once more he writes :
" Forget thy kinsfolk and thy father's house,
And live in Christ reborn !   The bridal Rite
Is venerable, holy the marriage bed ;

But high above the level of things good
Things better rise—things best.   In olden time
Command went forth, ' Behold, a man shall leave
Father and mother, cleaving to his wife ; '
But lo ! a lordlier challenge greets us now :
' Soul by God's Hand created unto God
For His sake count as dross all lesser things
So shall the King have pleasure in thy beauty.'
Unworthy art thou ?   Such unworthiness
Is worth with God.   He, choosing from all lands,
Elects the Ethiopian, bids her sing,
' Dark am I, dark yet fair.' "

                       Mother, methinks
I scarce had liked that praise of convent life
Save that he speaks with reverence too of marriage :
The life of nuns must be a kind of marriage,
Marriage to One unseen.

                  He writes once more :
" In the old time blest was he whose field was rich,
Whose flocks were large; the poor are blessed this day :
Blessed of old who laughed ; to-day who weep :
Blessed of old the man whom all men praised ;
Blessed this day who walks despised by all :
Blessed of old the man who stood secure
Palm-like beside still waters ; blessed now
The Runner in God's race.   In ancient time

Blessed that Hebrew maiden changed to wife ;
Her babe might prove the Christ.   Now Christ is come :
In sorrow Eve brought forth : Mary in joy :
Virginity brought forth not death but life,
The Lord of Life, and won thenceforth for Woman
The restful hymeneals of the skies.
Our loves are loftier than of old, our wars
Sublimer ; not with flesh and blood we strive,
But princes of the darkness of this world :
God calls thee, not to heights, but to the highest :
Preserve God's sanctuary.   The Ark of old
Held these two things, the tables of the Law ;
Held these and naught besides."

                              Mother, my Mother !
How dear to this high Teacher she had been,
That girl, the glory of Rome's earlier day,
Virginia !   Ofttimes I have seen her face
Clearly as now yon apple-tree dew-bright !
O chaste as all the Vestals, with what joy
She met her father's knife !   Unstained, untouched,
She reached the mansions of the holy Dead
That flocked to her as doves to haunts well known.
Christians methinks there lived that knew not Christ,
Baptized in death by Powers unseen !   Our Master
Writes sternly : " Touch not thou a Pagan book :
Stand not anear it, lest a demon leap

Forth from gilt page, and light upon thy heart :
For their sake penance nigh to death was mine."
Mother, where sweetness is must needs be goodness :
All other Pagan legends may be false ;
That tale I know is true !

        Our Master spurned
Not Pagan books alone ; he left, he fled
The lands they boast. " Hail, holy Waste," he writes,
" Bare, yet enamelled with the flowers of Christ !
Hail, Solitude immeasurable ! to thee
We fly, not shunning aught but seeking all :
Thy Face we seek, Thou conqueror who o'ercam'st
The Tempter in the desert ! Worldly toys
Here rise not 'twixt our spirits, Lord, and Thee :
We see Thee tread thy loved Judean fields
Helping the sick, the blind ; and hear Thy voice,
These words, ' Her sins, though many, are forgiven,'
Or those of kindred tone, ' Lazarus, arise ! '
Far off we ken the City of Thy Saints
And gates of sunset gold." Yet through that waste
Portents there roamed which shook that kingly soul,
Temptations we can guess not, spared, no doubt,
To ill-resisting weakness. Burning sands
Drank up those flaming suns and sent their glow
On through his body and soul. Whole days, whole nights
He beat his breast at some cold cavern's mouth,

Fled thence to deserts lonelier.   Lion and pard,
Or demon-foes imaged in dreadful shapes,
I trembled here too much to understand,
Passed him fire-eyed.   Benigner visions soon
Healed his tired being with assuaging light,
Memories, it may be, of yon Alban hills
Or choirs dance-woven of Rome's young, fair maids;
And when that storm had left him angels sang,
"We follow where thou goest."

　　　　　　　　　　Mother beloved!
I should not read you more.   You kept, last night,
Long vigil: leaning now 'gainst yonder stone
Your head, your eyes alternate flash and close;
And sometimes ere the smile has left your lips
A momentary sleep sits on your lids.
Hear but one passage more: " Humility
Learn from humiliations; these are sent
To spare us degradations ours through pride:
Be humble thou; yet boast not humbleness:
Be ignorant rather than, through knowledge, vain.
Then when the trial finds thee, as a seal
Let Christ be on thy heart and on thine arm;
Walk on: fear naught: pure foot shall tread secure
Adder and serpent's crest."   Again he writes:
" What!   Wouldst thou tread the lilies only?   Nay,
But paths empurpled by the Feet divine,

And daily ways of death."

                  I think—I doubt not—

Our stern, rough Teacher had a sister once!
He knows that praise, though undeserved, alas!
Helps girls to merit praise. Again he writes,
"Give thyself wholly to the Lord of all:
Wholly for thee He died. What wife would couch
On silks while bleeding lies her warrior lord
On snows far distant? Shun the festal haunts:
The Spouse of Souls is near thee: seek Him not
In crowded ways. The watchers of the night
Will meet thee there, and rend from thee thy veil:
Pray thou within: He stands without and knocks:
Then when thou hear'st 'My sister and my spouse,'
Fling wide thy door, or soon thy song shall be,
'I opened: He had passed! Yea, lightning-like
He passeth; and His footsteps are not known.'"
   Thus he concludes: "The Mother of thy God
Make still thy pattern; in thy heart of hearts
Thus shall her Babe be born. She, she alone,
The Inviolate One, was fruitful in herself,
Parent—sole parent—of Incarnate God,
In this an image of the Eternal Sire
Parent, sole Parent of the Eternal Son.
The stem is she from Jesse; He the flower
That, burgeoning from that stem, satiates with sweet

Both heaven and earth.   The soul that loves her well
Should be God's night-bird singing all night long
With bleeding beak the Passion of her Son.
What are the voices of the earth beside?
Wouldst hear His Voice?   Be wise in sacred lore:
Read well God's Book, to noble hearts how dear!
It is God's Eden: yea, He walks therein
In the coolness of the day.   What find we there?
The record of the Making of all worlds;
The record of Deliverance for His own;
The record of the giving of His Law
On Sinai amid thunders: after these
Soarings of regal or of priestly psalm,
Next, warnings of sad seers from Carmel's steeps,
Or moanings of that far, prophetic sea
Wide as man's heart, that, heaved by breath divine,
Yearns round the bases of the Mount of God
With groans unutterable.   Later came
That second Tome—the Four Evangelists:
There lives, fire-breathing like the stars of God,
There lives that vision of the Creatures Four
Seen by Ezekiel!   Full of wings and eyes,
Man-faced yet lion-faced and eagle-faced,
Forward they rush, yoked to a fiery car;
Forward they rush where'er the Spirit wills;
Yea, for the self-same Spirit is in those wheels:

Throned in that car, above God's hills for ever
On sweeps the Son of Man."
                              O mother mine !
I read, unweeting how the moments passed,
And louder read as yonder garden choir
That first but piped, each bird a note, then slept,
Rewakening shook the blossoming boughs, as though
God loved no praise but theirs !   The ascended sun
Shoots o'er the pavement now a longer beam,
A warmth how grateful, for the unsandalled foot
Chills soon upon these marbles.   Hark a sound !
Swift steps in street and courtway.   Why, O why
Hate men our Master ?   Fierce in fight they call him :
Methinks there might be wars with mildness blent ;
They say that turtles fight, and yet, one dead,
Its little mate heart-stricken dies of grief.
What know I ?   Mother, you have heard his letter :
Needs must I write my thanks upon my knees ?
And yet not thus : my tears might blot the page ;
And "keep," he said, "in youth thy tears for God :
Drop them in age for man—less dangerous then."
I must write gaily lest my scroll prove irksome :
I must write briefly for he ends, " Few words !
Mine hours with tasks are laden."
                              Hark that chime
Rolled from St. Peter's !   'Tis Saint Peter's Day !

Listen !   Again that rush of countless feet !
All Rome makes speed to greet her great Apostle !
Hasten we, too :—my letter first : 'tis writ !
Irené, take these tablets to my Master :
These lines—there are but three—may win his smile :
Likewise these presents three ; the *Armillæ* first,
War-bracelets clasping none but conquering arms :
Doubtless some warrior of our house, long dead,
Won them by merit.   Heavier blows by far
This athlete of God's church hath dealt her foes,
Too fiercely dealt them Roman priests aver ;
But then they fear his haughty strength and looks
Still heated from the desert.   Give him next
These two young doves so loving and so mild ;
And, last, this basket heaped with early cherries.
The hour he sat here first I gave him such !
Three years have passed since then.   Smiling he spake :
" The gift is meet : cherries, like little maids,
Are fresh and pure ; a blushful gleam without ;
Hard heart within."   I think he will remember !

THE DEATH OF SAINT JEROME.

(A.D. 420.)

ARGUMENT.

After many years spent on his translation of the Sacred Scriptures into Latin, and the introduction of the Eastern Monasticism into the West, Saint Jerome returned to Jerusalem. In Bethlehem that great warrior of the Faith died. He had lived a man of controversies and of labours, of wanderings and of solitudes, of stern resentments, of impassioned friendships, and of sore griefs, the sorest of which was that caused by the fall of Rome beneath the sword of Alaric — although he saw in that fall a righteous retribution. Saint Jerome had loved Rome with a vehement and faithful, though not with a servile, love. His death-bed at Bethlehem was solaced by the filial devotion of the " Second Paula," the granddaughter of the " Earlier Paula " and the niece of Eustochium, both of whom had died at Bethlehem.

A WOFUL night !   My sleep was storm not rest :
The death-cry of great Rome rang over it.
Ten years are past ; yet still I hear that cry,
　And loudest oft in sleep.   Who comes ?   'Tis Paula !
I know that voice ; I know that hand.   In mine
The hot, hard bones and ropy veins grow cool

Touched by its snows.   Paula ! I see thee not :
Mine eyes are dazzled by the matin beam :
Those Hebrew scrolls, those characters minute
Have somewhat tasked them.   All night long in fire
They glared upon me.   "Sedet Civitas "—
Incipit Jeremiæ Lamentatio :
" Lo, solitary sitteth now the City : "—
As dead men in the streets, so lie her sons.
I dictated in dream : I dreamed my scribe
Dropped on the parchment down his youthful head ;
I laid my hand thereon and sent him forth
With blessing to his couch.   His rest was sweet :
But I—my bed is watered with my tears,
For night by night I hear the self-same cry,
" Esuriunt Parvuli : the suckling's tongue
Cleaves to the small roof of the suckling's mouth
Because his drought is sore."   That Hebrew Seer
Lamented Salem's downfall.   Rome, great Rome !
I that rebuked thy wanderings was thy son.
Dalmatia called me by that name : I heard ;
But, even in childhood, standing by her waves,
And gazing on her mountains near the sea
That o'er it glittered 'gainst the orient ray,
For me my Rome beyond them rose, seven-hilled
Fane-crowned.   I cried, " My Mother ! "

                               Fling it wide,

Yon casement ! Let the sea-breeze cool my brow !
No, not sea-breeze ; this is not Aquileia
Where lived Crostatius and Eusebius, mine ;
I left my young, sad sister in their charge—
Was that well done? I know not ; ne'er shall know —
Then passed myself to Chalcis 'mid the sands :
It was a fiery prison to the sense,
A Patmos to the soul. Let in the breeze !
There died my dearest then upon the earth,
Hylas and Innocentius. Still at times
I weep them, though I trust to see them soon.
Thanks, Paula, thanks ! Hail, pure reviving airs
That blow from me the mist of evil dreams
And bring me healing memories. Once again
O child, I read the tidings of thy birth
By Leta sent to greet her husband's mother,
That earlier Paula, here that time recluse.
" The child of all thy prayers is ours at last !
Mother, thy name shall be our infant's name,
A younger Paula pledged before her birth
To live like thee the handmaid of the Lord,
With thee and thy Eustochium, my sweet sister."
I wrote in turn : " Leta, I share thy joy :
Train up thy child to God : her little hands,
When first they travel o'er her mother's face
In wondering love, press on those letters small

Q

Ivory or ebon, spelling God's great name :
Let Hallcluiahs be her earliest song :
See she be humbly clad and tend God's poor :
When womanhood draws near her, but ere yet
Childhood has left her, send her to this spot
That, kneeling where the cradled Child-God slept
She learn His service.   I will be her Teacher."
She sent thee.   Say, have I belied my pledge ?
    Another pledge, not yet fulfilled, remains.
I promised thee the story of my life,
Now near its close.   Twice I began to write,
Then flung to the earth my pen.   Sit down and list
Of that poor life some fragments ; thou hast claims :
It owed to thine and thee its best of days.

    O holy, sweet, and gracious Company !
O Household dear to God !   Their feet to us
Who trod this vale of tears shone beautiful
Upon the mountains ; for where'er they moved
'Twas mountain land, the mountain of the Lord,
To them : they bore God's Gospel on their brows
And flashed it forth to men.   O happy day
That gave them to me !   I had dwelt five years
Alone in deserts lodged 'mid ravening beasts ;
And when I saw man's face once more therein
Ferine was mixed with human, though in some

Valour, and gleams of rude barbaric beauty,
Illumed that aspect ruthless.   Back to Rome
I passed : I found not in her what my youth
Half-spurned, yet half-admired.   The Prince of Peace
Held there a place that feared to claim its own :
The spoils and trophies of a thousand wars
Bade Him defiance.   Palsy-stricken long
The old Pagan Rite lifted a brow still crowned,
A sceptred hand, though shaking.   Proud in death
Like Rome's old emperor it "stood up to die :"
Well-nigh two hundred temples laughed in scorn
From summits seven.   The Imperial power itself
Trembled to front the rage of popular vice :
Feebly it trod and waveringly as men
In cities earthquake-jarred.   A Past there was :
Authority, Tradition still survived :
The dignity of these things was gone by :
To shameless spectacles the people rushed :
The gloom of wearied lusts was in their eyes :
The Coliseum's blood-stained sports, though dead
Left dark their foreheads.
                    Sweet as music-strain
Dawned on me then that vision strong and fair
Of Romans true at once to ancient times
And loyal to God's truth.   Heroic Houses,
The great patrician races of old Rome,

The Anician, Claudian, Fabian, yea the Scipios',
Before me stood, but consecrate to Christ:
The pristine "Virtus" now was spirit-crowned:
The instinctive chastity of early days
Had learned its meaning in the heavenly spousals:
The patriot's soul had found a native land
Worthier than that for which Attilius died—
God's church.   The hearth has won its rights.   True
    wives
From Lucrece on to Portia; holy mothers
From her whose son captured Corioli
To her that reared the Gracchi, stood once more
With loftier stature.   Senators were Christian
And, garbed in peasant's cloak of homely brown,
Filled with God's poor the palace of their sires:
"Rome is forgiven!" I cried; "the wrong is past:
The blood that cried for vengeance cries no more:
Maro's old vision of a realm world-wide
Which only smote the proud to raise the weak
Shall find at last fulfilment."   Woe is me!
I saw but half.   Morals depraved long since
Had paved the way for heresies in Faith:
God's Truth was bartered for Imperial favour:
Vainly God's Prophets thundered 'gainst the crime:
Fate trod behind it close.

               My lips are parched:

How fresh that water ! Thanks ! Holiest and best
Of all those holy ones to me so dear
Thy father's mother was—that earlier Paula :
Beside a daughter's grave I saw her first :
The trials others shunned to her grew dear ;
They brought her near the Man of Woes.   Her mind
Was all of ardours and of soarings made,
Winged like the Greek ; unlike it soft and sacred :
Greek she knew well ; Hebrew she learned ere long :
She thirsted for that land the Saviour trod
And thither fled.   Weeping, yet glad, she traced
His steps from north to south, from east to west,
Then chose this site and here her convents raised :
She ruled them twenty years, then slept in Christ.
In death she lay as one restored to youth
The while close by in Hebrew and in Greek
Bishops and priests chanted her requiem psalms,
And o'er the bier that black-robed mourner lay ;
Her lips were on her mother's brow, her face
Hid on that mother's bosom.
                                      In a cave
Close to that spot where stood the Sacred Crib
We laid the Dead, expectant of that day
When God shall raise her.   On the rock hard by
I graved her name and lineage :
                                      " Here in Christ

Paula finds rest.   The great Emilian race,
Cornelia's blood, the Scipios, and the Gracchi
In her lay down the pride of ancient Rome
Before the cradle of Incarnate God.
She was Eustochium's mother.   All, save her,
She left to worship here."

                    Eustochium's mother!
Eustochium—those who looked upon her face
Believed perforce.   Amid the virgin choir
She stood, men said, Virginity itself:
They thanked her less for all she brought of good
Than all her presence slew.   The shames of life
Vanished, and memory's book laughed out in light :
Lethè ran o'er it.   Paula wept at times ;
Her child shone out as from the weeping cloud
The all-radiant arch.   In her the Virtues Three
Began with Hope—for what is Hope but Faith
Mounted on wings?—passed on to Charity,
And ended in some grace to man unknown.
A child she wrote me letters, sportive, brief,
Yet serious 'neath her sport.   Childhood in her
Lived till her mother died.

                    She too is dead !
That whole great race hath passed from earth away :
Pammachius, of Camillus' mighty line,
And Leta and Toxotius.   All are gone !

When died the last I registered a vow :
I vowed their names should live till mine had perished.
Those names are welded with that Tome which clasps
My life's long labour.   It is gone, that life ;
Yon sun new-risen is my latest sun :
Be near me, child !   Thank God, another Paula
Remains to close my eyes.

               As death draws nigh,
Peace-maker best, men turn to those who made
Their peace on earth.   Mine was a life of wars ;
Was that my fault?   I know not.   Roman half,
Barbaric half, I was not made for peace ;
My blood rushed fiercely as Dalmatian floods
When thunder shakes our hills.   I knew in youth
A house among those hills ; on stillest days
Close round it reeled a tempest of its own,
Whirlwind of confluent winds whose course was shaped
By distant mountains.   Like that house was I.
Strange hands far off had shaped me unto storm :
Storm sang the dusky matins of my life ;
Storm sang my vesper psalms.   Others have fled
To wastes in search of peace : to such I rushed
To fight with fiends whose chief had warred on mine
Then late baptized, in the great wilderness.
Five years we battled.   Victory doubtful seemed :
God spake ; then ceased the winds, and fell the waves,

And there was a great calm.   New foes succeeded,
Foes from Christ's household, anchorets of the East
That ground their teeth against me.   " Ho," they cried,
" Impostor of the Gentile world far West,
Tread'st thou our East?"   Then shook I from my feet
The burning sands in testimony against them :
I passed to Antioch ; to Byzantium next
Better so called than by his arrogant name
Who made God's church an appanage !   Next I saw
That great Thebais and its hermit sons,
And wrote their deeds.   At Rome Pope Damasus
Loved me ; and all her saints.   So much the more
They hated me without a cause, those priests,
Ill-tonsured heads, obsequious ; men who trod
The rich man's purples whispering to his leech,
And eyed the miser's will.   I pointed 'gainst them
This finger now so stark.   Ascetics false ;
Solitaries whom envy not their fasts made lean ;
And, noisomer culprits, priests that ate from gold,
That, sinning with the people sinned against them,
That prophesied illusions and deceits
And therefore won no vision from the Lord :
On such I hurled God's bolts.

                             Erred I in this?
My mother said of me, " His hand is hard,
Though not his heart."   The boy was hard ; the man.

My chief of battles was with Origen,
That Greek whose airy fancies, unbaptized
Save in Castalian springs, if spared had changed
The solid lands and seas of Christian Faith
To mist of allegory.   Rufinus next—
Ah, false, false friend !   He walked with me in youth :
In age with parricidal hand he wrote
That book against God's church.   With him he drew
Salem's unholy bishop, Barnabas ;
Later, by night that base Pelagian crew
Full fain had burned me in my monastery
Whose site, foreseeing, I had chosen for strength.
I shook this hand against them from its roofs,
Then 'scaped to yonder tower.

                    How unlike these
That youthful priest, angelic more than priestly,
Nepotian !   Standing in the imperial court
He wore the hair-cloth hid.   A soldier once
A soldier's simpleness was in him ever;
He was the outcast's help, the orphan's hope,
The strength of all the oppressed.   Like pure, cold airs
Launched from white peaks on one that tracks hot sands
The casual thought of him had power to cheer me.
Once more I see him with that child-like smile
Brightening his grave and sacerdotal stillness
Each holy widow " Mother " still he called,

Each maiden "Sister."   With what care he clothed
His own high thoughts in garb of teachers old :
"Saint Irenæus argues ; Cyprian hints— "
Shunning all self-assertion !   Ah ! great God !
That lily, which the right hand of Thy pureness
Had shaped to be an image of itself,
Struck by the noontide ardours, drooped, and died !
Here, far away at Bethlehem, I sat :
"I shall have letters from him soon," ·I mused :
A stranger entered, sad of face : he laid
A young priest's garment on an old man's knee ;
He spake : " Nepotian sent it thee in death ;
'Go thou,' he said, ' to him, my friend, my father,
Through whom I, nothing then, became a priest ;
Tell him that by God's altar day by day
This was my tunic as I ministered.' "
Paula, since then it lies athwart this couch :
Spread it above me dead.
                              He died in youth :
So best !   How fair a thing is youth like his,
Yea, how complete, from Innocence to Death
Wafted unstained !   How beautiful to him
Whose age is but a maimed and mangled weight,
Whose life a long frustration !   Such is mine :
They that most hated, they who fain had stoned me,
Belike too high esteemed me.   All that life

Was conflict fierce of random purposes,
Poor nothings which the Hand that made all worlds
Alone could shape to good.   I strove to plant
The convents of the East o'er all the West
Yet never was at heart a man recluse :
I said : "No choice is ours : dead Paganism
Breathes from its shameful grave a mist that slays :
Christians must flee the infected world."   To me
Not high, not pure, a restless spirit ever,
Travel world-wide, strong studies, rule of men
These things were welcomer thrice than convent-cells :
In these I had large share.   My books were acts ;
I sent them forth to toil.   The thoughts heaven-born
That, angel-like, dropt by Augustine's tent—
I love that man the more for conflicts past—
Sought not my cavern.   Vowed to holy church,
'Twas yet against my will they made me priest :
I knew myself unworthy.   Once alone
I offered Sacrifice.

           And yet this hand,
So soon to mingle with its native dust,
Transferred God's Oracles from tongues long dead
To Rome's which cannot die !   Was this my praise ?
Not so; I toiled, at first to shun temptations :
The task that lulled my youth brightened mine age :
Book after book took shape beneath my hand

Not preordained by me.   God wrought the work :
Through God alone His great Book of the East
Shall live the great Book of the West, the world,
The Church's Holy Book, which, like that stone
Hewn from the mountain, that became a mountain,
Shall singly in its majesty make null   .
The books of all the nations, heaped albeit
Cloud-high by each, yea, lost in cloud, and thence
Oft shedding ruin on the vales below.
This is God's Book : in it the Church of God,
While myriad Errors round her rise, shall see
Writ as in stars those Truths which in her heart
Live ever, seen or veiled :—the Church's sons,
Nurtured by it on heavenly food, shall walk
Not childish, not imbecile, but as men
In lowly strength of Faith.   If e'er man's race,
Its winter past, shall breathe a second spring,
The letters of the Nations shall not take
Their mould from barbarous lands that knew not God,
Or lands corrupt which, having known, forsook Him,
Nay but from words divine, the Lips of God
Parleying with primal man.   Earth's Homer new,
Her Phidias, her Apelles, themes shall choose
That change not soul to sense, but sense to soul :
That Maccabean Trump again shall peal ;
Ruth glean 'mid western fields.   Rebuke shall roll

From western Carmels on insurgent kings
Who o'er false altars hurl schismatic smoke
And filch the poor man's vineyard.   Casual texts
Shall slay yet make alive ; o'er western hearts
Sin-seared shall flash those dagger-points of light
That say, " Thou art the Man."   The Hebrew Spirit,
Yea, though o'er earth the Hebrew race walk bare,
Abject, down-trod, priestless and altarless,
Shall judge earth's orb secure.   Great Rome, herself
May share in this with Sion.   Centuries hence
Broken like her, her fragments too may pave
A causeway for those Feet which bore the Nails,
And theirs His followers' up to Eden's gate.
I say not this shall be, but this may be.
" Prophesy, Son of Man, can these bones live ? "
The Prophet answered thus : " O Lord, thou know'st."

   Too much of what is least.   Paula, I seem
To dwell on self.   It is not so ; I linger
Beside each fount freshening my life's long road
Because its end is woe.   At last I face it.
Child, for thy sake it shall be briefly told.

   The Goth, the Hun, Vandal, and Marcoman,
Successive swept the world.   Cloudlike they rushed
O'er Scythia, Dacia, Thrace, my own Dalmatia.
The flaming churches witnessed their advance :

They dragged the old noble from his palace home,
The bishop from his flock.   They slew the babe
That smiled upon their sword.   The world's one flower,
Athens, they trampled 'neath a bestial hoof:
Damascus heard their coming : Antioch fell ;
Their steeds they watered in Orontes' wave
And Halis, and Euphrates.   We, not they,
Burned this great shame upon the brows of Rome :
Man sinned : God's judgment followed.

                        Near me, child !
'Twas in the night the crown of cities fell.
A thousand and a hundred years had passed
Since from that Capitolian height arose
Earth's throne permitted.   Rome, the Queen of men,
Had changed to Queen of slaves.   A cry was heard
Like cry of wolves that throng dark Dacian hills
O'erhanging some doomed village.   On the march
Of Alaric south, Alaric " the Scourge of God,"
Full forty thousand slaves of race barbaric
Had joined his standard.   Thirty thousand more
That night within Rome's fated walls uprose ;
They burst the Gate Salarian.

                        Paula, nearer !
The foe was in the city as a flood :
They thronged the Forum first, that Forum girt
With idol temples ; next that Coliseum

Where many a Dacian chieftain, many a Goth,
Had gorged the lion's maw.   'Twas there rang out
The second cry.   That was the cry of Rome—
Men say no other followed.

                O my child !
Thy tears which fall so quickly on my hand
Warn me to cease.   Not all was woe, was shame :
Alaric was Christian, and his Goths in part ;
They spared the maid, the nun ; one only perished,
Marcella ; she—her maiden pupil saved—
She, bleeding from the lances of the foe,
Made way into St. Peter's.   There arrived
The grey-haired Saint slept by the Apostles' tomb :
Beneath a gloomier vault the Conqueror lies.
His mission was fulfilled ; then on him first
Earthly ambition fell.   Southward he marched
To make a second continent his prey.
His Maker smote that proud one that he died.
Three days in wrath they mourned him; on the fourth
A counsel rose among them.   Swift and near
A river rushed : they forced a captive host
To sluice away its waters.   In its bed
They built a tomb trophied with spoils of Rome :
Therein they laid their Mighty One.   Once more
They rolled that river through its channel old,
Then slew that captive host.   " No man," they sware,

"Shall peer into the secret of the King ;
None trouble his remains."

His work was done :
No day but o'er the earth the exiles passed,
Exiles once Roman princes.   Every coast
Egyptian, Syrian, Pontic, watched them coming,
The old, the young, their purple changed to rags,
And followed far with sad, remorseful eyes.
The Christians of their number hither flocked ;
They yearned to die there where their Lord was born.
We gave them food at first : when none remained
We gave them tears.   The haggard phantoms trod
Awe-struck, the ways of Sion ; by that brook,
Cedron, and under groves of Olivet,
And Calvary, and beside that garden-cave
Where lay the Saviour dead.

The sight was strange !
These were the children of that Pagan race
Which wrought God's vengeance on His chosen City.
Their own had been the secular head of earth,
The Salem of the Unjust : their own was judged :
And now, like babes on some dead mother's breast,
They clung to her whose heart their sires had pierced,
Sought there a mother's aid.   Ah me ! Ah me !
Pilate and Caiaphas were one in sin.
Salem and Rome ! These might have been God's hands

Stretched forth in benediction o'er the world :
They met—those hands—one blood was on them both !
One judgment is on both.

There yet remains

A ruined fragment huge of Salem's wall :
A little Hebrew remnant haunt that spot :
They kiss those fissured stones and in their shade
Sing their lamenting psalms.   How oft hard by
Have I not heard our Roman exiles weep !
Antiphonal those dirges drear !   I thought
Each on the other railed reproach : first, Rome,
" Jerusalem, Jerusalem that slay'st
The Prophets :" next, the Hebrews' fierce retort,
"Art thou not in the self-same condemnation ?
Thy House is left unto thee desolate."

  Paula, these things lie heavy on my soul :
Last night Rome's judgment dealt with me so sorely
I scarcely know if months or years divide
Her death-day from my own.   I know but this ;
Her ending seemed the ending of a world.
If this our earth had in the flat sea sunk
Save one black ridge whereon I sat alone,
Such wreck had seemed not greater.   It was gone,
That Empire last, sole heir of all the empires,
Their arms, their arts, their letters, and their laws.

" 'Twas in the night the wall of Moab fell "—
Ezekiel sang that verse, the man who saw
The horrors of Sin's Chambers veiled by night.
Gone, too, is David's kingdom, Israel's House :
" Incipit Jeremiæ Lamentatio :"
" How solitary sitteth now that City
Which whilome was the joy of all mankind."
Begins the great lament that end hath none :
Then silence ; then that dirge predicted long,
The welter of that wide barbaric flood
Thenceforth earth's sable pall and universal :
The fountains of the nether deep are burst :
The second deluge comes.

                              And let it come !
That God who sits above the water-spouts
Remains unshaken.   Paula, what is earth ?
A little bubble trembling ere it breaks,
The plaything of that grey-haired infant, Time,
Who breaks whate'er he plays with.   I was strong :
See how he played with me ! Am I not broken ?
Albeit I strove with men of might ; albeit
Those two great Gregories clasped me, palm to palm ;
Albeit I fought with beasts at Ephesus
And bear their tokens still ; albeit the wastes
Knew me, and lions fled ; albeit this hand,
Wrinkled and prone hurled to the dust God's scorners,

Am I not broken? Lo, this hour I raise
High o'er that ruin and wreck of life not less
This unsubverted head that bent not ever,
And make my great confession ere I die,
Since hope I have, though earthly hope no more :
And this is my confession : God is great ;
There is no other greatness : God is good ;
There is no other goodness. He alone
Is true Existence ; all beside is dream.
Likewise confession make I that His Hand,
Which made all worlds, and made them to His glory,
Which touches earthly greatness and it dies,
Shall touch one day the dead within their graves
And lift them to His life. The Death Divine
Hath raised mankind above all fates and fortunes.
Paula, when thou hast closed these eyes in death
And laid this body in this holy land
Close by thy kinsfolk whom in life I loved,
Record of me, not dangers, labours, triumphs ;
Record alone that in the day of death
Christ was my stay ; He only ; that on Him,
Bending above the imminent grave, I leaned—
God's penitent not less than confessor—
My total being, body, soul, and spirit,
His liegeful servant. Holy is the feast
He keepeth ; and His truth remains for aye.

STILICHO.

(DIED A.D. 408.)

ARGUMENT.

Stilicho, though a Vandal, had fought from his youth under the Emperor Theodosius the Great, and conceived for Rome a veneration heightened by compassion for her fallen estate. That Emperor's sons having been left in his guardianship, he devoted all his energies and genius to their defence and that of the Empire, and had conceived a scheme for its complete regeneration. When on the point of executing that scheme, he was put to death through the jealousy of the Roman nobles, and the treachery of the Emperor Honorius.

A Gothic Chief appears suddenly at a banquet of the Roman nobles. He upbraids them with their falsehood, enumerates the successive occasions on which Stilicho had saved the Empire from destruction, and announces that Alaric is within two days' march of Rome which he has vowed to destroy, and that he himself is issuing forth to Alaric's camp. He departs, no man daring to bar his way.

NOBLES of Rome—I scorn to call you Romans—
Ye bade me to your banquet; I have come,
Not therefore trencher-guest. I come to strike
A dagger-worded edge of just revenge
Far on through treason's heart. My sword, you see it—

Too long, like Stilicho's, it served your State—
Is snapt in twain.   I brake it as I passed
Upon the stone head of that idol Jove
Which, ten years prostrate, shames your Capitol,
That Capitol whose gates Stilicho shattered,
Burning your Sybil's books.   I come to tell you
That which was writ within that Sybil's books
In the last page, unless that Sybil lied.
There sit two hundred of you : ye can slay me
If my discourse—I think it will—molests you.
What then ?   I shall have told the truth and died.
Lords, would ye learn who taught me those two lessons ?
The man a week since murdered, Stilicho.

   Lords, let me tell you somewhat of that man
By you perchance—a week is long—forgotten :
I knew him well and owed him my advancement.
Stilicho was my friend : behoves it, sirs,
Ye learn his history from first to last ;
So shall the dead man be his own avenger.
That man was Vandal.   In her later years
Your Rome has needed oft Barbaric aid :
Great Theodosius never marched without him ;
His counsel on the battle-field was law,
His presence inspiration.   Victory
Dawned on the face of every Roman soldier
When came the tidings, " Stilicho is near : "

I heard the Emperor say, " This Vandal Chief
Is Roman of the Romans."   As he passed
A shout rang out, " Fabricius," or " Camillus : "
Never they named him with your later names !
In every province he had held command,
Yet no man taxed him with an " itching palm."
    The Emperor linked him with the imperial house
By marriage ; dying, placed him o'er his sons,
Regent of East and West.

                                Attend and learn :
I but record plain facts: these stab the deepest :
That Emperor's son, Arcadius, was a lackwit :
Rufinus ruled his realm, the East : this aim
Was his, to bring to naught the Western Empire
Where reigned Honorius, not through hate of him
But hate of Stilicho, the youth's protector.
Rufinus was a Gaul, astute and pliant :
Rufinus was a traitor.   From afar
He beckoned to the Hunnish tribes that roamed
The Caspian coasts : with Alaric next he trafficked :
He placed, in secret, Greece within his grasp :
By open pact he throned him in Illyria,
And pointed thence to Rome.   What help was hers ?
Nobles of Rome, reply !

                        A man—one man !
Stilicho crossed the Alps alone : alone

His hand he lifted upon Rhenus' banks,
A hand that raised a standard.   Round it flocked
The wrecks of ancient Roman legionaries
The Gauls, the German tribes late linked with Rome
By treaties, first-fruits of his rule sagacious.
With these, as with an army from the clouds,
He dropp'd on Greece astonished.   Alaric fled
To far Thessalian hills.   He girt him round :
In one day more, but one, Alaric had perished :
That noon, the assault commanded, rode in sight
A horseman by the Eastern Emperor sped,
The bearer of a missive : " Leave this land :
War not on Alaric : Alaric is my friend :
Send back mine Eastern Legions."

                         He obeyed :
Nobles, ye know his act, but not its sanction :
He called to him a Goth, by name Gainus ;
He gave command ; all heard it : none forgot :
" Lead thou those legions to the Bosphorus ;
There slay Rufinus ! Slay him with thy hand,
In the Emperor's sight : in sight of all his people :
Rufinus is a traitor proven."   Ere long
Rufinus' plot was ripe.   That self-same day
Which saw the legions of the East return
Was chosen to make Rufinus Emperor.
Arcadius and the Upstart sat enthroned

With all the nobles of the court around :
The legions made advance ; Rufinus rose ;
Their standards he saluted : he began—
Gainus smote him through the heart, with shout,
" From Stilicho ! "   An eastern warrior cried,
" Say not from Stilicho, but Theodosius !
The brave old Emperor smote him from the grave."
Stilicho saved that day your Eastern Empire.

    Two years went by.   Feasters of Rome, give ear !
The tale of Stilicho is your history's last ;
With Romulus it began : 'tis worth your knowing.
Gildo, the Moor, descended from king Juba,
Raised in revolt the total Lybian coast,
Recalled its corn-fleets ; sentenced Rome to famine—
From ports unknown or hostile, Stilicho
Launched corn-fleets new to Rome ; trod down rebellion :
Stilicho saved that day your Afric Empire.

    Attend once more : this matter touches you !
Six years went by : the Goths o'erflowed your land :
What course was theirs who boast their Rome ?   They
     fled !
Their roads were choked : their harbours crammed : their
     galleys
Took wing to Corsica and Sicily.
Where then was Stilicho ?   His voice went forth
From Rhetia's vales : his name subdued the indwellers.

A Race barbaric saved you : some had served
Beneath his standard : some had felt his steel :
As though by magic moved they turned and joined him.
Your legions breathed again.   A man—one man—
Had stamped upon the earth, and raised two armies !
He freed Honorius then at Asta sieged :
He met the invaders on Pollentia's field ;
Later he broke them 'neath Verona's wall—
Stilicho saved that day your Western Empire !

A danger worse than these beset you soon :
From Asia's farthest north and farthest east,
Beyond Sarmatia's bound, a race unknown
By hunger driven for centuries on had crept
Slow as an ice-stream in some Alpine vale ;
At last they reached the West : the German tribes
Your foes of old beyond Danubius, pressed
By irresistible might o'erswarmed your bounds,
And marched t'ward regions of the setting sun
By Radagast led.   No Alaric he—an Asian—
Nothing ye knew of him save this, his vow
To offer to his gods for hecatomb
Rome and her sons.   Before Florentia's wall
That portent sat.   Ten days had lodged his host
In Rome.   Who saved that Rome ?   The man late
        murdered !
Florentia all but yielded, at her gates

A sudden apparition he appeared :
By miracle of strategy he conquered :
Their monarch fell : their myriads starved : once more
Our Stilicho redeemed your Western Empire.

   It willed not to be saved.   The terror past
Your pagans cried ; " What man is Stilicho ?
To him no God gave help ! His wife, Serena,
Wears still that circlet snatched from Juno's brow ! "
Your Christians cried ; " What ! Stilicho a Christian !
Claudian, his poet, is a pagan vowed :
So are his sons' preceptors. If a Christian
Why breaks he not the statues of false Gods ?
The victory was miraculous : 'twas not his ! "
Thus raved the inept.

                The man they scoffed replied not :
Lonely he mused on Rome's far destiny
By him since youth foreseen :
Events to him unwelcome brought the crisis.
He met it prompt, not glad.   " By Rome," he said,
" Confugiendum ad Imperium est :
Till now she ne'er was more than half an Empire."
But there was greatness in his scheme : and Rome
Could rise no more to greatness.

                   Came the end :
One half the tribes that passed Danubius' flood
In Radagast's time had crossed the frozen Rhenus :

They burned the stately cities on its banks;
The glories of the old Roman Colonists;
Levelled the nobles' halls, the poor man's hut;
Down trampled Gaul; o'erran Iberia; clasped
Your Rome's unshielded throat with stifling arm :—
The man not murdered yet addressed me thus :
"Rome might have borne great loss, the loss of realms :
The blow is this; they fell without a struggle!
Britain will fall in turn : the sires were men :
The sons are slaves.   Dishonour means destruction :
How meet this shame? The East is false, and hates us :
The Roman knows to boast; but not to fight."
    One hope remained.   An honourable foe
Is better than false friend.   Alaric had served
Like Stilicho in Theodosius' armies :
They knew each other's worth : to each the course
Held by the other was intelligible.
The King of Goths, the Regent of the Empire,
Had proved—each knew it—faithful to his trust :
Rivals they were in youth : war followed war :
Stilicho twice drave back the Goths : that done
He spared the German blood : the noble foes
Changed to true friends.   Some Eastern plot detected
Stilicho cried; "Would God, Alaric and I
Might march like brothers to the Bosphorus
And drown therein the traitors!"   One who heard

Whispered that word to Alaric.

                              Who is Alaric?
One swift in love in hate!   Freely he proffered
To join his warriors with the Roman force,
And to the Roman realm revindicate
Gaul and Iberia lost.   That task achieved
His people were to hold, secure from wrong,
Some space unpeopled in the Western Empire
Thenceforth its friends.   No secret pact was this.
When Stilicho discoursed with me thereon
The Emperor stood beside us.   Loud of voice
He praised the compact : he had late espoused
The Regent's daughter, that domestic tie
Sealing their life-long union.   Secret league !
Stilicho loved no secrets.   He himself
Deliberately divulged it to the Senate :
Some loud ones in that Senate stormed and raved.
Placid as power no petulance can shake
Stilicho rose : at once the tumult ceased :
He might have said ; " For centuries, Senators
Phantoms were ye gibbering in cave and crypt,"
(Methinks I see among you such this hour)
" 'Twas I that raised again the buried Senate."
Not thus he spake : he laid the facts before them,
The West o'errun ; Rome powerless to redeem it ;
They signed and sealed that league.

                                    There are who swear
" That treaty would have flung the Empire's gates
Open alike to Roman and to Goth."
That was its chief of merits !   Stilicho
Had faith in Rome her children feel no more,
Faith in her destiny, faith avouched, proclaimed,
Her destiny to raise not some few nations
But earth itself to her imperial height
And there in deathless majesty sustain it !
This was the dream, not work, of Constantine :
Augustus, Trajan's self, not even in dream
Had grasped the thought.   Rome ruled the East and
          West :
She might have won the North not less and held it :
A century had sufficed.   The work, though hard,
Had nerved the conquerors like their earlier wars,
Ere civil conflicts had denaturalized them.
Yet Stilicho still added thus : " That work
Is not the sword's alone.   In Gaul, Iberia,
'Twas work ill done.   Conquering, Rome civilized them,
But conquered first ; and bondage means corruption ;
The Germans she must civilize first ; then rule ;
Help them to fell their forests, fence their fields,
To bridge their floods, in every noble art
Ungrudgingly initiate them, invite
Their Chiefs to Rome ; as princes there receive them :

By intermarriage blend their race with hers ;
Teach them to love her laws, to share her wealth,
And draw them thus, unvanquished, incorrupt,
To seek admission to that world-wide Empire
Centred in Rome." There lived a man Elect—
He loved the race barbaric—he was of it :
He loved your Rome—since youth he fought its battles ;
The aim persistent of that man was this
Twofold to magnify your Roman Empire,
And make its rule perpetual. Fools ! fools ! fools !
The man ye hated was your last of friends :
The warrior whom ye dreaded was, in head
A politic Sage, in heart a man of peace.

It came—the end. The vilest of your vile ones,
Olympius, won your Emperor, made him dream
The Father of his Wife, his second father,
The saviour of his Empire—of his life—
Plotted against that Empire and its lord.
The Goths for Gaul designed were at Bologna,
Among them Stilicho. The Roman host,
Their brave compeers on many a well-fought field,
Camped at Pavia. There the Emperor joined them :
Three days irresolute he sat ; the fourth,
Addressed them thus : " Legions of Rome, ye march
To Gaul, the host barbaric at your side ;
No wish was this of mine." Drugged by Olympius

Those legions rose in mutiny : they slew
The friends of Stilicho round Honorius ranged,
The chief ones of the army and the State ;
The streets ran red with blood : the fires rushed up :
Honorius hid disguised in slave's attire :
Olympius sought him out : he bore a parchment :
"The head of Stilicho :"—Honorius signed.
Bologna heard : then rose the cry of "Vengeance :"
Stilicho spake : "The Emperor is deceived :
I served his Father : never hand of mine
Shall war against his standard ; never dash
Goth against Roman."
       Late that night the Goths
Assailed him in his tent : they slew his guards :
He rose not from his desk ; those Goths departed.
  Next morning Stilicho rode forth alone,
Rode to Ravenna 'twixt the pines and sea.
He slept that night in the Basilica,
Sanctuary inviolate. At earliest dawn
A royal herald at its portals stood
With soldiers girt. He held a Rescript high
Signed by your Emperor. Stilicho went forth :
In vain the old Bishop cried, "Keep sanctuary !"
The gates fell back : the herald read that scroll,
"To Stilicho, a rebel 'gainst the State,
Immediate death." Some few, that hour arrived,

Advanced to shield him.   Haughtily he stood :
He waved us back : he willed to live no longer :
He faced the soldiers.   In a moment more
He sank upon that fane's ensanguined step :
His strong white head propped on this breast he died.

　　His boy escaped to Rome ; your Emperor slew him :
His daughter, to that Emperor wedded late,
That Emperor drave forth.   His wife, Serena,
The stateliest offshoot of the imperial stem,
Saved by the savagery of Roman mercy,
Exiled in solitude laments her lord ;
These things to you are nothing.   Be it so.

　　He died : Rome lives : how long ye Roman nobles ?
This matter touches you.   Alaric draws nigh :
Alaric and Stilicho were veracious men :
Stilicho kept his word : Alaric will keep it.
Alaric stood pledged to march with Rome to Gaul,
But found no Romans at the trysting-place.
Alaric has changed his name : the title sole
He claims to-day is this, "the Scourge of God."
No death-cry from the lips of Stilicho
Made way to Alaric's ear.   Not less thereon
A cry there rings, a cry of babes barbaric
And bleeding mothers on whose breasts they died :
These were your hostages : your legions slew them,
Mad with their triumph o'er that great one dead.

That day full thirty thousand of the race
Barbaric, to the Roman service vowed
Their standards broke and marched to Alaric's camp :
Alaric is five days' march more near to Rome
Than Radagast when he sat before Florentia.
I go to meet him. Roman Lords, farewell !
I think that none of you will bar my way.

THE LEGEND OF SAINT GENEVIEVE.

(DIED A.D. 512.)

ARGUMENT.

Saint Germanus, of Auxerre, reaches Nanterre, near Paris. Among the Christian people there he notes a child of seven years old, by name Genevieve, and knows by divine inspiration that she is a Saint. He enjoins upon her a great faithfulness to her Lord, the Spouse of Souls, and lifting from the ground a small iron relic, with the cross graven thereon, commands her to wear it round her neck till death, and to wear no ornament besides. Lastly, he announces that God will, through that child, draw many from their sins, and that she will one day be honoured as the Patron Saint of Paris, which predictions were fulfilled.

GERMANUS, Saint and Bishop, who erewhile
   So glorious made his sacred see, Auxerre,
Journeyed to Britain, then " The Northern Isle "
   Styled by the Gauls.   Heretic sin raged there.
The Church of God had sent him for that cause
To vindicate Christ's Faith, His Church's laws.

One eve he reached, as slowly sank the sun,
    A tree-girt hamlet loud with children's sport
His resting-place, for wont was he to shun
    Those cities huge where wealth and pride consort.
Lutetian Paris stood not far : but he
Loved men of lofty heart and low degree.

Red on the church-roof hung the sunset fire ;
    Thus spake he : " I in yonder church must pray
To Him, its Guardian, 'mid the angelic choir—
    Great joy that Spirit should thus keep watch o'er clay ⊢—
First for that hamlet's children ; next that I
Though weak, may prosper in my mission high."

That place was Pagan half and Christian half ;
    Its Christian half swarmed forth to meet their guest
Matron and elder leaning on his staff
    Young men and maids in crimson kirtle drest ;
In front a priest with brows to earth inclined
Paced with slow footsteps : children ran behind.

The Sire of men with lifted hand and heart
    Sent forth his blessing o'er that gladsome throng,
Then moved among them zealous to impart
    The lore they loved. That time, Christ's poor among,
A bishop still was greeted with such zest
As when the callow fledgelings of a nest

What time they hear the mother-bird returning
　　Make gladsome stir and open beaks uplift
For needful food, her foray's harvest yearning ;
　　Then grateful feed, unquestioning of the gift :—
Sudden that bishop's piercing eye was stayed
Upon a child hard by, a seven-years' maid.

A heaven-like beauty triumphed in her face,
　　A beauty such as vulgar souls pass by :
Visibly on her beamed supernal grace :
　　The whole sweet-moulded form, like lip and eye,
Shone out in gracious meanings, made appeal
To men who think aright because they feel.

Germanus watched her long ; then, downward sped
　　From heaven upon his spirit, there fell a beam ;
O'er his worn face that inner splendour spread ;
　　And thus he spake : "O friends, we walk in dream :
Far glories fancy-born, for these we sigh,
For that cause miss God's marvels ever nigh.

" See ye that child with eyes fast fixed on heaven ?
　　Elect was she ere sun or moon had birth !
I tell you that, besides that angel given—
　　Seraph perchance—her Guardian here on earth,
Thousands this hour are following from above
That creature's steps this hour with gaze all love.

"I tell you that while wolf and wild boar trample
   God's Church, His Eden through all lands diffused,
Within that infant breast God holds a temple
   That ne'er by man or fiend shall be abused;
That sinners many she shall save, and bless
This land, its mother-city's Patroness.

"Look up! Once more God writes His Name in stars!
   Now two, now three they glimmer through yon skies
No longer veiled from earth by daylight's bars;
   Each night they rise to set, and set to rise:
Ye know the righteous shine as stars; and I
This night a star till now unseen descry."

Germanus ceased: then to that child he drew
   And straight she turned, as one who wakes from trance,
Her dusk eyes from that heaven of deepening blue
   And fastened them on his. No transient glance
Was hers, but fearless gaze and frank, the while
All round her quick red lips there ran a smile.

He spake: "My child, if God should spare your life,
   In what sort would you live it when full-grown?
In convent or in house; a Christian wife
   With babes, or spoused to Christ, and His alone?"
She mused; then answered softly; "I would bide
With Christ alone, His handmaid, child, and bride:

" For where the convent rises from yon grove
   Spouses of Christ there dwell ; and glad are they ;
From morn to eve their life is peace and love ;
   And still they tend His poor, and still they pray :
Me too, though stammerer yet, they teach to sing
His praises.   Hark !   Their vesper bell they ring !

" Beseech thee, Man of God, to lead me there !
   Beseech thee, bid those sisters in their choir
To place me grown to maid-hood."   Unaware
   She stretched to him both hands.   That child's desire
To that grey patriarch seemed as God's command :
T"ward that still convent paced they hand in hand.

Behind them thronged that concourse wondering much :
   Not few among them censured sore that child
Unweeting how she dared that hand to touch.
   Not so the Nuns : they saw from far, and smiled ;
Then near the altar raised a rustic throne
And clustered in the porch with myrtles strewn.

Germanus entered : on that throne he sate :
   Unawed beside him stood that little maid ;
And ever, as the legends old relate,
   His wrinkled hand upon her head was stayed ;
His eyes were downward bent : upraised were hers
As though the roof she saw not, but the stars.

Some say that, heavenward while that anthem soared
　Which Mary made, knowledge of things to be
Fell on him in the visions of the Lord,
　Those visions spirit-eyes alone can see ;
Such as the Hebrew Prophets saw of old,
And Paul and Peter in the later fold.

He saw her chase those spirits that stain with sin
　Precincts which Poverty, God's gift, was sent
To cleanse like rocks rough sea-waves sweep and din :
　He saw her frustrate Attila's intent :
Up from the city's ramparts rose her prayer,
Where then his Huns?　His threatened vengeance where?

He saw her climb, her lantern in her hand,
　Nightly Montmartre, piercing the midnight gloom ;
He saw the Church that rose at her command
　Thereon, and hallowed more Saint Denis' tomb.
Bright was that lantern : brighter far that light
Which later from her grave made glad each night !

He saw her, one slight finger raised, discourse
　With steel-clad Clovis on the Christian Faith,
And t'ward it draw him with magnetic force :
　Lastly he saw her laid in happy death
Near him and his Clotilde.　For centuries fame
Gave to that church wherein they slept her name.

The sweet chaunts ended, with them died the day:
    Staff-propp'd, the Saint drew near the threshold low:
He beckoned to her parents: wondering, they
    Obeyed, and thus he spake in accents slow:
"Severus and Gerontia, blest are ye
Since great among God's Saints your child shall be.

"Full oft, I deem, her slender hand and arm
    Ye raised, and with them traced the Sacred Sign
To shield her infant brow and breast from harm
    Ere she that ritual's meaning could divine:
It gave her timely help: this day she knows,
Few better, what that Cross on man bestows.

"Liegeful I know hath been your wedded life,
    And that ye reverenced God's high sacrament
Marriage, that rite which husband joins to wife
    With mystic meaning and benign intent:
Reverence His Saint that 'neath your roof doth tarry
As He, that Patriarch Husband, reverenced Mary.

"She seeks that 'better part' fitted for few:
    Nurse ye that hope; shield her from all things base;
Rule her, and keep her holy, humble, true,
    For great the prize she claims, and hard the race:
Farewell!   Return at morn when heaven grows grey;
With her return.   Far hence I take my way."

Next morn, an hour ere light, her parents led
    Their child to where that Sire of men had slept,
Who, kneeling now, his matin office said :
    Throngs gathered near : round eastern clouds there crept
A fiery fringe ; next kindled hill and wood ;
Then, lo ! before their eyes Germanus stood.

The Blessing given, he turned him to that child—
    " Child, hast thou memory of thy wish last eve ? "
The maid once more that smile bewildering smiled,
    Then spake ; " I wished that I might never leave
That house where Christ's sweet spouses dwell in bliss,
But still, like them, be His, and only His."

Then fixed the Patriarch on that child an eye
    Tender and strong and edged with boding quest :
He spake ; " The woman's snare is vanity ;
    When older, bar to it thine eyes, thy breast :
Shun them who praise thee ; bid them keep that praise
For God : wise men it scares ; the unwise betrays."

That moment through disparted mists a beam
    Shot from the circlet of the ascending sun,
Flashed from the pebbly path a spark-like gleam :
    The old man stooped, and from the shingles won
A pilgrim's roughest relic. Thereupon
Burnished like brass the Sign Redeeming shone.

Silent he lodged it in that infant hand ;
   Then closed her fingers. Next he spake with breath
Low-toned ; " In future years no gems demand
   Save this : this wear till death, and after death."
She knelt : he laid his hands upon her head
In blessing ; kissed it last ; then northward sped.

She kept his gift. That wish, fair as a flower,
   To live for Christ might as a flower have died—
A flower by March winds blighted. From that hour
   Solid it grew like stream-growth petrified
Or like that relic which,—amid her dust—
Guards still perchance its memorable trust.

A people hath, like children, instincts sage :
   Significance in trifles it discerns ;
Keeps faith with vanished things from age to age ;
   Drains heaven's nepenthé from earth's frailest urns :
In faithful hearts, though rude the race, that hour
God dropp'd a seed : the plant held healing power.

That people knew what lived in Genevieve
   Like Saint Germanus when he saw her first ;
Knew it more late ; they most the wise and brave
   They best who felt for heaven the heavenliest thirst,
Whose heart was deepest and whose hope most high :
Nearest they felt to God that creature nigh.

They marked that things they dimly saw were clear
　　To her as trees to them, or hills or skies ;
They knew that sensuous things to wordlings dear
　　For her existed not, her ears, her eyes :
Inmate of alien worlds she seemed ; and yet
Who saw her least of acts could ne'er forget.

One half of Europe then the darkness covered ;
　　Night held its own ; yet morning was at hand ;
Dubious betwixt the two her country hovered
　　Like bird that half belongs to sea, half land.
To France, sin's cripple, others preached the Word ;
Her life the Angel was Bethesda's well that stirred.

The way of words is the way round-about :
　　Good-will believes ; and words lack power to give it :
Die for thy Faith ! then dies the good man's doubt :
　　If Faith is tried no more by death, then live it !
A great, true Faith expressed in life as true
Lifts hearts to heaven as sunbeams lift the dew.

She lived her Faith : she walked the waves of life
　　Like Him who trod that Galilean sea ;
The temporal storm, the worldly strain and strife
　　Quenched not her gladness: from her, fair and free
It hurled its beam o'er seas by tempest tost ;
A ray surviving fresh from Pentecost.

Her valour 'twas that taught in later times,
  The Maid of Orleans taught, to love her well ;
For centuries household bards in honest rhymes
  To breathless throngs were wont her deeds to tell
Ere yet the Troubadour had tuned his song
To hymn base loves and crown triumphant wrong.

One sang how Childeric his Franks had led
  From that huge forest of the northern sea
Where Varus lay with all his legions dead :
  How Childeric's hosts frenzied by victory
Girt Paris like a wall :—no food remained ;
On the dead mother's breast the infant plained.

Louder he sang how dear Saint Genevieve
  Had launched her bark and faced that downward flood,
She and her four ; beat back the insurgent wave ;
  Baffled the shafts from bank and rain-drenched wood :
She steered ; they rowed while night was in the sky :
Back sailed the Saint at dawn, that bark with loaves
    heaped high !

Still blew the gale : that bark rushed down the river ;
  A rock—all knew it—split the midway tide :
She stood upon the prow ; serene as ever
  She raised the standard of the Crucified :
Full many a corse had strewn that rock of yore :
Thenceforth no eye of man beheld it more.

As oft he sang to them in hut or hall
  A sister legend of their favourite Saint :
The Frank was throned in Paris : fled the Gaul,
  Fled, save that band by foul and fell constraint
Long weeks in dungeon vaults alive entombed,
Their country's bravest sons : for that cause doomed.

Childeric had seen the Saint ; had heard that none
  Had power her strength and sweetness to resist :
Wary the man : he vowed that face to shun :
  The power of female beauty well he wist :
The power of Virtue he had yet to learn :
That king had instincts high, though proud and stern.

Paris, that time Lutetia named, most part
  Secure within its high-tower'd island lay :
A wooden bridge the river stretched athwart
  Fenced by the fortress of the Chatêley :
To them that held its gate Childeric sent word
"Obey, or die ! Entrance to none accord ! "

Propt by that gate at noon the warders slept :
  Sudden in trance they saw Saint Genevieve :
Nearer she moved : strange music o'er them swept
  As when through portals of a huge sea-cave
Makes way the organ anthem of the sea ;
Touched by that strain, those gates opening gave entrance
    free.

That hour, that moment by King Childeric's throne
  Saint Genevieve stood up !   If words she spake
Those words to angels, not to men, are known :
  The king sat mute,   As one that half awake
Sits blinded by the matin beam he stared :—
This only know we ; that the doomed were spared.

Such acts survive : as age to age succeeds
  Man's sequent generations, mountain-wise,
Reverberate echoes of heroic deeds :
  Each echo dies yet lives, and lives yet dies :
And still, as on from cliff to cliff they float
The strain remotest yields the tenderest note.

These be the lesser things of Christian story
  By some o'er-prized.   To o'er-prize them or impugn
Alike is littleness.   Faith's ampler glory
  Sits higher throned.   There waxing as the moon,
Strong is the sun, it lights the Christian sky :
More great than miracle is Sanctity.

Yet worth of Saints attested stands by time
  When great love, capturing thus a people's heart,
Sustains therein its royalties sublime
  And cheers alike low hut, palace, and mart,
Virtue's meek handmaid.   Who dare scorn that love
Which wafts a nation's hope to worlds above ?

This was that love which, 'mid those ages wild,
  France in her virgin breast, though rough yet true,
That vernal morn conceived for that fair child
  On whom his long, last gaze Germanus threw
Checking, as northward forth he rode, his rein,
And looking back.   That twain ne'er met again.

This was that reverence which in France increased
  As Christian Faith deepened therein its sway ;
Which gladdened Lenten fast and Paschal feast ;
  Inspired her Trouvére's tale, her harper's lay ;
Brightened young eyes; on wounded hearts dropt balm
And lit from Honour's heaven her Oriflamb ;

Lit it when high from Clermont soared that shout
  " Deus id vult," and Godfrey of Bulloign,
From Europe's loyalest princes singled out,
  Led forth his France that kingly host to join
Which knelt when first on Salem's towers it gazed,
Then knelt, and on her walls *that* standard raised.

In later wars, when riot filled the tent
  One name sufficed to lull it—Genevieve :
In peace to maids on girlish sports intent
  One thought of her a hallowing sweetness gave :
They looked like those she led at dawn of day
Before the Baptistery's shrine to pray.

Ofttimes a Saint dear to his natal place
    Elsewhere is ill-remembered or unknown :
But she, wherever spread her country's race,
    Was loved : the Loire revered her as the Rhone :
Three names for aye blazed on that country's shield—
Saint Genevieve, Saint Denis, Saint Clotilde.

AMALASUNTA.

(DIED A.D. 535.)

ARGUMENT.

Amalasunta was the daughter of Theodoric the Great, the Gothic King of Italy. On her father's death she became Regent, the King, her son, being a child. Through the violence of the Gothic Chiefs, whose oppressions she had held in check, she was sent a prisoner to an island in the lake of Bolsena, to perish among its pestilential marshes. In that island she was murdered.

There she revolves the career of her father—the spell which the greatness of Rome, though past, had exercised over his mind in youth; his desire that her Empire should be enlarged and perpetuated by including within itself the Barbaric races; his equal treatment of Goth and Italian, the restoration of Italian prosperity and letters. Lastly, she remembers in anguish the crimes which stained the close as well as the initiation of his reign; the judicial murder of Boethius and Symmachus, and the persecution of the Catholic Faith, which, till then, though an Arian, Theodoric had treated with respect; his remorse, and unhappy death.

It is a tender and a gracious morning,
A morning peacefuller than the calmest eve—
Some meaning there must lurk in such a quiet.
Tells it of death, or something after death?
The grey lake hath its gleam and naught beside :

T

If it had wrong last night, to-day it plains not ;
No ripple prints its sands ; no sailing cloud
Is imaged in its bosom ; not a bird
Flutes 'mid the reeds or streaks the level mere.
The autumn-reddened copses lose their red
In vapoury distance.   Nature's latest sigh
Is breathed—like mine—and now for both is stillness.
Lasts it for aye, that stillness?   Lo! I drop
A pebble o'er the water.   Hark, a sound!
The pebble sinks : some petty bubbles rise :
Twinkle ; then break.   When this, our Gothic realm
Built by my Sire, Theodoric, named the Great,
When this fair kingdom meets its final term
Like yonder pebble it will sink, send up
That bubble from the waters of oblivion
Which men call Fame, and in a moment more
Be gathered to the dark.

                           How strangely now
That buried past returns to me !   My Sire !
With what a puissant hand and mastering brain
Didst thou build up that kingdom !   For thy sake
I ruminate its fortunes !   With what joy
I, then a child, my hand upon thy knee,
Mine eyes upon thy face, listened the tale !
Thy youth in Constantine's more beauteous Rome
Washed by Propontic waves ; thy sedulous study

Of that once-splendid polity then grey-grown ;
Thine early vow—how like to Stilicho's—
To prop that ruined realm, our foe of old—
Sustain her, not destroy.   I hear thee speak :
" The Empire's power survived the Empire's self :
Albeit a wreck she ruled.   My youth gone by,
I roamed amid her wrecks of greatness dead
Kingly, Republican, Imperial greatness ;
In them the history of the world was writ :
All men saw that ; but something was there deeper :
Alone I marked that cradle 'mid the tombs,
The cradle of whatever greatness God
Reserves for future earth.   A sin it seemed
To snatch the sceptre from that wrinkled hand
Now feebler than a babe's."   He ended thus ;
" Only when long experience painfully proved
That Rome, old Rome, lay choked in her own ashes,
I said, ' A Gothic kingdom I will rear
Cast in the Roman mould.' "   I heard him speak it
With that deep voice and leonine !   My tears
Fell heavy on his hand.

              His rival dead,
He too of race barbaric—Odoacer—
Ah me !   How dead—by whom ?   I feared to ask—
The throne was his.   He rent it not from Rome,
Nor styled himself the Emperor of the West :

His race he deemed the noblest of the north:
He strove to blend it with the Roman, strove
In vain, alas, to breathe its manly pureness
Through that dead Empire.   Equal laws, when King
He gave to both the races ; portioned forth
Justly the Italian lands betwixt the twain.
Dead learning lived anew, and letters flourished ;
In them he trained me.   " I," thus spake he once,
" Can rule an army and evoke a realm,
Yet scarce can write my name.   But thou, my child,
Purer than northern Odin's coldest daughters
Shalt pass in learning Egypt's amorous queen,
In beauty Grecian Helen."   I replied,
" Not Helen !   Call me that Antigoné,
Who led her blind old exiled Sire through Greece,
His living staff."   My Father smiled.   Alone
On face so rough can rest a smile so sweet !
That smile went slowly by : again he mused :
" Thank Heaven, the father dies before the child !
Girl ! I have chosen even now thy future husband,
The noblest of our royal race, the Amali :
See that your child and his be fit for rule—
If hot his blood, as mine, he'll need much training—
To him, that child, the crown of earth shall pass.
Then when the Roman Empire, not extinct,
Girdles the northern as the midland sea

And wars on far Sarmatia."

                  O my Sire,
Much, much of that high vision was fulfilled !
To dwell upon that thought is still my peace.
This Italy was but thine Empire's core,
Rhætia, Dalmatia, Norieum, Pannonia,
The West was thine.   Iberia, southern Gaul,
Earth from Danubius to the Atlantic pillars !
The Italians held the civil offices,
The Goths the warlike.   Peace returned—then gold ;
In desolate cities glorious structures rose ;
Fair villas smiled above the Larian lake ;
The waves Lucanian : classic song revived :
Philosophy looked up once more to heaven :
The Goth less ravined on the Roman : he
In turn lived cleaner life—
Hope ruled again the world.

                  These things I learned
Less from my Father than from Cassiodorus :—
How writes he now ?   " The realm I served is doomed,
Thy Father's thirty years and three of greatness
Make dismal end.   I, like the deer in death,
Crawl to my forest lair.   Calabria bore me :
There will I build to God a monastery ;
There 'mid the ocean thunders find my rest ;
There on Boethius muse.   Pray that my life,

Too blest, too peaceful for heroic virtue,
May there make holy end."

                        But thou, my Sire,
What end was thine ?   If not a happy one
'Twas penitent at least ; and that is peace.
Ah, had that end but earlier come ! With most
Age shows in weakening brain. In thee the omen
Was wrath more fiery ; lessened self-control.
Diversities of Faith began the woe,
Diversities whereof thou said'st so oft,
" Battles are these of fools !" That Eastern Empire
Warred on our Arian Faith. Then rang thy shout,
" I on that Western Faith will war in turn !
I never loved that Apostolic Throne."
Thy people which had loved thee learned to hate :
Thenceforth suspicions gnawed thee ; and thy sword
Smote that great twain, Boethius, Symmachus,
Like lightning wrecking palace-towers of kings
When shepherd huts escape. Informal death
May be as just as death with forms of law ;
But these high victims died without a trial :
They loved thee though they scorned to fawn on power.
Then came remorse. I see thee yet again
Start from the banquet board, confront the spectre
That held his eye upon thee night and day :
Again I hear thee make distraught demand,

" Who sent thee hither?   Was it Odoacer?"—
Alas that day when Odoacer died !—
Again I see thee hurl from thee thy crown,
Hear thy last word ; " The Frank shall have the Empire."
My Father, what to thee are Empires now ?
    The sun rides high though hid in mist ?   'Tis strange !
But late 'twas morn.   Methinks I must have slept—
Not lately ; for those fire-flies of the waters
Still stung me into fevered wakefulness :
I must have slept new-risen : 'tis then I sleep
Forth issuing to cool air from that high prison
Whose roof sucks in the noontide flame and makes
My midnight cell a furnace.   Be it so !
    I built his Tomb : that was my first of cares,
My care as daughter and as Regent both :
The gold it cost had fee'd a body-guard
And lopped betimes treason's unnumbered hands.
'Twas better spent.   That Tomb o'erlooks Ravenna,
Its harbour, and the pine-woods far away :—
I built that Tomb, a wonder of the world ;
Above it hangs that dome, one granite block
Whereof the like shines not on Tiber's wave,
Or where beside the Ganges or the Nile
Far-shadowing rise the hundred-columned fanes :
Inurned o'er all repose my Father's bones :—
So long as Adrian billows lash Ravenna

Pilgrims shall stand before that Tomb and cry,
" There lies Theodoric, King of Goths : he ruled
Half earth ; yet scorned to bear the Imperial name."
    Are there not those who say that Love is gladness ?
I never found it such.   Love for my Sire
To me, a motherless child, meant ceaseless fears
Of swords barbaric or Byzantine poisons ;
And oft in the grey dawn behind his door
I listened for his breath.   That year of marriage—
Thank God, my Husband lived to see his son !
Had he survived that son had lived this hour !
How beautiful he was !   How like a fawn
He bounded through the woods !   And yet—and yet—
How suddenly that fawn would change to pard !
Wayward to most, to me he still was loving,
Save once when some rough Chief that passed us growled,
" Warrior he'll never prove."
                              What sound is that ?
They change, methinks, my dungeon's guard.   Ah me !
I never hear the tramp of armèd heels
But that black hour returns !   Once more as then
The palace courts grow dark with frowning brows ;
The palace corridors ring : those footsteps reach me :
Around me stand the steel-clad mutinous Chiefs,
Each with drawn sword.   Again I hear them cry,
" We brook no more this female government :

Thy son shall rule ; not thou ! " They hated me :—
A woman reigns not in a Gothic realm :
I stood too near the throne. They hated me
Because my people loved : they hated me
Because I stayed their ravage on the poor.
That day my son had struck his grey-haired tutor ;
To the feasting chiefs he rushed : denounced his wrongs :
Gladly they heard : 'mid that revolted throng
He stood—my son : a cloud was on his brow
Down bent. Not once he looked upon his mother.
Thus to their taunting speech I made reply ;
" It is the strong rule, not the weakling rule,
Sirs, which ye hate. Theodoric, late your King,
Governs his grandson through his daughter's hand :
Beware, sirs, what ye do." Frowning, yet mute,
They passed me with the boy. Then fell mine eye
Upon three daggers which beside me lay
Bought for my ladies from a merchant Mede :
I held them up and spake : " Sirs, I impeach you
This day of treason 'gainst my son and me !
Your sins will taint my son : his own will slay him :
When that day comes, albeit I stand this hour
A queen deposed, those daggers three shall find you,
Lawfully sentenced by these lips this day,
Sentenced, though now the execution halts."
They led him forth : he passed me without word :

They gave him foul ensample and he fell :
The wine-cup was his teacher, not his Mother.
I never saw him more.   Too much I heard
Of riot, of excess, of sickness last.
His sixteenth birthday came : a step approached :
It was not his : a man drew near and spake :
" The king's physicians say all hope is o'er !
Even now he dies."   I rose from where I sat ;
I took those daggers three.   Three faithful men
I sent to where upon the kingdom's bound
Those three the foremost in that murder ruled :
On the third day they cumbered earth no longer :
Justice was done that day ; my child avenged.

    This is, methinks, my latest day on earth,
Else why should memories of a lifetime past
Wrong me with crowding on me—from that night
When shrilled that voice, " Thy Mother is no more,"
To that dread morn when in the galley's hold
Bleeding I woke, and bound—why force me thus
To track, against my will, from point to point
A chronicle of dead days, like one who reads
Not one who tells a tale ?   O wearied eyes !
How heavily they cling to you this hour
Those images of all things loved and lost !
How sweet will be your closing !   Of God's gifts
Methinks that sleep should be accounted best,

Sleep, or, it may be, Death ; but not that Death
Whereof the plaining pagan poets babbled
With petulant yet luxurious iteration,
Ignorant that Life was made to fit for Death
And Death to lead to nobler life through woes
Endured with courage.   Here I sat at dawn ;
Dawn's virgin twilight now is changed to eve's
Dusty with sad experience.   Yonder cloud
Like some far mountain closes all the West :
Beyond it lies the world.   Within yon lake
Fair shines the evening star, and seems to clasp
The bright and silver key of mysteries hid,
To make, one day, man's peace.   Hail, evening breeze '
O what a weight of sighs must load thy wings
Travelling man's world !   They stifle not thy freshness !
See, I unloop my vest !   Find, if thou may'st,
And cool this burning heart !   They sent me here
Knowing my people would avenge my wrong,
They sent me here not stabbing me to kill,
Choked by yon mist.   Its work is sure yet slow :
Unmannerly it seems to task their patience,
A trick of queens.   They'll wait not long—I think—
Justinian spake me fair yet will not aid me,
Much less that Emperor's wife who loves not beauty
In others, dimmed albeit.   Cassiodorus
Writes thus : " The men of death are on thy track."

That sentence I forgot. I like it well :
Their daggers quicklier than their mists will give me
Those whom I ne'er forget. A Christian true
Would say, "Will earlier give me to my God."
    I fear our Gothic Faith hath lacked a something ;
Have thought at times those Catholics with their creed
Transcendant more than ours, their mystic rites
That seem to lift our earth so nigh to heaven,
Their friendly ways with Mary and God's Saints,
Were born beneath a happier star than we,
And on a soul of sweeter, silkier grain
Take the celestial impress. Arians we :
They that baptized our nation made it Arian :
That suits rough hearts. The ignorant cannot choose
'Twixt creeds : the faithful may not quit old friends—
My father failed. The imperial reign o'er earth
It may be is reserved for one who holds
His crown from Christ ; believes He reigns in heaven.
I fear I never had a full devotion :
Yet this I sought ; to act as God commands,
Bear bravely what He sends : and this I hope,
Death past, to meet my Sire—my Son—my Husband,
Meet them unstained. If my own blood should stain me
Beforehand I forgive my murderers.
—The Frank shall have the Empire, not the Goth :
In death he spake it ; and his word is true.

SAINT BONIFACE.

(DIED A.D. 755.)

ARGUMENT.

Saint Boniface, first called Winfrid, belonged to Wessex. When
a child, he was taken by his father to see Saint Cuthbert, and ever
afterwards desired to evangelize the heathen, and to seal his testimony by his blood. Both wishes were granted. For forty years he
preached Christ in Germany, of which country he is revered as the
Apostle. That work accomplished, he was slain with all his
fellow-labourers near the stream Borduc in Friesland.

While his companions take their noontide rest, the Saint meditates
the events of his long life—his first failure in Friesland—his sojourn
in Rome, where Pope Gregory changed his name to Boniface—his
daily labours and sufferings in the great German forest, and the
benignant dreams by which those sufferings were nightly assuaged.
He praises the German races, and adjures them to remain for ever
faithful to Christ.

WHAT is it makes the Universe of God
So wondrous seem this day ? 'Tis always fair,
Balm-breathing, glorious, like a monarch throned
Or priest who kneels gold-vested by God's altar
Offering all creatures' praise. 'Tis always great :
Through sin we note its greatness but in glimpses ;
This day that greatness grows to palpable ;

This day anticipates those heavens and earth
That shall be when immortalizing Death
Removes for us their veil.   Even now I feel
The germination of those spiritual senses
Which in our body glorified shall show
Creation as it is.   Lo! where it beams
Like countenance of a Saint whose lips long mute
Break forth at last in psalms.   That was the gift
Of Pentecost.   If fiery tongues this hour
Sat on the brows of yonder hills and woods
I scarce should wonder.   Is it the glad new year
Which works this marvel?   Scarcely—but in part;
For thrice I saw that glory, when the hand
Of winter bound the earth in iron chains,
While rushed the frost wind o'er that boundless forest
Which, where the storm had cloven long lanes of wreck,
Showed but some river broad with rafts of ice
Toiling to ocean's marge, and high o'erhead
The dusk cloud onward streaming.   Those three times
Martyrdom seemed close by us.   Now 'tis summer:
Spring flowers are dead: but dog-rose buds remain
Flower-bubbles blown by Nature, loved by her
Who smiles to see them die!   She fears not death,
She sees in death new birth, in earth a wheel
That, circling through the under-darkness, lifts
Dead night to dawn.   Painless her children die:

'Tis well; but death for Christ were something better,
Something more precious; something worthier men.
What? slink we out of life when Christ bore all?
May not this joy be prescience of His coming?
Is there who fears that hour?

From earliest youth
The passion of my life was one and sole
To die for Christ. What argues love, like death?
Next to that great desire my hope was this,
To free our brethren in the flesh who roam
These German forests like our Saxon sires
From thraldom blind to Odin and to Thor.
This was my childhood's dream on Wessex' coast:
This was my boyhood's vow at Escancester:
That vanished life how strangely all this day
It haunts me! Why reject its pleading looks?
My brethren take their noontide sleep: to me
Such memories may waft a rest more healing.
'Twas well no doubt my earliest effort failed:
It humbled me.

To Friesland I had gone;
Wrought nothing there: my fault it must have been:
Later I passed to Rome: a Roman noble
Showed me its pagan glories. What were they?
The sum of all that virtue counts for naught;
That Faith esteems as loss. A nightmare 'twas,

A bad man's wickedest dream—such dream as stands
Near him, belike, death past, his plague forever
In bodiless worlds where sin is known as sin.
From trophies of proud wrong I fled to where
The houses of Cecilia and Prassedé
Now churches stand ; the prisons profound where sat
The Apostles chained.   Men spake of later days ;
Saint Gregory, named the Great ; his acts his words ;
Born of the old stock ; stately ; profound in lore :
With lands in every province far and near :
Their increase went to God.   To him they owed
That psalmody severe and piercing both
Which one time shook the Solomonian temple ;
Shook then their huge basilicas.   'Twas he
Who, noting English children sold in Rome,
Exclaimed, "Not Angli—Angeli," and to England
Commanded great Augustine our Apostle.
The "Servant of the Servants of the Lord"
He styled himself; and when in Roman streets
They found one morn a beggar dead from cold
He from the Offering of the Sacrifice
Restrained himself three days.   A tale they told :
Each day within his huge ancestral palace,
He fed twelve pilgrims.   Once, at Whitsuntide,
Those twelve were round his board.   Repast surceased
A guest departed : all the rest abode :

Ere long the eldest spake like one in fear :
" Twelve guests here sat we late ; and one has gone :
Yet twelve remain !"   They counted : twelve remained.
Who then was he, that uninvited guest ?
Be sure none other than the same Who said
" That help ye gave to him the least of these,
That help ye gave to Me."
                      Three months I dwelt
At Rome : that later Gregory then the Pope
Probed me with searching question of the Faith ;
Next he ordained me Bishop ; smiling, last,
He changed my name to Boniface from Winfred,
And bade me to the heathen.   I made vow
To guard Christ's Faith from wrong, His Church from
      schism ;
The scroll whereon that vow was writ I laid
Upon Saint Peter's tomb.
                Nigh forty years
I roamed from realm to realm that German land,
Pannonia, and Thuringia, Dacia, Rhetia,
Bavaria, and Burgundia.   O how oft
I longed for that high grace, the " gift of tongues,"
Then when the natives crowding round me came,
Each with his woes—and sins—and none to help him !
I looked at them and wept ; yet thus I mused
Forward ! great Love suffices, Love can teach :

                              U

And thus I spake; "Demand thou light from God:"
Those words I knew in all their languages;
And still I pointed to the heavens; and still
Taking the hand of each, three times I drew
From brow to breast the Venerable Sign:
That gave them help.   They knew my heart: they said
"This man brings tidings good and cannot speak them!"
God spake them in their hearts.

                      It was not strange:
There is an instinct which precedes all knowledge,
Uses, yet knows it not.   The body hath it:
Through it the new-born infant knows to feed,
Else who could teach it?   Reason hath its prescience,
High yearnings for the True, the Just, the Good;
These shape the way for knowledge more distinct
Which else a life's experience had not brought:
'Tis thus with Souls: their instincts lean to God;
Reverence makes way for Faith; humblest affections
For charity divine t'ward God and man;
Heart-cleanness clears the way for spirit-vision:
There where the Virtues hovering o'er man's heart
Have cleansed that mansion, angels entering in
Will lay—perhaps in death—the Bethlehem Babe:
A word suffices: thousand words avail not:
Where confident most, I failed; where shamed the most
Reaped harvest late.   The younger of these Gentiles

With shrewd, sly smile—tasked me by questions hard :
I answered thus ; " No theologian I !
I bear a message ; I divulge the Tidings : "
The unanswered question was forgotten soon ;
The Tidings welcomed.   Marvellous was their Faith :
How oft I cried, " the single eye is theirs :
Venturous are they to seek for Truth, then use it :
That fineness which prevaricates with God
Is none of theirs.   Like storms, passions may rend them ;
Then comes the counter-passion of Remorse
And burns away the stain."

                        Transitions swift
O'er-swept them.   Once when, axe in hand, we hewed
An oak to Odin vowed, they closed around us :
Circles they made : the inner raised their clubs,
The outer, lances level with their shoulders ;
They stood; they glared:—we smote with stroke o'er
    stroke
The stem ; that shivering 'mid the boughs thick-leaved
Increased : the strong root shrieked ; the crash suc-
    ceeded :
We looked for death : their rage had changed to awe :
Kneeling they cried ; " Great Odin then is dead ! "
Next day they sawed from that dismembered tree
The planks that walled our church.

                        God only saved me !

All were not mild and loyal like the best:
Of them who joined our following some betrayed us:
That was our worst of trials; next to that
Hunger and frost-wind fanged with death, and cry
Day-long of wolves echoed from woods and rocks,
And death of good men from our English shores
That yearly joined my toils.

            When times were worst
This thought recurred; the woes we face, what are they
Compared with that wild dread which shook the world
Three hundred years gone by?   Then man to man
Whispered death-pale, "The Barbarous hordes advance:"
And in the bridegroom's hand the hand of bride
Shivered ice-cold.   "Where plants my horse his foot
Grass grows no more;" thus cried King Attila:
Huge realms became as lands the locust-cloud
But late o'erswept: where temple and street had stood
High as their horses' chests the conquerors rode
Through ashes strewn.   Civility was dead.
That day the sage and peasant side by side
Watched from the city-wall the advancing woe
As when the fountains of the mighty deep
Had open burst, and tremblers on hill crests
Eyed the great Deluge with its watery wall
On moving t'ward them.   Faith alone remained,
That Faith a weeping Faith.   A record old

Consoled my comrades oft.   The greatest man
And best that time on earth was Saint Augustine.
He saw that Terror reach the Afric coast :
He heard the echoes of the falling cities :
At last the Vandal reached his sacred See,
Hippo : for fourteen months the siege endured :
He said, "The shepherd with his flock should die :"
Daily, though broken, to his church he crept :
Daily he taught the poor.   When sickness smote him
He said, "Remaineth Penitence :" he spread
His pallet midmost in his little cell :
He gave command to trace upon its walls
In letters large the Penitential Psalms
Which evermore he read till ceaseless tears
Dimmed the strong eyes nigh fourscore years had left
Like eagles' eyes.   At last he gave command
" Henceforward leave me, friends, with God alone :"
In holy sorrow thus Augustine died.
Ah me ! man's sorrows are his chief illusions !
One half those Tribes Barbaric now are Christ's,
Our Kingdoms Seven among them !   That Dismay
Was but God's storm scattering the infected mist,
Winging God's seed o'er earth.
                              A second help
My God vouchsafed to me.   The dreadfullest day
Ofttimes the compensating night retrieved

Through dreams that left me bright a week.   The first
Was granted me the night I reached this land
Friesland, there ending where my work began.
Methought I roamed o'er Wessex shores; the sun
Reddened, late risen, the broad trunks of the oaks,
Or fired their mossy roots.   The fair green lawns
Swelled up 'mid bosky knolls of beech o'er-dewed
And orchards whence sea-scented breezes rapt
White bloom o'er azure waves.   Onward I passed
To where a river, widening, joined the sea.
There on a promontory stood a house;
The ripple lapp'd its basement; gladsomer sounds
Allured my footsteps; 'twas our garden old!
My brothers and my sisters trod its grass!
No feature, gesture, voice mocked my remembrance:
Passed like a mist were sixty years, and more!
There stood that girl with hair half brown half gold;
A spirit of love she stood with yearning eyes
All light; close by, that vestal child, her sister,
Slender and stately, and with look severe.
I leaned upon the gate; a sweet voice said,
"That ag'd man is wayworn: bid him rest:"
They drew a bench beside me; kissed my hand
Honouring white hairs, and then resumed their game.
There midmost sat my Father and my Mother:
Delight of health and strength within them glowed;

Around them all was fortunate; joyous all;
Misgiving lived not.   Half my present years
Seemed theirs, or less.   The strangest of emotions
Is his methinks, who from the heights of age
Regards his parents in their day of youth
'Mid some remembered scene—their day of youth !
That day with him was childhood's day; his love
Was childhood's loving reverence; still 'tis such,
But reverence which, commingled with a love
Foreboding, half parental, prompts that prayer,
"Shield, Lord, their inexperience."

                        Oft in youth
I taxed my heart with coldness to my kin:
At times I marked them not when near: the door
Had closed not when I cried with chiding pang,
" Perchance—who knoweth—they may ne'er return : "—
Our Father died : we met around his death-bed :
Those severing weights of flesh and blood were gone :
There, soul with soul, we touched as spirits in heaven.
'Twas so that hour.   I raced among those children ;
With them I rushed into our parents' arms
Myself a child.   That dream dissolved.   Once more
Alone, a grey-haired man I woke : I wept ;
I felt as if some sin had been forgiven :
I said, "the end is near."

                     Dream heavenlier yet

Was mine last night.   Alone I paced a cliff:
That Wessex height it seemed whereon, a boy,
Nightly I walked—its name the cliff of Torre—,
Not distant from a blue south-facing bay.
I saw the Hyads and the Pleiads rise
And the dim seas star-gemmed. ˙A sudden glory
Drank up those lesser lights.   Aloft I gazed:
Downward and onward both, lapsing it moved,
With exquisitest cadence nearing earth,
Yet sinking as some shape that condescends
Conquering its heavenward yearnings.   Nigh at hand
At last it stood, a mystic fabric fair
All golden, needing neither lamp nor torch,
Self-radiant and serene.   High-towered it stood
Like minster's portal triple-arched.   Within
I saw a wondrous company, and knew
Each one by name.   These were the Saxon Saints,
My country's, and, one family with them,
For kindreds in the skies are spirit-linked,
Erin's and Rome's that drew our race to Christ:
High Kings of Peace they stood, yet wearing, each,
God's armour, and the Truth's, the Spirit's sword
Breast-plate of Faith, and helmet of Salvation.
There stood our great Augustine; by his side
King Ethelbert, Queen Bertha, hand in hand;
Saint Laurence glorying in God's rights restored;

King Sebert gazing t'ward Saint Peter's Church
New-risen on Thamis' bank ; Northumbrian Oswald
Beckoning Columba's sons to bless his realm ;
Those three great Bishops, Aidan, Finan, Colman,
Iona's lights shining from Lindisfarne ;
Bernician Oswy by his consort's tears
To penance won and peace. Apart I saw
Heida, the prophetess of dark woods, who found
In Odin's faith our Christ. With beaming brow
Stood Hilda as she stood on Whitby's rock
Listening from Cædmon's lips the immortal song ;
Cædmon stood near her—silent ; for his ear
Had heard the song of angels. Frideswida
Mused on her future Oxford. Cuthbert smiled
As when beside that river near Carleol
I fixed on him mine eyes, and heard him say,
"Of men the greatest is that man who draws
To God, God's creatures." Venerable Bede
Sat central there in stillness of great love
Brow-bent above his scroll. From these remote
And taller far a monarch stood, with front
Monastic but the sceptre-wielding hand :
Again I stood in Wessex' banquet hall,
And heard Birinus thus to Kenwalk speak,
" From Wessex soil shall England's hope arise
Two centuries hence : and Alfred is his name."

Then raised those Saints their hymn, and with that
    hymn
Onward and up that glory rose to heaven ;
And as it rose they stretched to me their hands :
Therefore 'tis certain I shall die ere long,
Perhaps to them be joined.
               Eternal Power
That called'st me forth from nothing, I return
To Thee, my Maker. Sinner though I be
My life has not been barren. Manhood come
I burst the snare of dreamy youth : I said
" Henceforth my life is work." The coral worm,
I' the dark laborious, buildeth continents :
Shall we, Thy creatures of the hand and head,
Leave naught for God or man ? Through help of
    Thine
I laboured to be worthy of that help ;
Yea, tremble ofttimes to have wrought some tasks
Fitter for cleaner hand. Cædmon bewailed
" In youth I shamed to sing amiss : in age
To have sung, impostor-like, some strains too high
For minstrel scant of grace—some strains that won
Praise but for virtue meet." At best I made
Beginning only : perfect, Thou, that work
Lest, lacking roof the rain corrode the walls.
My People want not zeal, but they are heady :

Imaginations wild take hold of them
As sensual lures on men of southern climes,
Yea, with a subtler might; for thus 'tis writ,
" Our wrestling is with Spirits in high places,
The Princes of the Powers of the air
That rule in Darkness." Teach my People, God,
Humility! When those tempestuous fires
That swell this day their hearts, to the brain ascending
There kindle storm of thought—bid them that hour
Revere his voice, the Gentiles' Teacher sage,
The man for measureless wisdom scorned as mad,
Who, raised at times to Visions of the Lord,
A mystic walking ever in the Spirit,
Was instant thus: " Be sober, and keep watch:
Be not o'er-wise, for knowledge puffeth up,
Charity buildeth up." Temptation comes
To men of zeal through scandals gendering wrath:
That I foresaw betimes; I scattered wide
Convents and Bishoprics; but laboured more
To overawe abuses, strengthen discipline:
I cried, " Decay beginneth at the head:
If he who, being Master, for that cause
Should most be servant, beats his fellow-servants
What doom for him? The salt o' the earth, forth cast
O'er all the earth, shall generate o'er the earth
Fumes that make mad the nations."

Race high dowered !
Through nature's hardness nurtured unto God
Consummate thy great destinies, subjecting
Valour to Virtue, and the Mind of Man
To Faith, the shadow of God's Mind Supreme
Down cast upon Man's Mind unmeet to bear
As yet His beam.   The shadow of God's mind
Is radiance unto man's.   Be true; be just !
Transmit thy gift !   Erin to England sent—
Erin and Rome—the Faith ; England to thee :
Transmit it thou to that dark North sea-dinned
Whose mountains, leaning far o'er frith and fiord,
Change day to night ; whose isles are funeral pyres
Making night dreadful with eternal flame ;
Whose sons, wilder than waves or lava rivers,
If left in the dark may plague the unhelpful lands
For slothful fraud which napkin-hid God's Talent,
Christ's Faith, amercing man of those two worlds,
Heaven and   our   earth,   since   earth   divorced   from
    heaven,
Is earth in name alone.
                        Brethren, awake !
'Tis time we were afoot !   What sound was that
In yonder wood?   'Twas like the clash of arms ;—
Men spake of bandits near.
Brethren, awake !   'Tis Eve of Whit-Sunday :

Three thousand late baptized in Borduc's stream—
Thanks to this balmy June nor girl nor boy
Nor sire grey-headed shivered in the water—
We bade to meet us in yon wood this day
For the Confirmation Rite.   Arise !   'Tis time.

THE CROWNING OF CHARLEMAGNE; AND THE HOLY ROMAN EMPIRE.

(A.D. 800.)

AN ODE.

I.

THAT God of Gods the universe who made,
 Who spake, and from the void rushed forth the stars,
He, too, their orbits shaped, their movements swayed,
 Wrote on their brows in shining characters
"God's flock are we : our freedom is to go
That way His finger points, with motion swift or slow : "
 That God spake Law not less to Man : He said,
" Revere your kings ; Good-will, and Order cherish :
Live like Mine angels ; not like beasts that perish : "—
  Primeval man obeyed :
Those earlier Patriarch kings were shepherds true :
 Bad kings came next : on rival kings they preyed :
From ancient wounds the blood welled forth anew
  Till swelled the cry
" One king should rule on earth : One God there reigns
 on high."

II.

Then Empires rose ; then subject kings
   Like children chidden lived in peace
Cowering beneath the imperial wings
   Of Assur, Babylon, Persia, Greece.
Yet those four Empires to the world
   Bequeathed not *growth :* the wheel round ran ;
The sighing vans around were whirled ;
   They stored nor wheat nor bran :
The windy towers shadowed a barren strand :
   The sea-gales ground but the sea-sand—
Rome rose at last ; her Empire stretched o'er all,
   A firmament at first—at last a pall.

III.

   What changed that Empire's good to ill ?
Ignorance that nations shrine—like man—a Spirit ;
   That sowing to the flesh their hope they kill,
Renounce that spiritual crown true States inherit.
   Material good sufficed Rome's Empire old :
   No God believing, every God it served :
   Whate'er it touched its gold hand changed to gold :
      Full-gorged it starved :
   The pampered body throve from scalp to sole ;
   But on the spirit God sent leanness and bitter dole.

IV.

Not less in one thing was that Empire great ;
It gave one Law to all ; made earth a single State :
A citizenship it reared in every city
Better than lawless freedom, fruitless fame :
They that at home nor justice hoped, nor pity
Found still in Rome refuge from bonds and shame :
Fabricius, Regulus, Scipio fought
For ends above their limit-line of thought :
The Rome-girt Sea shone out man's palace floor ;
Peace reigned from western Atlas to the Colchian shore.
More late that Empire Christian was in name :
It slipp'd the worn skin of Materialism
Friendship with disanointing Faiths to claim,
Falsehoods, not Faiths, that mocked at crown and
chrism :
Not David's was its throne, but that of Saul :
It fell : it spurned the chairs of Peter and of Paul.

V.

Our Rome again is risen !
She lay for centuries three in chains of Fate
Far down in earth's dark prison :
She roamed on coasts unknown, sunless and desolate

Where frozen seas make dumb the ghost-thronged shore,
Nor answered priest or king who cried, " Return once
more !"
    First Odoacer came ;
   Theodoric next with more majestic aim ;
     But still, " Where is she ;—where ? "
The Earth incredulous cried with ever new despair—
    Silence, astonished lands !
   She lives ! The great, true Rome among you stands !
  That Empire old was but the statue's base :
This day the statue's self assumes its destined place.

VI.

   What functions gird this Wonder new
  That stands a-gazing on the sun ?
This Empire's Head Elect to whom must he be true ?
    Kings have their realms each one :
    He need have none :
His course, a glittering meteor, may have run :
  He may have lived unknown, or known to few.
  His sphere of action is the earth's wide sphere :
  No personal ends hath he ; no interests small and
near :

               x

His first great function is to shield
From caitiff hand Christ's Bride ;
From Schism, whose sword would cleave her sacred side
Severing God's bond with man in Christ's own blood
close-sealed ;
From Heresy whose lips
Before them darkness spread ;
Whose breath, to tempest swelling, would eclipse
Star after star, those lights which crown her queenly head.
I saw in heaven a Sign ;
I saw a Sceptre and a man Divine :
Beneath I saw a Dragon that pursued
A Woman o'er the earth, still raging for her blood.

VII.

That Emperor's next of functions is to guard
Justice, God's Attribute
Which stamps distinction prime 'twixt man and brute,
In each man sees God's ward.
God's mercy to God's Church belongs ;
Through it she lifts His people to His height ;
The Emperor wields His justice ; tramples wrongs ;
Renders man's life on earth the triumph of the Right.
The Emperor metes that justice among kings :—
Justice and Mercy are the sister wings

Whereon God's new Creation issues forth,
New Heavens, new Earth—
Things old have passed away ; things new have come to
birth !

VIII.

Not one of woman born
Divined the sequel this great Christmas morn
When paced Rome's mitred Sire to where,
That spot beside
Where hung of old Saint Peter crucified
The Frankish king knelt on his tombstone stair.
Silent that Pontiff stood : silent dropped down
On that high kneeler's brow the Imperial Crown—
'Twas not his work alone ! his hands he raised :
The Church o'er earth, the popular Heart at Rome
They crowned, through him, a Head for Christendom!
The crowned one gazed
Round him like one by sudden lightning mazed ;
Took passively that crown ; and then resumed his prayer.

IX.

Darest thou to claim, base Empire of the East,
Our Rome's supreme and universal sway,
Tyrant yet slave that hold'st ignoble feast,
Thy forehead brazen and thy feet of clay,

Far fenced from honourable war,
By mountain walls, and waves that near them roar?
To thy great Mother of the West
What help from thee at need? Her death-cry was thy
jest—
To Rome a traitor in the ages past!
To God a traitor turned Iconoclast!
A woman * hugs the realm she stole—
Our Strong One hath it half, and soon will have it whole. '
The Chair of Peter, fixed like Fate,
Raises this day a Holy Empire's Throne:
In her celestial Unity that mate
Terrestrial imaged sees its own!
The Pontiff's mitre and the imperial globe
Are one; not one as was that "Seamless Robe;"
But one as two great powers in one accord;
Two servants of one Saviour Lord.

X.

The Frank was chosen not the Goth,
Though potent both;
Though widelier far the Gothic race had spread;
At times for Rome had bled;
To politic wisdom had an earlier claim;
Had boasted first the Christian name.

* The Empress Irené.

Tell us, high-favoured, what was that which won
    The birthright for the younger son?
The Frank long since had shown his right to rule :
Our Charles it was who smote that Idol, Irminsûl ;
    Yea, though that Idol centuries eight had cried
    " 'Twas here that Varus, with his Romans died,"
    The Goth was Arian : Christ, if less than God,
Had only earlier raised the Arabian Prophet's Rod.
    —What mean those silver trumpets in mine ears
        Blown from the summits of St. Peter's fane?
They mean not mad ambitions, widows' tears ;
They mean the warbling of celestial spheres
        Echoed in Earth's glad strain ;
           The Jubilee
    Of every race and order and degree,
The Kingdom of the Just, the God-man's endless reign.

XI.

Rise, then, thou chief of Empires and the last
      Later there can be none :
Rise, *first* of Empires, since the whole world's Past
      In thee lives on !
Ride forth, God's Warrior, armed with God's command
To chase the great Brand-Wielder with the brand
To the Asian deserts back, and wastes of burning sand.

In one brief century from the Impostor's death
Past Mecca's gates the fiery flood had rolled
  In ruin o'er the Church's land of gold :
    Bethlehem and Nazareth
The Sepulchre of Christ, were hers no more :
The Alexandrian Empire, Egypt hoar
The gem-crowned realms that held the south in fee
Dazzling the Afric limits of the Midland Sea,
  Were lost : Iberia followed : trembled Gaul :
And Arab Horse were seen from Rome's eternal wall !—
  Islam shall die ! the Faith shall burst its chain !
  Who smote the turbaned host on Poitiers' plain ?
  Charles Martel, grandsire of our Charlemagne !
  Not East and South alone :—to Christ give thou
Those northern shores whereon ne'er grated Roman
    prow !
  Show thou how great a thing Empire may be
When founded not on sanctities downtrod,
    When not by greed and guilt
    Ingloriously up-built,
  But reared to be a fortress of the free,
    A temple for our God.

THE END.

PRINTED BY WILLIAM CLOWES AND SONS, LIMITED,
LONDON AND BECCLES.